At Every Turn

ANNE MATEER

BETHANY HOUSE PUBLISHERS
a division of Baker Publishing Group
Minneapolis, Minnesota

© 2012 by D'Ann Mateer

Published by Bethany House Publishers
11400 Hampshire Avenue South
Bloomington, Minnesota 55438
www.bethanyhouse.com

Bethany House Publishers is a division of
Baker Publishing Group, Grand Rapids, Michigan

Printed in the United States of America

Library of Congress Cataloging-in-Publication Data
Mateer, Anne
    At every turn / Anne Mateer.
        p.   cm.
    Includes bibliographical references.
    ISBN 978-0-7642-0904-8 (pbk.)
    1. Young women—Fiction. 2. Automobile racing—Fiction. 3. Charity—
Fiction. I. Title.
PS3613.A824A93 2012
813'.6—dc23   2012013124

This is a work of historical reconstruction; the appearance of certain historical figures is therefore inevitable. All other characters, however, are products of the author's imagination, and any resemblance to actual persons, living or dead, is coincidental.

Scripture quotations are from the King James Version of the Bible.

The internet addresses, email addresses, and phone numbers in this book are accurate at the time of publication. They are provided as a resource. Baker Publishing Group does not endorse them or vouch for their content or permanence.

Cover design by Dan Thornberg, Design Source Creative Services

Packard Runabout automobile on cover art courtesy of John D. Groendyke, Enid, Oklahoma

12   13   14   15   16   17   18   7   6   5   4   3   2   1

For Jeff
Words cannot express the depth
of my love for you.

1

August 1916

$\mathscr{M}$y foot pressed the pedal on the floor, shifting the Packard Runabout into a higher gear. A slight nudge lifted the lever on the steering wheel. Gasoline gushed into the engine. Already engulfed in a cloud of smoke and dust, the motorcar jumped forward over the rutted dirt road, bouncing me above the leather seat. My hands gripped the steering wheel, keeping my auto on the road and me within its confines. But even the jolting of my body couldn't dampen the thrill that electrified me as the world raced past.

My Bible danced on the seat beside me. I imagined the look of horror that would appear on stodgy Mrs. Tillman's face should I drive into the churchyard at upwards of thirty miles per hour. Trapping the book with one hand, I slid it beneath my thigh. My grin fell away. As much as I loved the swiftness of the machine beneath me, I owned no desire for scandal. And an overheated engine wouldn't get me to church on time, either.

Shifting gears, I pulled back on the gas. The world slowed, and the white steeple of Langston Memorial Church came into focus. By the time I pulled into the churchyard, the Packard was creeping along at the pace of a fast walk. The first deep note of the bell tolled across the quiet Indiana countryside.

A horse munching grass raised its head and stared until I set the brake and stopped the engine. The mare went back to her breakfast while I pushed my door open and stepped out among the few autos dotting the field beside the clapboard building.

I shrugged out of my linen duster before unwinding the swath of netting covering my head and face and fluffing the short brown curls that peeked out from under my small hat. Dirt marred the fingertips of my white gloves as I pushed the door shut, but few would notice the testament of my indulgence on the open road. The windscreen and top kept most of the dust and oil smoke from my clothes.

"Good morning, Miss Benson." Mrs. Tillman's purposeful stride carried her past me, her family struggling to keep up.

"It's Alyce. Remember?" I tried to banish the disapproving picture of her I'd imagined and instead hurried to draw even.

She glanced in my direction. "Hmm. Yes."

"I've been thinking about ways in which the Women's Mission Auxiliary could raise funds to help with missionary efforts both at home and abroad. I wrote down some ideas." I opened my handbag and withdrew my list as Mrs. Tillman halted at the bottom of the steps leading into the church.

Her eyes widened a bit as she studied my dress, my hat, my gloved hands. She tugged at her floor-length skirt and then at the high collar of her blouse before reaching for the paper I held out to her. My cheeks flamed with the realization that my exposed ankles and square neckline rendered me suspect in Mrs. Tillman's eyes. What if she noticed the dirt on my gloves? I whipped my hands behind my back.

"Mrs. Swan said you had ideas." She skimmed the piece of stationery in her hand, mumbling as she went. "Bake sale. Quilting bee. Picnic with games and concessions." She folded the paper and tucked it inside her Bible. "Of course we can bring these up for a vote at the next meeting."

"I would like that very much, Mrs. Tillman. I think we can—"

"Just remember that this isn't Chicago, Miss Benson. It's Langston, Indiana. We have humble means, though our hearts are large."

I rocked forward on my toes in excitement. "Exactly. That's why I thought—"

Mrs. Tillman's lips pressed together, and her eyes narrowed. I straightened my shoulders, feeling altogether like a schoolgirl again.

Her daughter sidled up next to her. Mrs. Tillman laid a hand on the girl's head, her expression softening just a bit. "I'll put your ideas on the agenda. Next Sunday—a week from today."

I wanted to throw my arms around her right then, but the pinched expression returned. I nodded instead, wondering if I ought to curtsy, as well. "Thank you, Mrs. Tillman. I'll look forward to the meeting."

Her gaze raked over my attire again. I swallowed down a fear that she'd change her mind.

She sniffed once. "Seven o'clock sharp, Miss Benson." She pointed her fan at me to emphasize the point.

"Yes, ma'am. I'll be there."

Mrs. Tillman joined the others streaming into church, but I couldn't move. Joy surged up from my toes, tingling all the way to the top of my head. Using my ideas, the women of Langston Memorial Church would do something great, something *lasting* for the kingdom of God. Pressing my hands together, I gazed into the cloudless sky and thanked the Lord for answering the prayer of my heart.

"I saved you a seat, Miss Benson." A honey-colored mustache twitched a bit on the eager face of Father's new bookkeeper.

"Thank you, Mr. Trotter." I slid in next to him on the third pew from the front. An ache surged into my chest, a longing for Grandmother—the only person in my life who spanned the gap between my family and my church. Until Mr. Trotter's arrival.

"How is your grandmother?"

"The same. Her painful joints and faded eyesight keep her in bed most days."

"I could have picked you up this morning." Mr. Trotter's quiet words almost missed my ear among the surrounding chatter.

"That would have been quite inconvenient for you." I straightened my skirt and crossed my ankles.

"It would've been no trouble between friends, Miss Alyce."

My head jerked in his direction. Friends. I hadn't imagined they would be such a scarce commodity when I'd returned to Langston after two years at the Chicago Institute of Domestic Arts and Sciences. The friends I'd made growing up had moved away, gone to work, or caught a husband. Besides

Father's mechanic, Webster Little, I had no one my age to talk to. But perhaps that was changing. New people settled in Langston every day. Like this man who shared my faith.

I smiled.

His color heightened.

I averted my eyes.

Deep organ notes resounded through the room. The congregation rose to sing.

"Number thirty-six," Pastor Swan called out from the front platform.

Eyes shut tight, words of a new hymn rolled off my tongue. " 'Had I a thousand lives to live I'd live them all for Thee.' " A thousand lifetimes would never be enough to show my gratitude to my Savior.

We plunged into another song. And another. My spirit soared like when I let the spark plugs fire and the gas flow free.

I ducked my head lest such irreverent thoughts make themselves plain on my face. How dare I think of driving while in church? Yet perhaps the two experiences weren't totally incongruous. In both cases, I submitted to the control of something so much more powerful than myself.

The music ended. Pastor Swan invited us to sit. "Brothers and sisters, we have some very special guests with us today." His usually placid face grew animated, his step more buoyant. "John and Ava McConnell have spent the past five years living in a British colony called the Gold Coast in western Africa, sharing Christ with a people who have never heard His glorious name."

My breath caught. My body tingled. *Missionaries!* I leaned forward, hungry for every word, ignoring the escalating wail of a child, thankful that it soon faded into the distance.

"Please welcome Mr. McConnell."

A man stepped to the front of the church, his eyes downcast, his wrists extending beyond the cuffs of his jacket, a worn Bible grasped between his large hands.

Pastor Swan returned to the front pew and sat between his wife and the woman I assumed to be Mrs. McConnell. I couldn't pull my gaze away from her. A faded dress hung on narrow shoulders. Her bones must have been as fragile as a sparrow's. How did that kind of woman live five years in such a place as Africa? Had she trekked through a jungle? Encountered a witch doctor? Seen lives changed by the gospel?

What courage it took to board a ship for the unknown, to live among the natives of another land! What a thrill to be entrusted by God with such work! No matter what else happened this day, I knew I had to meet Ava McConnell.

My tongue whisked over my dry lips as I forced my attention back to her husband, his long fingers slowly turning the pages of his Bible.

"Mark, chapter six," he announced.

A familiar passage—Jesus sending out the disciples by twos, without money belt or extra clothes. Grandmother and I had journeyed through the Bible together many times, her reading to me as a child, me reading to her when her eyesight faded to black. My toes pressed against the floor as Mr. McConnell read the verses and then began to speak about his mission.

"Mrs. McConnell and I felt the call of God to go to the Gold Coast even before our marriage." He looked toward his wife. The love shining from his eyes twisted my heart. I'd yet to meet a man my parents and I both approved of, let alone one whose eyes reflected such adoration. Mrs. McConnell nodded sweetly. Her husband lifted his gaze to wander over the rest of us.

He talked of men and women mired in superstition and pagan rituals. Of punishment meted out to those who befriended the white strangers. One village chief fell ill after their arrival. The witch doctor blamed the McConnells for bringing bad spirits. My lungs refused to draw in air as he told how none of the witch doctor's potions and charms brought relief to the chief. Then he and Mrs. McConnell had entered the hut and prayed. The chief recovered, and though he hadn't yet embraced Jesus, he'd released his people to do so if they wished.

"Jesus has sent us to proclaim the gospel to the Ashanti people in Africa. We live trusting God to provide everything necessary to that work. Money. Food. Clothing. Even the words to speak in each moment."

My heartbeat quickened. Oh, to be called to be such a vital part of God's work! He wouldn't even have to send me to Africa, though the thought sent a shiver of excitement down my spine. No, I'd be content to work for Him here in Indiana. I glimpsed Mrs. Tillman closer to the front. Her face reflected the same rapture that pulsed through my veins.

"Thanks to a friend who secured some photographic equipment, you can see some of those who are part of our work in Africa." Mr. McConnell slipped several photographs from the pages of his Bible. He stepped to the front row and handed two to Pastor Swan and two to Mr. Tillman on the opposite end of the front pew.

"One picture shows the young man who came to help us the very first day we arrived. We call him William. He lives with us now, though he is almost a grown man. And the little children playing beneath the banyan tree are Mrs. McConnell's students. She has learned enough of their language to teach them English. We hope one day they'll be able to read and understand the Bible."

My eyes followed the pictures as they passed from person to person. Would they disappear before I could hold them? My fingers refused to stay still. I clasped them together and pressed them to my lap. For a moment. Then they wandered again, worrying over the folds of my skirt, the fringe on my purse, the pages of my Bible.

Finally the photographs landed in my hands. Breathless, I studied the dark faces. A group of men sat in a semicircle. A length of cloth draped the shoulder or circled the waist of each, dangling into a wrapped skirtlike garment. My cheeks heated. I told myself to look away from the scantily clad men who faced the camera. But I couldn't. The lack of hope in their steely eyes clawed at my heart.

I slid the photo to the back of the stack. Two little girls squatted at the edge of a trickle of water, bodies scarcely covered, faces serious. And William between them—at least I assumed so, given the toothy grin, the life-filled eyes. I swiped my thumb across his face, wishing I could see his joy in person. Joy that wouldn't be his if the McConnells hadn't gone to Africa in the first place. I pushed out my breath, trying to release the tight band of emotion constricting my chest. But it cinched tighter, surging into my throat and threatening to spill out of my eyes.

Mr. Trotter nudged my arm. I held out the photos. The minute they left my hand, I yearned to hold them again.

Mr. Trotter gave them a cursory glance and passed them along.

My mouth dropped open before it pulled into a frown. How could he part with them so quickly? Didn't he see what I saw? Didn't he feel what I felt? I craned my neck to follow the progress of the photos, reading other faces to see if their reactions mirrored my own.

Compassion cloaked many faces. Others gave them only momentary attention.

I turned back to the front, tried to concentrate on Mr. McConnell's stories of God's faithfulness in their work. But my thoughts returned to the pictures, to the people. How could anyone remain unmoved?

Perhaps the images stirred some people so deeply they had to relinquish them quickly. Perhaps if they gave close attention to the faces, they'd be unable to mask their emotions. My spirit brightened. That had to be the explanation.

Satisfied, I settled back in my seat to listen.

"Will you pray for us as we are away from our work? It is difficult but necessary. And by the grace of God, we'll return to Africa soon." He bowed his head, as did the others around me.

But I couldn't force my eyes shut. The earnestness that clenched his features as he talked to God held me fast—at least until my focus roamed to Mrs. McConnell. Clasped hands. Lips moving in silent supplication. Such obvious devotion. Such willing sacrifice. A lump rose in my throat as the pictures loomed again in my mind.

Pastor Swan stood before us again. I blinked my surprise. Had Mr. McConnell walked from the stage or been whisked back to his seat by the Spirit of God?

"What John will not tell you is that he and his wife are trusting the Lord to raise the money they need to return to their work among the Africans of the Gold Coast. They need money not only for their return passage but also to build a church for the new believers, to help educate the men who desire to lead the young congregation, and to feed and clothe those who have little resources of their own."

His gaze swept over the entire church, front pew to back,

one side to the other. "Will you commit to support them? Will you help the gospel go forth in word and in deed?"

My feet danced. My hands trembled. I squeezed my eyes shut, but African faces appeared before me, both the ones who needed Jesus and the one who had already found Him.

My eyes flew open. Money. I had money. Or rather, Father did. Why else would God have placed me in such a family if not to use its resources for His kingdom?

Like an automobile leaping into a full-throttled run, I sprang to my feet. My fingers clamped the back of the pew in front of me. "I can help, Pastor Swan."

His face tinged pink as he looked at me. My stomach somersaulted, but my mouth refused to stop. "I'll give three thousand dollars to Mr. McConnell's mission." I whirled to face the congregation. "Will you join me? Will each of you give something toward this important work of God? With our gifts together, we could present Mr. and Mrs. McConnell with a total of six thousand dollars to help bring Christ to the world."

Gasps sounded from every corner of the room. Wide eyes stared back at me, no less startled than if I'd declared an intention to travel to Africa myself. My knees shook under the weight of my words.

Three thousand dollars? Six thousand dollars? I doubted any of these people could fathom such amounts, though three thousand dollars would represent little hardship to my father. He'd spent near that amount on my Packard and his Mercer. Certainly Mother spent at least that much in a year on clothes and charity events and travel to and from Chicago. I peeked down at Mr. Trotter, anxious for his encouragement. But his jaw hung open, glazed eyes peering into mine.

"Such a . . . generous offer, Miss Benson," Pastor Swan stammered as I spun to face him again. Mrs. Tillman gaped back at me, her face seeming to reflect both admiration and concern. I brushed a cluster of curls from my face as I quashed momentary misgivings.

With a turn of my head, I found Ava McConnell's shining black eyes fixed on mine. The gratitude in them weakened my knees, until a tug at my sleeve drew my attention.

Mr. Trotter cleared his throat, patted my place on the pew. I eased down, eager for the service to be dismissed. I needed to meet the McConnells and explain how much I admired and appreciated their service to the Lord.

"You've landed yourself in quite a quagmire, Miss Alyce." Mr. Trotter's whisper tickled my ear. "Have you forgotten that your father despises all things religious?"

I turned in his direction. "Except for his daughter." I kept my voice low as my lips curled into a smile. Mr. Trotter appeared unmoved. I shook away his concern. He handled Father's accounts. Yet I knew my father far better than he did. Father supported Mother's charitable causes without question. I couldn't think of a reason he'd refuse to support mine.

2

Mrs. Tillman beat me to the McConnells. She gushed out details of her own work facilitating the spread of the gospel through the Women's Mission Auxiliary. I tapped my foot. Stared out the window. Blew an errant wisp of hair from my forehead.

Mr. Tillman crept up behind his wife, a mask of doubt covering his pasty face. When he tapped her on the arm, she hesitated, her mouth puckering with displeasure for a split second. Then it smoothed into a smile.

"If you'll excuse me?" She nodded to each McConnell in turn. "Such a pleasure to meet you."

I stepped forward before she'd finished her exit, extending my hand first to Mr. McConnell and then to his wife. "I'm pleased to meet you both."

Mrs. McConnell's plain features lit with joy as our eyes met again. Without hesitation, I threw my arms around her slight body. She chuckled as she pressed her small hands against my back. When I pulled away, Pastor Swan stood beside me.

My cheeks heated. "I never meant to disrupt the service. Will you forgive me?"

"No need to apologize, dear." The pastor's eyes wrinkled at the corners. "I see you've met John and Ava."

We all answered yes.

"Good. Good." His head bobbed a period at the end of each word. "Then I guess we ought to discuss the details of your generous offer toward their work."

"Of course." I glanced over my shoulder. Mr. Trotter hovered behind our group. I stepped aside, motioned him into our circle of conversation. "Mr. Trotter, please meet Mr. and Mrs. McConnell."

While the men shook hands and exchanged greetings, I gave closer study to Ava McConnell's face. Despite her sallow complexion, her eyes shone with energy and delight.

She inched closer to me. "I pray the Lord will richly bless you, Miss—"

"Alyce." I grasped her thin hands as if she and I had already shared years of friendship. "Alyce Benson."

"Alyce." Her smile warmed me to my toes. "But surely you didn't intend to offer such an exorbitant sum."

I glanced at Pastor Swan, a grin playing at my lips. "Oh, but I did. How could I not after seeing those faces?" I pressed my hand over my heart.

Tears welled in Mrs. McConnell's eyes. She reached for her husband's Bible and slipped one of the photographs from its pages. She stared at it for a moment and then held it out to me. "These are three of my favorite children in the village."

I smiled down at them, wishing I could wrap my arms around their little bodies. "They are beautiful." I pushed the photo back in her direction.

She held out her palms. "No, please. Keep it. Pray for them—and for us."

I dropped to the pew as my heart burst into a million pieces at such an extravagant gift. "Oh, Mrs. McConnell! Are you sure?"

She perched beside me, nodding. "I'm sure. I would only give those precious faces to someone I felt cared about them as I do. And please, call me Ava. We're friends now."

I pressed the photo to my chest, unable to voice my gratitude on both counts.

Her spindly fingers rested on my knee as she lowered her voice. "But Alyce, are you sure about the money?"

Laughter spilled out of my full heart. "Please don't worry on that score, Ava. My father owns Benson Farm Machinery here in Langston. He'll be happy to help with your work in Africa."

Joy radiated from her face. "Then we must thank him personally." She pushed up on her toes and stretched her neck to search the thinning crowd.

My stomach clenched as I rose. "My father doesn't actually . . . attend church."

Ava's heels settled back onto the ground, but her smile never wavered. No pity sprang into her eyes. My twinge of anxiety fell away.

"Be assured, then, that I will pray for your father, Alyce. His generosity will accomplish much in our small corner of Africa. And I know the Lord will reward His faithful steward for sowing an abundance into the work of the Lord."

My smile sagged into a frown. She didn't understand. Father wasn't a steward of the Lord. He didn't yet recognize his need for a savior, let alone a Lord and master. I knew myself to be a servant of the Lord, but I had nothing of my own to give. Nothing but what I received from my father.

"How long will it take to arrange the transfer of money, Miss Benson?" Pastor Swan asked.

Mr. Trotter cleared his throat, gave me a pointed look. I tried to dismiss him, but he cleared his throat again. More loudly this time.

What if it took some special action to retrieve the money—something I didn't understand? Was that what Mr. Trotter was trying to tell me? I certainly didn't want to look foolish in front of these men. "I don't know. I mean, it might take a little while."

Mr. Trotter relaxed. There. I'd read him correctly. I'd speak with him to understand the details, and then we could move forward. I sucked in a breath, ready to excuse myself from the gathering to confer with Mr. Trotter.

Mr. McConnell waved one of his large hands. "I can provide you with our bank's information. I assume there wouldn't be a problem with a wire transfer." His gaze landed on mine.

I turned to Mr. Trotter. His eyes stretched wide as red splotched his face. I stepped in front of him, blocking his agitation from my new friends. As I did, my mind whirled with other possibilities. A celebration of God's provision. A way to expose others to the work of the gospel around the world. "I'd hoped we could present the money to you in person. Couldn't you stay a few days longer?"

Mr. McConnell wagged his head. "I wish we could. I sincerely do. But we haven't time to spare. We are expected at another church, in Illinois, this evening." He pulled out his pocket watch. "We must catch the train in less than an hour."

My excitement wilted. I didn't want to send the money to a bank. Not when I'd felt such a connection to the McConnells and the people they served in the Gold Coast. I wanted to feel the transfer of funds from my hands to theirs.

Pastor Swan's face brightened. "Perhaps you could stop by on your way back to New York, at the end of your visit to the States. That would allow my congregation time to meet Miss Benson's challenge to match her generous offering. We could boast publicly of the Lord's faithfulness and provision."

Mr. McConnell's deep laughter rumbled through the almost-empty room as warm breath spewed down the back of my neck. Fingers jerked my elbow. I turned my head just a bit, my voice low, my lips barely moving. "Thank you for your help, Mr. Trotter. I'm sure I can handle things from here."

Mr. Trotter's eyes narrowed as he stepped away, his shoes echoing up the aisle and out the door.

"I think that's a fine plan." Mr. McConnell slapped Pastor Swan on the back, nearly catapulting him into the front pew.

I fought back a giggle as the missionary pulled a diary and pencil from his pocket. "September twenty-fourth should work," he said. "We hope to be on a ship back to Africa by the end of that month."

"Lord willing," Ava breathed.

September. I counted quickly. Seven weeks for the people of our church to raise three thousand dollars. Father would provide our part and then I'd help the others raise the rest. How providential that I'd just offered a list of ideas to Mrs. Tillman that very morning. Bubbles of joy tickled laughter from my mouth.

The Lord had obviously prepared me for this day and this day for me.

Now I just needed to speak with Father.

My heart soared as my foot pressed the pedal on the floor, urging the car homeward with small adjustments to the throttle and spark plugs. Moments later, I turned off the main road and motored down the brick drive running beneath the porte cochere of our Italianate home. The doors of the old carriage house stood open at the end of the path.

I motored inside. Father's Mercer, silent and clean, sat to my right, beside a shell of a racing car Webster Little was building. I parked the Packard between the Mercer and the workbench attached to the wall. My engine fell silent. I gathered my things, banged the Packard's door shut, and grimaced. Earth clung to the paint of my car, transforming its gleaming white to the color of my morning toast and muting the bright red trim. I latched the carriage-house doors shut with a grin. Webster would likely shake his head and ask how fast I'd traveled before scrubbing every inch of the motorcar and checking it for damage.

Handbag swinging from my wrist, I sauntered through the ornamental gardens at the back of the house. Velvety petals drew my nose to their sweet scent and reminded me again that a sacrifice of obedience such as I'd offered that morning rose as a pleasing fragrance before the Lord. I hurried up the steps and into the kitchen, grasped our cook around the waist, and spun a circle before letting her free.

Clarissa shook her wooden spoon at me, but I recognized the smile tugging at the corner of her mouth.

"It's a glorious day, Clarissa!" I dashed into the hall, up the curved staircase, and into Grandmother's bedroom, my feet almost dancing.

I placed my Bible and handbag on a small table and leaned down to kiss Grandmother's soft cheek before thudding into my usual chair beside her bed. She reached for me. I clasped her hand tight.

"I wish you could have been at church today, Grandmother.

A missionary came and spoke about his work in Africa. He and his wife live in the Gold Coast. They teach the people about Jesus, as well as meet other needs in the remote villages. It was the most wonderful thing I've ever heard."

Releasing her hand, I fumbled through the pages of my Bible for the photograph. "I wish you could see this picture Ava gave me." I leaned in, elbows sinking into the mattress. "Two little girls and a little boy, all sitting in front of a massive tree, its arms spread out over them, shielding them from the sun. Their faces are dark, but their eyes and teeth gleam white. There are grass huts in the background. Ava teaches them. She said these are some of her favorites."

Grandmother's mouth curved upward, as I knew it would.

"I've never heard such wonderful stories in all my life. And the photographs! There were several more. I feel so honored that they let me keep one. To remember." With a sigh, I leaned against the back of the cane-seated chair, wishing I could loosen my stays and be more comfortable. But sharing my enjoyment of the photograph eased the pinch of my corset.

"I can just imagine those sweet children, Ally. But your enthusiasm over them worries me a bit."

Laying aside the photo, I scooted my chair closer to the bed.

Her head tipped to one side as she stared unseeingly at me. "What have you done?"

I crossed my arms in a huff. "How do you know I've done anything at all?"

She giggled, her wrinkled face transforming into an expression of childlike wonder. "Because you've been on a desperate search for adventure ever since you were a tiny thing. Remember when we had to get the fire wagon's long ladder to help you down from the old oak by the creek?" She shook her head. "No one ever imagined you'd climb up so high."

I smiled in spite of myself. Mother had swooned right there under the tree.

"And when you put yourself between those two ducks, one wing in each hand, and jumped out of the old hayloft? That time you were certainly old enough to know better!"

The doctor had shaken his head, too, as he fastened a harness around my arm to keep it still while the bones healed. But those few minutes in the air had been worth all the pain. "Scoot over, Granny. I'll tell you everything."

Grandmother felt her way to the far edge of the bed. I sat beside her, feather pillows propping us upright, her head not quite reaching my shoulder.

"As I said, Mr. McConnell explained to us about his and his wife's work in western Africa. Such splendid work. Then he passed around photographs of the people there, and my heart cracked like an old mirror. I knew I had to help."

Grandmother sucked in a sharp breath. "Tell me you aren't going to Africa, child."

My heart leapt. Would the Lord see fit to bring me a missionary man some day? We might sail far across the ocean, to lands I knew only as a spot on the globe. Closing my eyes, I could almost feel the hot breeze of Africa, smell the loamy jungle.

I rested my cheek against the top of Grandmother's head. "I wish God did have some exciting work for me to do. But no, I'm not going to Africa. Though it does sound . . ."

A lump in my throat halted the words. Tears stung my eyes as I felt her nod. We sat in silence, as we so often had, neither of us needing to speak. Grandmother read my heart like no one else. She'd understand what I'd done. I drew in as deep a breath as my clothing would allow. "Pastor Swan asked if our congregation would give to the McConnells' African mission."

Mr. Trotter's face appeared in my mind, suddenly leaving me wary and desperate for air. Grandmother's tiny hand lay near mine. I laced my fingers through hers. "I told them I'd give three thousand dollars."

Grandmother bolted upright, head knocking my chin, hands groping until they held my cheeks between them. "Three thousand dollars?"

I nodded.

"Ally, honey. Where are you going to get that kind of money?"

I pulled away. "I'm going to ask Father, of course."

"*Your* father?" Her hands released my face and kneaded into each other.

I tilted my head, fingers raking through the curls that bobbed above my shoulders. Grandmother had great faith. Always. For everything. Most of all, she had faith that her son and daughter-in-law would do the impossible—see their need of Christ before their days on earth ended. So why did she not have the faith that Father would give me the money?

I hiked up my skirt and folded my legs beneath me. "The Lord will soften Father's heart. I know He will. After all, this is for His work."

Her face didn't change. Her hands didn't stop. "I don't know, Alyce. I'm not sure—" Her voice faded as I climbed from the bed. Touching the photograph now lying atop my Bible, I sighed. "I might as well tell you the rest."

"There's more?" Her voice trilled higher, like the treble keys on the piano in the drawing room downstairs.

"I asked the church members to match my contribution."

Grandmother fell back into the pillows behind her, her unseeing eyes staring at the ceiling. "Three thousand dollars? Most of those people can barely provide for their own families, Ally."

A smidgen of doubt wiggled in my belly. "Some will be able to do more than others. And I know the Women's Mission Auxiliary will take this on as their special project. God will provide. I know He will."

But even I recognized the lack of conviction in my voice. Three thousand dollars. Most of the families couldn't afford the three hundred dollars that would buy them a Model T. What had I been thinking?

Trembling hands pressed against my souring stomach. I'd done what the Lord had desired me to do. I knew I had.

Or at least I believed I had.

Until now.

3

"Ally!" Father's voice boomed up the stairs the next morning as I pulled on my shoes, silencing the chirping birds outside my windows. But in spite of the volume, his tone conveyed affection, not a flash of temper.

Good thing, too. For I'd opened my eyes at dawn and reached for the photograph of the African children. Sitting up in bed, I'd pulled my knees nearer to my chest as their young eyes pierced my very soul.

"Draw them to Yourself, O Lord. Bring light into their darkness. The fields are white unto harvest and Your workers are willing." A tide of emotion shut my lips. I knew John and Ava McConnell would strive to meet these children's physical and spiritual needs. But they needed money to aid their endeavors. And I could provide that. Had Father ever denied me anything I'd asked?

But the timing hadn't seemed right yesterday, during our customary Sunday drive. So I rehearsed my speech as I dressed. I hurried downstairs, met Father in the foyer. His hand tapped the banister. The minute he saw me, a grin covered his entire face.

I kissed his cheek. "Good morning, Father. Ready for Clarissa's good breakfast?"

His sniff of the air in the dining room as we entered told me all I needed to know.

"Where's Mother?"

"I imagine she'll be down soon." He took his place at the head of the table while I filled a plate for him from the sideboard before filling my own.

He tucked a napkin beneath his chin and then sawed off a piece of steak, stabbed it with his fork, and raised it to his mouth. His eyes closed as he chewed and then swallowed.

"Clarissa!" His voice echoed through the room, shaking the crystal droplets on the wedding-cake chandelier above the table. Clarissa charged in from the butler's pantry, her freckled face blazing as red as her hair.

"Somethin' the matter, Mr. Benson?" Her slight Irish lilt made her words seem polite, though I recognized her irritation.

"A fine breakfast." He chuckled, his ample stomach shaking.

She pursed her lips, bobbed a curtsy, and returned to the kitchen.

Nothing more than their usual morning interaction. As a child I'd cried when he shouted her name. But over the years I noticed that in spite of the abruptness of his tone, not once did he criticize her cooking. In fact, several times he'd upped her pay on the spot.

I slipped into the chair on Father's right. My mouth watered at the sight of the fluffy scrambled eggs and strips of crisp fried bacon on my plate. I bit into a biscuit and let my napkin catch the butter dripping down my chin.

"Alyce, did you learn nothing at that school?" Mother seemed to float into the chair at the opposite end of the table from Father with a grace I could never manage for myself. She sighed as I reached for the coffeepot and filled her cup. "And what in heaven's name are you wearing?"

I shrugged. "I picked it up in Chicago."

"Really, Alyce. Where on earth did you find a frock so drab?"

"It's quite the fashion, Mother." I smoothed my skirt over my legs. White crepe with sprigs of pink flowers, a pink sash at the waist, and pink shell buttons up the bibbed front. I liked this dress, liked how I felt . . . normal in it. At least as normal as the daughter of the wealthiest man in town could feel.

Mother's manicured eyebrows seemed to rise as high as the ornate ceiling above our heads. "Fashionable with your church people, I suppose. I can't imagine your classmates succumbing to such an ordinary costume." She rested her elbows on the table, her chin alighting on her clasped hands. The Venetian lace at her wrists fluttered like butterfly wings before settling on the sleeves of her silk dress.

I fought the downward tug on my lips. What she'd paid for her dress might feed a Gold Coast village for a month. A dress she didn't even deem worthy of a public wearing. And yet she constantly devoted her time to the charitable efforts of her ladies' club, so I had to believe she cared about someone besides herself. She'd had nothing when she became Father's wife. Couldn't I excuse a bit of self-indulgence?

"Leave her be, Winifred." Father spoke from behind Saturday's edition of the *Indianapolis Star*. He reached for his coffee, took a long draught, and returned the cup to its place on the table. "We don't want to run her off after we've just got her home again."

Mother opened her mouth to reply.

"Anything interesting in the paper?" I jumped into the silence as I watched Mother from the corner of my eye. Then I popped a bite of scrambled eggs into my mouth.

"War in Europe. Presidential election. The usual." He turned another page. "Oh—here's something you'll like. They held an automobile race in Tacoma, Washington, on Saturday."

I ceased to notice the food I forked into my mouth. Instead, images of speeding motorcars and swirling smoke filled my head and quickened my pulse. "Who drove?"

"Rickenbacker. De Palma. A few others."

"Board track or dirt?" I gulped down half of my tepid coffee in excitement.

"Board. Cracks filled with gravel instead of left open."

"Wonder if that was to Rick's disadvantage."

Father snorted and turned another page. "Doubt it. Eddie Rickenbacker's a natural. Guess the results will be in the paper today."

Thanks to the interurban, the *Indianapolis Star* arrived in Langston just a few short hours after the ink dried.

"Alyce." Mother sighed my name.

My stomach tumbled, regretting its desire for food. Why did her disapproval affect me so?

She turned her irritation on Father. "Really, Harry. Do you think it proper for a girl of her age and station to converse about such things? It's bad enough that you allow her to drive. And then keep us in this backwater town with no eligible men to court her. Must you fill her head with auto racing, as well?"

I couldn't quell my grin. I felt sure merriment twinkled in my eyes, too. So I kept my gaze pinned on Father.

He chuckled. "Say what you will, Winifred, but if her

attention to racing keeps your Chicago dandies away from her, all the better."

My silent mirth gave way to heated cheeks. I pressed my linen napkin to my mouth. Oh, to escape the conversation that replayed like a phonograph record in my head. It had started the day of my thirteenth birthday, Mother insisting I learn feminine accomplishments and leave off diving from haylofts and climbing trees—and driving my own motorcar and talking about auto races. Those things, she insisted, invited scandal, not suitors. Without Father's indulgence all these years, I imagine I would have suffocated long ago.

Father folded the newspaper and set it aside. "I don't intend to give my girl to just any young swell that comes along. And I won't let you foist on her a man who's only interested in her inheritance."

Money. Africa. I folded my napkin and stared into my lap, preparing to make my request. Father had championed me once this morning—would he do so again? I shot a quick prayer heavenward before addressing him.

"Yes, my girl?" He hummed a bit of a tune as he finished his breakfast.

I took a deep breath. "I need some money."

"Money?" He reached inside his jacket, pulled out his wallet, and tossed a bill on the table. "Will that do you for a few pretties?"

President Grover Cleveland's face stared up at me, *Twenty Dollars* inscribed beneath his name. "Actually, I need a bit more than that."

He chuckled and wagged his index finger at me. "I knew you'd catch on to your mother's schemes one of these days."

Mother rolled her eyes and excused herself from the room as he picked up the money, slipped it back into his wallet, and returned the wallet to his pocket. "Just charge what you need. I'll cover the bill."

I jumped from my seat, my hand restraining Mother's exit. "Wait, Mother. You should hear this, too."

She stopped, returned to her chair, and pushed her half-empty plate toward the center of the table.

I clasped my hands behind me. "It isn't clothes, Father. Or anything like that."

His left eyebrow rose, giving his face a lopsided look. "Not tired of the Packard already, are you?"

I shook my head.

His eyebrows sank into a deep V. "Smashed it up, did you?"

"Alyce!" Mother bolted upright.

Father shook his head. "I always knew you would one day. Can't drive as fast as you like to without losing control at some point."

"My Packard is fine. It's just that I need . . ." My throat constricted around the largeness of the number. "I need three thousand dollars."

Mother gasped.

"Three thousand dollars?" Father pulled the square of linen from its place in his collar. "What in heaven's name for?"

"Wait here. I'll show you." Before either could protest, I dashed up the stairs, grabbed the picture from my Bible, and scurried back to the dining room.

I slapped it to the table. "There."

Both of my parents moved closer, peered down into the faces that lived vivid in my memory.

"Why, they're children." Concern etched itself around Mother's painted lips.

"What does this mean, Ally?" Father's grumble stirred the breakfast in my stomach once again.

"A man and his wife who work in Africa came to our church yesterday. They live among the people in a place called the Gold Coast. In Africa. People with little to wear, little to eat." I held my tongue before mentioning their need for Jesus. "I want to give three thousand dollars to help advance their work."

Silence.

Mother dropped back into her chair. Father paced in front of the tall windows.

"That charlatan Swan put you up to this." Tight words, portending a storm of great force.

I flinched but didn't retreat. "No, sir. This was my idea."

He stopped pacing and faced me. "Well, it was a blame-fool one. I hear what you're not saying, Ally. They're over there touting religion to those unsuspecting people. I won't be a party to it." He stalked toward the door.

I hurried after him. "But, Father, everyone's expecting it."

He froze, then turned. "What do you mean everyone's expecting it? Who thinks you have that kind of money?"

"Everyone at church." I moistened my lips. "I told them I'd give three thousand dollars to help fund the work."

"You did what?" His face turned the color of a ripe strawberry as his voice rose, the full fury of the storm lashing out. "Let me tell you, missy, not one cent of my hard-earned money is going toward this foolishness. Do you hear? If you're so all-fired determined to participate in this scheme, you'll have to scavenge for that money yourself. And don't even think about wheedling it from your mother!"

My mouth dropped open as he charged out of the room. Not since the day when Grandmother told him of my walk down the aisle at church had I seen him so angry.

The front door slammed shut, tinkling the chandelier overhead. I sank back into my chair and groaned as Mother swished from the room after throwing me a disapproving look, but whether she resented my request or my making Father angry, I couldn't tell.

The silence made my thoughts loud. Where in the world would I find three thousand dollars? And how would I ever face my church again if I didn't?

The swinging door creaked open.

"You can come in now, Clarissa." I slumped a bit toward the table, my chin resting in my upturned hands like Mother's had not long ago.

Clarissa bustled into the room, shaking her head and *tsk*ing under her breath. "You barely ate a thing." She whisked my plate from the table and set it atop my father's empty one.

"I'll work up an appetite for lunch. I promise. Maybe Grandmother will even feel up to coming to the table with me."

Silverware clinked against china. "Don't you worry, Miss Alyce. The Lord will provide, especially once your grandmother gets wind to pray." A broad grin lit Clarissa's freckled face as she pushed her backside against the door into the pantry, hands piled high with dirty dishes.

Grandmother's prayers. Normally a comforting thought. But even Grandmother didn't have the faith to believe the Lord would change my father's heart this time.

4

My shoes clicked across the stone path leading through the back garden and around the small gazebo in its center. The varied blooms didn't catch my eye, though their scents trailed after me. Questions zipped through my head like cars racing around a track, demanding my attention. But I couldn't think. Not here. I needed the wind knotting my curls, fields and trees whizzing past in a blur. Then my mind could relax. Then I'd hear the voice of the Lord explaining where I'd gone wrong.

The trunks of waving green-leafed tulip poplar trees stood guard around the end of the red carriage house—Father's long-ago concession to Mother's insistence that the building's presence, however necessary, ruined the ambiance of her garden. Leaving the path, I traipsed across the grass, dew wetting the ankles of my stockings.

One of the large double doors angled open. I slipped into the dim interior, shivering in air still tinged with cool from the darkness of night. In my girlhood, the pungent smell of horseflesh hovered over this place. Now the perfume of gasoline and oil filled my nose. Instead of a pony, my Packard Runabout sat in the shadows. A kitten of a car. This morning I needed a tiger.

"Webster?" My eyes searched the shadows. An empty spot told me Father had left for work. And there, huddled next to the far wall, sat an unpainted auto body covering a powerful engine. I drew in a deep breath. Father's racing car. He'd hired Webster to build it and to maintain our other autos, as well as to repair broken machinery at the plant.

I ran my hand over one of the leather straps holding the engine's cover secure, stroking it like the back of a well-loved cat.

"A beauty, ain't she?" Webster Little wiped the grease from his fingers before shoving the dirty rag into the back pocket of his overalls. He pushed up the flat brim of his cloth driving cap. A lock of dark hair escaped, sweeping across his broad forehead, above his dusky eyes. His wide mouth split into a grin, coaxing one from me, as well.

I wondered how many hearts that grin had broken. Not intentionally, of course. Webster didn't seem to be that type. But for a man I suspected to be near my age and unmarried, it wasn't hard to fathom.

My fingers curled around the steering wheel and then slid onto the crude seat. "You got the body on her."

"I did. Once we hit a hundred miles an hour up that hill, I knew it was time."

I frowned. "I wish you'd have let me drive it that day."

"With just the engine on a frame and a crate wired to it for a seat? I don't think so. Your father would have killed me with his bare hands if he'd found out."

I ran a hand around the circle that would steer the powerful car. When I looked up, he stared down at me, his visage open and honest. Would he be willing to risk Father's ire now? "I could drive her today."

Webster's head swayed like a disapproving schoolteacher's. "Ally, I told you. Your father's not—"

"I need to drive her. Please?" I clasped my hands in front of my chest, knuckles whitening. "Father needn't know."

One of his eyebrows rose. "Because no one will notice a half-built racing car tearing up the roads. Or a woman behind its wheel."

"Not if we take her out to the track." I plucked an old duster from a nail on the wall, thankful I'd traded my Sunday corset for a newfangled brassiere. I buttoned the duster over my simple dress before settling a pair of goggles on top of my head. "You coming or not?"

"Ally, you can't—" His nostrils flared, but his eyes twinkled. He grabbed another pair of goggles. "I'm certainly not letting you take it out alone." He jogged to the doors, pushed them open wide, and met me behind the car. We rolled her into the open before he cranked the engine to life. The roar reverberated through my head. And with every rumble, my excitement climbed.

Webster shut the doors of the carriage-house-turned-garage and hopped in beside me. I eased the auto into gear and puttered down the brick drive. We moved slowly at first, past the house and onto the hard dirt road out front. I turned left, away from town.

"Hold on." I eased off the clutch and let the gas out a bit.

"Don't let 'er go till we hit the track," Webster called out over the engine's noise.

I nodded, both hands on the wheel.

"So what happened?" Webster laced his hands behind his head and slouched lazily in the seat beside me.

I raised my voice above the din. "I asked Father for some money."

"Money for what?" he shouted over the motor and the wind.

A small gap appeared in the tall grass of a fallow field. My foot jammed down on the brake pedal as I jerked left, into the wheel ruts. The uneven path threatened to jolt me from the car. I gripped the wheel more tightly, focused all my effort on maintaining control of the car as the path carried us toward the back of Father's property.

A clump of trees to my left drew nearer. Waving grass obscured the half-mile dirt oval from any but those who knew of it. Father. Me. And Webster.

No errant stones or holes marred the surface of the track. Webster must have been here recently. I motored onto the more level surface. Spark plugs firing fast, gas flowing without restraint, we surged forward.

The first turn came quickly. I eased off my speed and held us steady, eyes locked on the straightaway. Then we gained speed again.

Three laps around the oval. I shifted gears once more. We flew forward, the speedometer inching up toward fifty miles per hour as Webster squeezed the bulb of the pump beside him to send more oil to the engine.

The sun rose higher, transforming the moist coolness of morning into sultry summer air that slammed against my cheeks and tangled curls about my face.

"Sixty-seven," I yelled, glancing at Webster and pointing to the speedometer. A grin stretched across his face, shoving his round cheeks closer to his goggled eyes. I hunched over the steering wheel, head low, eyes on the path slipping beneath my tires.

"Watch the curve." Webster's voice sounded far away. I

eased back just a bit on the gas and pressed the brake as I rounded the far end of the track.

Then, with another straight stretch before me, we shot forward, even faster than before. I peeked down. The needle quivered at seventy-two. My breath caught in my throat as a thrill shivered down my spine. Could I go faster? Heart pounding, I rested my thumb on the lever in the center of the steering wheel.

Webster's hand appeared on top of mine. He wanted me to slow down. Rounding the track once more, I moderated the spark plugs, the gas, employed the brake, until finally, after another lap, we ambled off across the field and arrived at the real road once more. I turned the car opposite of home and tooled along at a respectable twenty miles per hour.

I looked at Webster. He raised his eyebrows in question as he slung his arm across the back of the seat. "What'd it register?"

"Over seventy. I had to look quick."

He whistled. "Felt like it. Turn here." He pointed to a small trail on the right.

I eased the auto onto another bumpy road. Little more than wagon tracks, really. The trees thinned, opening into a small clearing on the bank of a brook. I killed the engine, tore off my goggles, and unbuttoned my duster as the roar in my ears gave way to the soothing sound of water gurgling over rocks. As soon as my limbs quit trembling, I intended to make good use of the liquid on my dirty face and parched throat.

As if reading my mind, Webster climbed from the car and knelt at the edge of the stream. With a cupped hand, he drank from the clear water before splashing it over his face and hair and neck and shaking himself dry like a common mongrel. He slapped his cap against one leg. Dust flew up in a cloud before he settled himself at the base of a tree and leaned against the wide trunk. "You never did answer my question, you know."

"Your question?" My muscles tensed. I stood at the edge of the creek and removed my duster. Relief flowed over me as a breeze cooled my skin and rustled the leaves that shaded me from the sun. I drank the clean air into my lungs and then leaned down to scoop cold water into my mouth.

"About the money." A handkerchief dangled in front of my face.

I reached for it, but it fluttered away. Then it appeared again—along with Webster's laugh. My fingers caught the edge, gave it a playful tug. He yanked back, but I held firm, both of us grinning. I rocked back on my heels, ready to push to my feet. His smile disappeared. He let go of the handkerchief and returned to his place on the ground.

Confusion twisted my face as I soaked the cloth and swiped it over my grimy skin. Had I done something wrong? I rinsed the cloth and wiped my face a second time, less to make myself presentable than to give me time to think, to compose myself, before facing my friend again.

A fish wiggled by, hurrying downstream, making me think of God and His creations. Above all that He had fashioned, He loved mankind most. White and black. American and African. I wrung water from the handkerchief, concentrated on the droplets returning to their source. Would Webster censure my impetuous donation as Mr. Trotter, Grandmother, and Father had?

I folded the saturated fabric and stood, staring down at the rushing current. "The money's for a missionary."

"A missionary? How much did he get you for?"

I whipped around, fury pursing my lips and filling my chest. "He didn't 'get me' for anything. I offered it."

Silent laughter danced behind his eyes. He seemed to be enjoying my discomfort. Thoroughly.

My frustration melted. Dropping down on a patch of grass near him, I pulled at a blade that stood higher than the rest. "You should have seen the pictures, Webster. Men and women and children—especially the children—looking at the camera with such sad eyes. You could see their need so clearly. Need for food, for clothing. But mostly their need of Jesus." I bit my lip and looked up at him, wondering if my shattered heart showed plainly in my eyes.

His gaze held mine for only a moment. Then he looked away, cleared his throat, scratched the hard ground with a stick. "So how much?"

My hands fidgeted in my lap. His head rose and tipped to the left.

"Three thousand dollars." I leapt up and headed for the automobile. Webster had probably never held together more than a few hundred dollars in his life. Maybe not that much. If he had, wouldn't he have an automobile of his own by now?

He snorted. I glared in his direction.

"And your father wouldn't give it to you?"

I shook my head.

"So that's why you needed to drive."

A long breath streamed out through my mouth as my chest grew tight. I nodded. He knew me well.

"Just tell them you made a mistake. The money wasn't yours to give."

"I can't." I shrugged into the filthy duster and scampered back into the driver's seat.

"Why not?" He pushed up from the ground, swiping the dirt from his behind before positioning himself near the crank at the front of the car.

I studied the large driving gloves as I pulled them over my small fingers. "Because I told everyone I'd make the donation."

"Everyone, as in—?"

My fingers curved around the steering wheel. "The whole church." My voice fell to a whisper. "And I asked them to match my donation."

He whistled long and low. "That's some kind of predicament. Did you really think your father would give you that kind of money—for a missionary?"

"I hoped so. But obviously I was wrong." I yanked the goggles in front of my eyes before he cranked the engine. But my vision fogged. I lifted them again, wiped the moisture from the lenses, and breathed another prayer.

Webster plopped into the seat beside me. His face had lost its laughter.

"Oh, Webster. What am I going to do?"

He pressed his full lips together, the edges of his mouth fighting a rare downward turn. "Either tell them you don't have the money or find a way to get it."

I groaned. "That's what Father said, too." I rested my forehead on the steering wheel. "I can't get those kids out of my head. I see their little faces, and I know I have to help them." I raised up and looked him straight in the eyes. "I have to do this. It's more than just wanting to be part of God's work in this world. It's an aching hole in my heart. I don't know any other way to fill it."

My shoulders lifted and fell as the idling engine jiggled us. "How can I raise such an amount—and in only seven weeks?" I shook my head. "Father's money is the only thing I have. I must find a way to convince him to give it."

"Are you sure?"

Of course I was sure. My foot cramped on the brake. I put

the car in gear, motored down the little path, and turned onto the main road. I oughtn't to have expected more, I guessed. In the course of our two-year friendship, Webster had never mentioned God or attending church, though he'd never belittled my faith, either. He had no idea what it meant to obey the voice of the Lord. And yet he did seem to believe I could raise the money on my own.

The idea turned itself over in my head as we bounced up the drive beside the house and through the porte cochere. When we reached the garage, I pulled the handbrake, let the engine fall silent.

Webster unfolded himself from the car. "Leave it here. I'll need to clean 'er up a bit." His long legs carried him into the carriage house, out of sight.

The silence jarred, as unfamiliar as the new thoughts swirling around my head. Raise the funds myself. Was such a thing really possible? Behind the wheel of a motorcar, any goal seemed attainable. Just another challenge to meet.

Stripping off the coat and goggles, I returned them to the nail on the wall inside what used to be my pony's stall. And I remembered. Every time I fell from that pony's back, I brushed off my dress and climbed back on again. Was this really any different?

On my way back out into the light of day, I stopped beside the Packard. A girl couldn't spend her entire life behind the wheel of a car with the wind in her face. Sometimes she had to move on the strength of her own two feet.

5

After another quick wash of my face and hands and a change of clothes, I cajoled Betsy, the upstairs maid, into helping me maneuver Grandmother out of bed. With one of us on each side, we propped her upright. She weighed little more than a child. Either one of us might have carried her. But we both knew she'd hate that. Instead, she shuffled through the hall and down the stairs at a pace even a turtle would find tedious.

"Come now, Mrs. Benson, we're almost there." Betsy's childlike voice belied her forty-plus years.

Grandmother grimaced but nodded. I winced to see the pain so clearly in her face. Maybe this hadn't been such a good idea.

When we reached the dining room, her frail body relaxed into a chair, her hands searching for the table's edge. I took Mother's seat at the foot of the table rather than my usual place across from Grandmother.

"Thank you, Betsy."

Grandmother's head whipped toward the door, as if searching for the maid's location. "Yes, dear. Bless you for your help."

The woman bobbed a quick curtsy and returned to her work as Clarissa bustled in from the pantry, skirts swishing. She set a plate of delicate sandwiches before each of us, like the ones she served for Mother's occasional card parties. Grandmother groped for Clarissa's hand.

"Stay with us, dear, as we bless this good food."

Clarissa's face pinked, but she stayed. I bowed my head and dashed off a prayer.

Grandmother echoed my amen. "Thank you, Clarissa." She squeezed Clarissa's hand before letting her disappear into the kitchen.

My stomach suddenly felt as empty as a summer rain barrel. I finished off three small triangles of chicken salad slathered between slices of fresh-baked bread before Grandmother managed to eat even half of one. Without waiting, I dove into my saucer of fresh blackberries and sweet cream and almost licked it clean.

While Grandmother nibbled, I pushed my dishes away. "I talked to Father this morning."

Her face brightened, then fell. "About the money?"

"Yes. It didn't go very well."

"I'm not surprised." She took a long drink of the sweet lemonade beside her plate. I watched her feel the spot before setting the glass back down again. "I suppose you'll just have to explain it to Pastor Swan. Such a shame. But I'm sure the Lord will still provide for His worthy servants."

I fingered the rim of my own glass, staring at it as if it held every answer I longed for. "Maybe there's another way."

"Oh?" Her face turned toward me like a flower seeking the sun.

"I could raise the money myself." I picked up my lemonade, let its coolness slip down my throat, which burned as if the words had scorched it on their way out. Grandmother's face flickered through emotions, finally settling on excitement.

"I think it's a wonderful idea, Alyce. But what would you do? That is still a lot of money."

"I could ask people to donate, of course." I chewed on my lower lip. "Although they would have to be people who don't attend our church."

"That's true. Any other ideas?"

Twirling a short curl around my finger, I remembered the list I'd given Mrs. Tillman. Bake sale. Quilting bee. Even a picnic, complete with lemonade for sale and games set up to play at five cents each. I couldn't take back any of those ideas. Did I have anything else to offer?

My head involuntarily turned in the direction of the garage, even though I couldn't see it from where I sat.

The only other thing I knew how to do was drive.

My back stiffened, and I sucked in a breath.

"What is it, dear?"

"I just thought of something. What if I hired out my services as a driver?"

Her mouth turned downward. "Like a chauffeur?"

"Yes. Or even a taxicab, like in Chicago." I silently blessed Webster for watering the tiny seed that was now pushing through the ground of my mind and into the nurturing sunlight.

"I don't think your father would care much for that idea."

"Perhaps not. But he mentioned raising the money myself. I'd be acting on his instructions in the matter. Now if only I knew where to start . . ." My forehead crinkled as I demanded information from my brain.

"Start with your friends, dear."

"Right." Easier said than done. My few close friends in Chicago had no vast resources to seed my campaign. In spite of what Mother believed, I'd not befriended the society girls that came to my school to learn to run a household. I preferred the ones enrolled in domestic service courses. Hearty working girls. Friends who accepted me in spite of—not because of—my father's success. Girls with whom I often attended the Moody Church.

I rolled my fork through my fingers. "The girls I knew in high school are mostly married now, with little ones to tend and not much money or time to spare."

"That is true." Grandmother picked up another tiny sandwich, but then set it down again without a taste. "I wish I had some money of my own to offer you. Isn't there anyone else who would help?"

I pictured myself in town, sorting through faces as I would recipes while planning for a dinner party. One visage stopped me. Attentive. Concerned. Friendly.

Mr. Trotter.

He could help me advertise my driving services. After all, he and I shared a desire to see the gospel spread into all the world, did we not? Then again, he had seemed irritated with my pledge of money. Though perhaps he'd been offended because I hadn't included him in my scheme right off.

"Mr. Trotter will help me."

Grandmother's expression relaxed as she wiped her fingers on a napkin before pressing it to her lips. "See? I knew you'd think of someone." Her chair inched backward. "A lovely lunch, Ally, but I think I'm ready to rest now."

She wobbled to her feet. I reached her side in an instant, holding her upright, calling for Betsy to help me guide her back up the stairs and into her bed—though with the renewed energy of a solid plan, I probably could have whisked her up the stairs all by myself.

Gathering three thousand dollars still seemed a far-fetched prospect to me, but if Grandmother and Webster thought I could do it, maybe I could. And if it turned out I'd gone motoring down the wrong road, I'd trust God to step in and change my direction.

As I completed my household duties, I jotted down a list of businessmen in town who might be willing to pay for the services of a car and driver. Then on Wednesday morning I rang Father's office. But Mr. Trotter was out for the day. Replacing the earpiece on top of the wooden box, I pondered the options. Wait for his help or head out on my own? I scanned the list I held in my hand. Having Mr. Trotter's support would certainly boost my credibility. Or would he just make me feel less alone? As Harry Benson's only child, my name carried some weight in Langston. And the Lord would be with me, as well.

I charged upstairs and donned one of my more elegant costumes. A jacket-style dress with elbow-length sleeves and a feather-accented hat. At the last moment, I pinned Grandmother's cameo on my chest. If I couldn't employ her assistance, I could take some part of her with me.

The mirror confirmed my verdict. Feminine and refined, yet businesslike. Satisfied, I hurried to the garage and drove myself into town.

"What a generous heart you have, Mr. Morgan." I folded the bills that added up to a two-hundred-dollar donation and deposited them in my handbag. "You are storing up for yourself treasures in heaven, I feel sure. And don't forget, if you ever need to get somewhere in a hurry, just ring me up. Only fifty cents a mile and no hassle of driving your own motorcar."

Mr. Morgan, attorney and much-sought-after widower, shook as he laughed, his hands finding their way into his pockets and jangling the coins hidden there. "Does your daddy know about all this?"

My eyes stretched open wide. "Which part?" I'd approached Mr. Morgan precisely because I knew he wouldn't talk to my father. Mr. Morgan considered himself the most prominent man in town. Father considered himself the same. They'd circled around each other like two tomcats on the prowl ever since I could remember.

"Striking out into business on your own. And asking for money from me, of course."

I bit the inside of my cheek. Best to be honest. "No, sir, he doesn't."

Mr. Morgan's striking blue eyes gleamed like Lake Michigan on a summer day. "You can be sure he'll never hear about it from me." Then he winked.

Warmth stole over my neck and face. "Thank you, Mr. Morgan." *I think.*

He led me into the reception area before retreating back into his private office, shutting the door behind him. I leaned my shoulder into the wall and blew out a long breath.

"Did you get what you came for?"

I whirled around. A woman not much older than I stood beside the small desk. Had she been there when I'd arrived?

"What I came for?" Then I noticed her hand extended between us. I shook it.

"Lucinda Bywater. We go to the same church." The woman's voice turned shy, so different from the commanding question that had arrested my attention.

"Oh. I recognize you." And I did. Kind of.

Her lips curved upward, but more in a wince than a smile. "I'm not often in services. The baby's a bit fussy most days."

Baby. That's where I'd seen her. Whisking a wailing infant from the church, walking it outside after the service had ended. The baby I often wished silent.

She seated herself behind the desk.

"Do you work here, Lucinda?"

She nodded. "I'm so grateful Papa insisted I take a few courses in Indianapolis after high school. I learned how to run the typewriter and the telephone. I'd never have a job like this otherwise."

"But what about your baby?" I glanced behind the desk, expecting to see a pram with a napping child.

"She stays with Aunt LuAnn—my little boy does, too—at least until the other children get home from school."

"Oh? How many children do you have?" Maybe she was older than I imagined.

"Four total. Two girls in school, my boy who's three this year, and the baby, Teresa."

"You and your husband must be proud of them."

Her eyes took on the look of reflected light, shiny and bright. "Billy was right proud of his children."

Was? I swallowed hard, wanting to ask but not wanting to at the same time. I prayed she read the question in my eyes.

She glanced down, studying her clasped hands on the desk. "He was out chopping wood in January to make extra money to pay the doctor for the new baby. He took pneumonia. He was . . . gone in less than a week."

I wanted to throw my arms around her, tell her everything would be all right. But I couldn't. It wasn't all right. "How are you getting along?"

She shrugged. "This is a good job as far as that goes." Her gaze skittered to Mr. Morgan's closed door before turning on me again. "But with the burial costs and the baby bills, I can't seem to catch up."

I started to speak, but Lucinda's chin lifted. "Just before he passed, Billy told me not to worry." Her bottom lip trembled. She took a deep breath and seemed to find a real smile from someplace deep inside. "He told me God would make a way. And He will."

Lucinda would struggle to feed and clothe four children on a secretary's salary, I imagined. I guessed Lucinda's children didn't have enough of anything. Like the African kids in the picture that now resided in my purse.

But Lucinda stood in front of me, flesh and blood, her haggard face and shadowed eyes speaking more than her words. Could I relieve some of her burden? Wouldn't that be right? A cup of cold water in His name?

Peeking out the window, I spied my shiny Runabout waiting to whisk me to visit the next name on my list. But my heart wouldn't let me leave. The sun glinted off the brass headlamp like a wink. My fingers moved of their own accord, unclasping my handbag and retrieving the fold of bills her boss had handed me just moments before.

For the kingdom of God.

For Africa.

Or for Lucinda?

Giving to her was still giving to the Lord's work, I felt sure.

"Here." I shoved the bills into the palm of her hand, closing her fingers around them.

"But I can't—"

"Yes you can. Pay off your debts and put a bit aside for when one of the children gets sick. And make sure to get some good food into all of you."

"You don't have to—"

"I know I don't. But I want to. Let me be the hand the Lord uses to provide for your family today. Please?"

For a brief moment, tears stood in her eyes, on her lashes, but she blinked them back. "Bless you, Miss Benson."

I took both of her hands in mine. "We're friends now, Lucinda. Call me Alyce."

She gave a tiny nod and a shy smile. My own grin stretched as far as my face would allow. Next Sunday I wouldn't overlook her. I would even offer to help with the baby.

Minutes later, I sat behind the wheel of my car and let out a satisfied sigh. "Thank you, Lord, for letting me be a part of Your work today." I started the engine and chugged down the street, wishing my little Runabout would fly as fast as the race car—or at least Father's Mercer.

After rounding the corner, I eased to a stop in front of the pharmacy. The engine quieted, leaving me to sort out my thoughts. Mr. Morgan would likely frown on my giving his donation to his secretary. But that thought didn't bother me as much as another: My Africa fund had gone from two hundred dollars to zero in less than five minutes.

6

Two hours later, with one hundred sixty-two dollars in my handbag, I rolled into the empty expanse between Father's office and his factory. The Mercer wasn't in its usual spot, but that didn't matter. I preferred not to bump into Father anyway. It was Webster I hoped to see. Would he celebrate my success or scold my impulsive gift to Lucinda?

I tiptoed around my car and in the direction of the factory. Bangs and clangs littered the air. I held my breath, listening. A tap on my shoulder. With a squeal, I spun around. "Mr. Trotter." I breathed relief. "You frightened me."

His mustache lifted, fell, then lifted once more. "Did you come to see your father, Miss Benson?"

"As a matter of fact, I did not. I came because I—" I glanced back at the factory. Did I need Webster when Mr. Trotter was here? I laid my hand on his arm and smiled up at him. "I tried to call, but you were out. I'm in need of assistance, Mr. Trotter. Could we speak in your office?"

He grinned. "I'd be delighted."

Bare walls, a dingy window, and clutter on the desk defined his small space. He pulled out his handkerchief and swiped the dust from the seat of a straight-backed chair. I gathered up my skirt to keep the hem from brushing the floor as I sat.

"I guess you know why I've come."

He blinked at me in obvious discomfort.

"The Africans, Mr. Trotter. Mr. and Mrs. McConnell's mission in the Gold Coast?" I pulled the photograph from my handbag, smoothing out a small crease on one corner.

"Ah, yes. The money." His hazel eyes seemed to take on a new sparkle.

I nodded. "Father wouldn't . . . that is . . ." I pulled back my shoulders, sat up straighter. "I've decided to raise the money on my own."

His eyebrows lifted. "Three thousand dollars?"

I nodded again, more quickly this time, my head bobbing like tires rolling over bricked streets. "I've already begun canvassing businessmen in town." I slid the list across his desk.

He glanced at it and then back up at me. "And?"

"A few paid me to drive them from one place to another. Usually not far enough to collect more than the fifty-cent minimum. Some, like Mr. Morgan at the law office, gave an outright donation." I took a deep breath. "I collected a total of three hundred sixty-two dollars today—and I made known my willingness to drive for pay at any time." My chin lifted. Ten more days like today and I'd have all the money I needed.

"Quite impressive." His gaze strayed to my handbag. "So how may I be of assistance?"

"I need—" Staring into my lap, I wondered what I did need. Support? Advice? Help keeping the money I'd received? My head jerked up. "I'd be obliged if you could suggest a way for me to—hold on to the money."

He leaned back in his chair, eyes narrowed, lips mashed together, fingertips forming a tent.

"Could you open an account at the bank for me?" I withdrew the paper money from my handbag and thrust it in his direction. He cared for Father's money every day. No reason not to trust him with mine.

He took the money, counted it. His eyes widened. "But this is only one hundred and sixty-two dollars, Miss Benson."

"I know." I shrank back in my chair and swiped my tongue over my dry lips. "I gave away part of it."

He popped up from his chair, hands behind his back, the bills flapping in his fingers. He began to pace.

My heart pounded and my palms turned moist.

He stopped, faced me. "To whom did you give it?"

I intended to say "Lucinda Bywater," but her name stuck in my throat. "Someone who needed it."

He shook his head. "That just won't do." His pacing resumed. "No, it just won't do."

I gripped the handle of my purse. "So you'll take it to the bank for me?"

He stared out the cloudy window for what seemed like an eternity. "The bank would be one option. But perhaps, given the circumstances . . ." He whirled to face me. "I'd hate for there to be any hint of scandal, Miss Benson. And should it slip out that your numbers don't match what you've been given . . ."

I bit my lip. I didn't want any taint on this money. Nor did I want to rouse Father's ire any more than I already had. Perhaps Mr. Trotter had a point. "I guess I'll keep it with me, then."

I reached for the money. He pulled it back. "Would you allow me to hold it for you?"

Since I'd given away over half of what I'd collected less than two hours after receiving it, the idea had merit. I opened my mouth to accept his offer, to gush my gratitude for his help. But the words clogged in my throat. If the money went in the bank, I'd earn interest, some little part to make up for what I'd given away. I knew I had to replace that two hundred dollars. And every bit would help, no matter how small. Or perhaps I needed to be responsible for all the money on my own. Could I trust myself to guard it until the McConnells returned?

Lord?

No brilliant plan alighted. I stood, held out my hand. "Thank you, Mr. Trotter, but I'd like to consider my options."

His jaw seemed to tighten as his hand stretched to meet mine, to lay the bills in my open palm. Then he fell back into his normal ease. "I encourage you to make a decision quickly, Miss Benson. I'd grieve to find out your funds weren't available for those dear African children."

"Of course." I slipped the money and the photo back into my handbag, wondering at my indecision. Tonight I'd ask Grandmother for her advice. And maybe Webster, too. Above all else, I wanted to do the right thing.

Puttering home, I remembered the look on Lucinda's face when her fingers closed around the bills. In spite of the sinking feeling in my stomach, I couldn't convince myself that I'd done wrong, even if it meant Mr. Morgan's donation hadn't gone exactly to the place he'd intended. I felt sure Ava McConnell would have done the same after hearing Lucinda's plight.

I skidded around the corner and onto the brick drive that led past the back garden, into the garage. Clarissa was standing at the kitchen door, screeching at the gardener. Betsy and the day maids were hanging Mother's cleaned clothes from the clothesline on the opposite side of the lane, even though it wasn't Monday.

I jumped from my car and hurried inside.

"Mother?" Hanging my linen duster on the rack in the hall, I listened.

Voices drifted down the stairs, punctuated by thumps and bumps. I climbed toward the noise. Mother's bedroom door stood ajar. I pushed it wide. A trunk stood open in the corner. Mother was opening and shutting drawers in her desk, as if searching for something.

"Is something wrong, Mother?"

Her head turned in my direction. "Darling." She swept me into the room, led me to the tufted velvet couch in the corner, and kissed my cheeks before returning to her task. "Nothing's wrong. I simply need to run up to Chicago on club business. They can't seem to organize the charity bazaar without my presence."

In that moment, I envied my mother. Someone needed her. Needed her expertise.

"Here it is." She pulled a sheaf of papers from the back of one of the drawers. "I knew I'd kept those notes from past years."

I watched her bustle around the room, packing for her trip to Chicago. I glanced down at my purse. Mother would never blithely give away money entrusted to her for a specific cause. An ache started at the base of my skull and worked its way toward the crown of my head.

"Your father hated it when I left him alone when you were

away at school." Her skirt swished as she deposited the found notes in a soft leather satchel Father had given her for her work. "But I know you'll take good care of things now that you're back, Alyce."

"Of course, Mother." My head pounded in earnest now. I slipped from the room, wandered to the kitchen, and grabbed a handful of fresh blackberries from a bowl on the work table. Clarissa gave my hand a playful swat. I grinned and popped a berry into my mouth. As the sourness of the firm berry burst against my tongue, I thought again about Mother's charitable work. Did she truly care about helping those in need, or did she work more for the accolades heaped upon her for her successful efforts?

Pulsing pain tore through my head with every beat of my heart. If only I could go for one of my clandestine drives—sixty miles an hour with the wind slapping me in the face. That would cure the ache in my head—and maybe help me sort out the confusion in my heart, as well.

One more berry found its way past my lips. As it did, I looked at the few resting in my hand. Lucinda and her children would probably greatly appreciate some fresh summer fruit.

"Clarissa, could I take some of these to town? To a . . . friend?"

"As you like, but it will mean less for the cobbler."

I waved off her concern as I transferred half the bowl's contents to a small covered crock. "As long as you sweeten it enough, Father won't know the difference."

Her lilting laugh chased me from the kitchen.

7

Webster's familiar whistle lit the air outside the corner of the garage, pulling me to it like steel to a magnet. The moment he spotted me, his feet stopped and his tune faded.

"I looked for you at the factory this afternoon."

He wiped his hands on a rag. "I've been here." He flicked a glance toward the house as he shoved the dirty cloth into his back pocket. Then he motioned for me to follow him inside. My Packard sat in its customary place. I perched on a backless stool, the crock of berries in my lap, while he checked the tires and gadgets and fluids.

"I went seeking Africa funds today." I rested my hands on the lid, holding the berries inside, away from the temptation of my fingers and my mouth.

He cocked his head and rubbed at a place near his nose, leaving a streak of grease to decorate his face. "Any success?"

"Yes—and no." I sighed. "You might as well work while I talk."

He resumed his tasks. I told him of my idea to make money driving and my visit with Mr. Morgan and the others in town. Then I related my encounter with Lucinda. And Mr. Trotter. He didn't look at me through the entire tale. Just kept working. Washing. Drying. Buffing. Scraping splatter from the windscreen. Wiping down the soft black top and the leather seats. At the back of the motorcar, he cleaned the last bit of dirt from my spare tire as I fell silent.

He stepped away, admired his work or my car, I wasn't sure which.

I slid from the stool, suddenly afraid of his censure. "So what do you think?" I set the blackberries in the passenger's seat of my car.

"About which part?" He buffed one spot on the headlamp.

"All of it."

He pushed the bill of his flat driving cap a bit higher, revealing his dark eyes. "Why does it matter what I think?"

I clasped my hands behind my back and started a slow circle around my automobile. He was right. I acted for Jesus alone. What mattered was what He thought of me. I'd told Mr. Morgan the money would go to Africa. And it didn't. On the other hand, I'd seen one in need and helped. Like the Good Samaritan.

Or Robin Hood.

Which mattered most—telling the truth or doing the right thing? I wasn't completely sure. In spite of Webster's lack of spiritual direction, he'd demonstrated good sense in the few years I'd known him. "I value your opinion, that's all."

He shrugged. "Why? I just tinker with engines and machinery."

"You're the one who encouraged me to raise the money."

He snorted and turned away. "Did I?"

I blocked his path to the workbench. "It isn't that I need your approval. I just want to know what you think. So few people tell me the truth. My father might have more money than most around here, but I still need real friends."

His eyebrows rose. "More money than most?"

I cringed. "Okay, all. More money than *all* the people around here. Except maybe Mr. Morgan."

Webster stared into my eyes for a long moment. I squirmed, feeling as if my very soul lay bare beneath his gaze. Then he stooped to gather his scattered tools. With his back to me, he organized the workbench nailed to the wall. "Lucinda had it hard even before Billy died."

I held my breath, eager to hear every word over the clatter of his work. But the noise quieted. Webster turned, leaned against the workbench, arms folded. "Billy worked for your father, you know. Hard work. Small wage."

His words fell like a weight on my chest. "I had no idea."

"I know you didn't." His mouth settled into a hard line. "I guess you know you'll have to replace that money."

I stared at the ground. "I know."

He pushed away from the workbench and rested a hand on my shoulder. I shuddered. His hand lifted. "Go on, now. Your father will be home soon."

Heart heavy, I pulled open the door of my Packard.

"Ally?"

I stopped, turned back to him. "Yes?"

"You did a good thing for Lucinda today." The intense sincerity in his voice turned my knees weak. Webster approved of my actions. And he was one of the most considerate men I knew.

Maybe I'd actually accomplished something worthwhile instead of just messing everything up.

When I returned from delivering the berries to a thankful Lucinda, I sought out Grandmother.

"You did exactly right, Alyce." Grandmother sat in an upholstered chair in her bedroom instead of lying in bed. A good day. And I'd missed most of it.

I dropped to my knees beside her. "But now I have less than half of what I raised for the McConnells' work in Africa."

The little children's faces burned in my mind as the thin skin of Grandmother's hands touched my cheeks and lifted my face to look at her in spite of the fact that she couldn't see me. "It isn't just people in faraway places that need your compassion and your help. Sometimes it's those right where you are."

"But what am I going to do now?" I groaned as I laid my head in her lap once more. Grandmother's hand rested lightly on my hair, then stroked it back from my face. She didn't hurry her words. That was her way. She pondered, considered, prayed before she spoke.

A faint whistle drifted in through the open windows. I imagined Webster in the garage, that dirty rag hanging out of his back pocket, his cap pulled low on his forehead, fencing his unruly hair away from his eyes.

I'd driven a bit faster than normal on my way back from Lucinda's, but it wasn't like driving on the secret track in the field. I needed the wind to slap me in the face, steal all thoughts from my head—save those needed to keep the car on the road. I prayed best after those drives. Heard best, too. The voice of God seemed so clear in those moments.

"If the Lord desires you to help His work in Africa, He'll provide the means. You can be sure of that."

I lifted my head. "But what do I do about the money I've already given away?"

The growl of Father's Mercer sounded from the front of the house, drowning out Webster's whistle. "You'll have to make it up somehow. You told Mr. Morgan the money would go to the Gold Coast, and you must honor that."

A familiar refrain. Enough of my own troubles for the moment. I rose to my knees, kissed Grandmother's cheek, and lifted the worn Bible from the small table. Opening to the spot marked by a silk ribbon, I settled in my usual chair. "I think we ended yesterday in Isaiah."

One hundred sixty-two dollars. I spread the bills out before me and counted again. I tucked the money in a drawer in my desk and prayed God would multiply it overnight, like those loaves and fishes of old.

After washing my hands and face, I donned my nightdress and climbed into bed. The hum of insect life outside my open window seemed to sing *three thousand, three thousand, three thousand.* What had I been thinking to promise such an exorbitant amount?

I lay on my back and stared at the ceiling above my bed. I'd been thinking that Father would simply hand me the money, of course.

Maybe Father had been right not to give me the money. A good man had entrusted funds to me and I'd let them dribble out of my hands like creek water. I rubbed my forehead, trying to keep fingers of pain from compressing my scalp once more.

I considered again Mr. Trotter's generous offer to safeguard what I'd collected. But that felt like the easy way out. I ought to be able to protect the funds myself. I was twenty-two years old, a college graduate.

Climbing from bed, I plodded back to my desk and transferred the bills to my purse. In spite of Mr. Trotter's concerns, I'd march myself into Mr. White's bank tomorrow morning and open an account. Mr. White would whisk my money to a place where I couldn't touch it—at least not until the McConnells returned. And I'd earn a little interest in the process. Then I would transfer the entire sum into the hands of those worthy people for their noble cause and applaud my self-discipline in the process.

8

"Clarissa?" I swept down the main staircase just before noon, again wearing my most businesslike attire. "I can take you to your sister's now."

A clap of thunder rattled the glass above the double front doors as raindrops slapped against the tall arched windows in the drawing room and the parlor. Clarissa bustled into the foyer, her wide-brimmed straw hat obscuring her face. But I still recognized the tight mouth, the pinched expression of fear.

I pulled my duster from the coatrack before pressing my hand to her arm. "We'll arrive in one piece. I promise."

With a curt nod, she whirled around and marched out the door. I bit back a grin. The last time I'd driven her to town, she'd spent the entire trip crossing herself and praying that the Lord would preserve her life and sanity. But today I intended to drive like any other lady, slow and sedate. All the way to the bank.

And after I settled the money in Mr. White's keeping, maybe I could persuade Webster to let me take the racing car out for a celebration.

We motored into town, the spit of rain dissipating before we reached Main Street. But dark clouds remained overhead. Clarissa climbed down from the Runabout with a hint of a smile on her face. "Thank you kindly, Miss Alyce."

I resisted the urge to laugh at her obvious relief. She darted down the street and around the corner to spend her Thursday half day at her sister's house, surrounded by nieces and nephews and noise. I wondered if such noise would sound as lovely to me as the purr of an engine.

I puttered through town and spied an elderly couple on the sidewalk. I pulled near and lowered my window. The man startled. The woman looked wary. I put on my brightest smile. "I can drive you to wherever you are going, if you'd like."

The man looked at his wife.

"Is it safe, you think?" she asked.

He shrugged. "Best time to find out." He led her to my Packard. They settled in the backseat.

I twisted around so I could see them. "I'm playing taxicab. Fifty cents a mile. All the money goes to a missionary couple returning to Africa."

Their faces went slack. He reached for the door handle. My stomach tumbled. I wanted to bite my tongue in half. "No, wait. I'll drive you wherever you need to go. No charge. Just a friend doing you a favor."

The woman beamed at her husband. I faced forward, set the car in gear, and eased into the street. Keeping to a sedate speed, I followed their directions, finally dropping them off at a ramshackle house outside of town. Back toward the bank I went, asking for customers along the way. But once I mentioned money—even for Africa—few chose to ride. Thunder rumbled overhead. I parked the car near the brick bank building anchoring the strip of storefronts comprising the town of Langston.

Father chose this town long ago because he felt it would be a good location for his plant that manufactured farm machinery. As he found more and more success in his venture, Mother begged him to move to Chicago—or at least Indianapolis. But Father didn't budge. He liked being an important man in a small town. So he built Mother an extravagant house and let her take trips whenever she liked.

Though I'd enjoyed my two years in Chicago, I, too, preferred a more rural life. The slower pace. The knowing and being known. All the things Mother disdained.

The scent of rain lingered in the air. I savored it before stepping into the stuffiness of the bank. The tinkle of a small bell announced me, but Mr. White's familiar head, as smooth as one of Father's billiards balls, was nowhere to be seen. A young man smelling of hair tonic greeted me instead.

"I need to speak with Mr. White, please."

The young man's eyes darted one way, then the other, his Adam's apple sliding up and down his neck. "He ain't here."

"I can see that, Mr. . . . ."

The man stood up straighter. "Mr. Hill."

I stuck out my gloved hand. Pink crept into his face as he shook it. "Such a pleasure to meet you, Mr. Hill. I'm Alyce Benson. Are you new to the bank?"

"N-new. Y-yes," he stammered.

Was I responsible for his discomfiture, or did he always respond to people this way? "And how do you find our fair town?"

"F-fine. Just fine, Miss Benson."

"Good." I exaggerated my look around the dim room. Thunder growled. A flash of lightning answered. "Now, when did you say Mr. White would return?"

Mr. Hill nodded toward the door. "There he is now, Miss Benson."

Mr. White opened the door as another flash of lightning illuminated the bank. At the loud crack and bang, everyone froze. Then Mr. White wiped a handkerchief across his shiny skull, and we all returned to normal.

"Miss Benson. What a pleasure to see you." He hung his hat on the rack and returned his handkerchief to his pocket, his jolly face relaying the truth of his words. "Come to wheedle money from me again?"

Mr. White had reluctantly parted with fifty dollars after seeing those precious faces from the other side of the world, though he refused to let me earn it by driving him. He and I laughed. Mr. Hill stared at us, mouth agape.

"Actually, Mr. White, I've come to ask a favor of a different sort." I slipped my hand around his elbow. We started toward the back office as another peal of thunder drowned out our voices and our steps. Then we heard the clang of the fire bell.

Mr. White bolted out the front door. I followed close behind. The new motorized fire truck sped down the street, autos and horses crowding the far edges of the cobblestone path. Residents dashed out of storefronts and houses, heedless of the rain, following behind the truck like the wide tail of an unwieldy kite.

I joined the throng, my heart pounding with worry. Smoke billowed into the moist air, clouding my vision and sending spasms of coughs up my throat. I glanced at the clouds skittering across the heavens and prayed for a deluge instead of a drip. But the Lord didn't oblige.

Shouting sounded in the distance. Making my way through the crowd, I pushed forward into the smoky air, heedless of the sting in my nose and eyes. Finally I stood near the fire truck. Three men directed a flow of water toward towering flames reducing a house to cinders. And there in the yard stood Clarissa, arms circled around her sobbing sister.

By the time the fire shrank to a smolder, the crowd had dispersed, as well. I stood by Clarissa, our faces smudged with soot, our clothing damp. She took charge, parceling out her nieces and nephews to hospitable neighbors, but her sister refused to abandon the charred remains.

"All our savings went to buy that house. One wee roof of our own for shelter."

Clarissa soothed her sister as she would a small child. "There now. All your lads and lasses are well. Wood and nails can be replaced."

Flame-red hair framed the woman's tear-streaked face as she shook her head. "Wood and nails cost money we don't have. What will we do? What will we do?" She buried her face in the front of Clarissa's dress. Only then did I spy tears snaking trails down Clarissa's dirty cheeks.

I stared at the purse hanging from my wrist and gnawed on the edge of my lip. Then my eyes met Clarissa's over the top of her weeping sister's head. Before I could think, I pressed my money—one hundred sixty-two dollars—into Clarissa's sister's hand, telling her to use it to replace their things, to begin saving for a new house.

Before either of them could protest, I walked away. Without a look back, I climbed into my Runabout. Penniless. Again.

My knuckles turned white on the steering wheel as I bounced over the cobblestones and out onto the dirt road toward home. In spite of myself, I couldn't be sorry for helping Clarissa's sister and her family in their time of need. And just as the Lord had provided for them, He'd provide for His work in Africa. Grandmother believed it. So did I.

But please, Lord, couldn't You just provide it through me?

Not often did I shed my dress for a pair of knickers when I went for a drive. But this day I did. Late that afternoon, I pulled heavy driving gloves over my fingers as I strode into the cool, dark garage. My hands shook with the need to be behind the wheel. My foot itched to work the gas pedal attached to the floor of the race car.

An electric light flickered on the back wall of the garage, illuminating Webster's legs sticking out from under the racing car.

I nudged his foot with the toe of my tall riding boot. He scooted out, a cloud of dust arriving with him.

"Are you busy?"

He sat up and rested his hands on his bent knees as he surveyed my unusual costume. "More trouble?"

My shoulders hitched up and then fell again. "I guess you could say that."

He hopped to his feet, brushed his hands against his legs. "Your father again?"

I shook my head, noticing car parts strewn across the ground. "What's all this?" I poked a metal shaft with the toe of my boot.

"Tinkering a bit." He patted the hood of the racing car in much the same way Father patted my cheek.

"You can make it go faster?"

"Maybe." He looked me over once more. "You're serious today, aren't you?"

I nodded.

"So I guess your father told you."

"Told me?"

He blinked, a kind of fear hovering over his face. Running a hand through his dark hair, he disappeared deeper into the garage, his back to me, his attention glued to his scattered tools and spare parts. I followed, stopping within a hairsbreadth of his left shoulder.

I knew he felt me there. A minute passed. Then two. Finally he tossed a wrench to the ground. "He's entering the car at the Chicago Speedway next weekend."

For a moment, I couldn't move. Father's racing car. Competing. Then a squeal—my squeal—pealed through the garage. I flung my arms around Webster's neck. "We're finally going to race it!"

He pulled as taut as a clothesline, but he didn't move away. And neither did I. I savored the earthy smell of his neck, felt the warmth of his body next to mine. I eased back just enough to see into his face, to glimpse a look of tender wonder before he covered it over again. Or had I misread it?

One tentative hand reached up, cupped my waist. Then he pushed my body away from his. The fire of his touch seared to my very core. I fought to pull air into my lungs, to force myself to let go of him rather than cling more tightly.

With great effort, my arms returned to my sides. His did the same. I prayed the dim light of the garage hid the heat that was crawling up my neck, over my face, all the way to the top of my head. I'd thrown myself into his embrace. What had I been thinking?

I shook my head to clear away the confusion. Clasping my hands in front of me, I concentrated on Webster's shoes. The race at the speedway. That needed to be the focus of this conversation.

A deep breath, then I lifted my gaze to his face. He seemed to be laughing at me now, but I refused to acknowledge his mocking. Not when it appeared to be at my expense. "So, who's driving our car in the race?"

He shrugged, turned away. "Your father has someone lined up."

Jealousy flashed through me as quick and hot as lightning. To think of someone else behind the wheel of this car rendered her unfaithful somehow, though I knew that to be unreasonable. But if I couldn't drive, I at least had to be there to watch her moment of glory. In Chicago.

"Anyway"—Webster pulled the rag from his back pocket and wiped it across his forehead—"I wasn't supposed to mention it. And I have to get her ready." He clamped his lips shut and returned to work.

I leaned against my Runabout as he fit pieces into the engine—tightening, oiling, tinkering. I grabbed a clean rag from a shelf over the workbench to wipe the door of my dusty auto and remembered my desperation. What would Webster say if I told him I'd given *all* the money away?

I couldn't make myself chance his response. I had to find a way to replace the funds before anyone found out I no longer had them. My eyes caught on a simple gold bracelet circling my wrist. "Webster, do you think I could sell some pieces of my jewelry to raise the money I need?"

"What kind of jewelry?"

"Trinkets, really. Like this." I held out my arm. He barely glanced my direction. "I doubt they'd bring much, but then every little bit would help." I concentrated on a smudge of dirt that didn't want to let go. I rubbed harder, until it flaked to the ground. "But I wouldn't want to sell them around here. Too obvious. I don't suppose you could help me, could you?"

Clank. Clang. Tap.

I drummed my fingers against the body of the car as he worked. With a grunt, he pointed at a large wrench. I picked it up and placed it in his hand before tossing my rag onto the workbench and perching on the back fender of my car.

"Of course, selling a few baubles will only repay what I already gave away." My throat tightened, and my voice fell to a whisper. "Which would be three hundred and sixty-two dollars."

Webster bolted upright, banging his knee on the race car. Growling through gritted teeth, he massaged the spot before pushing to his feet.

"Say that again?"

I breathed deep. "I gave away the rest of the money."

He groaned.

"Clarissa's sister's house got hit by lightning. They lost everything."

His gaze burned into me, so intense it held me motionless. Then he piled tools in the toolbox and clamped the lid shut before securing the box to the back of the race car.

"I'll sell your jewelry for you. But you have to give it to me before we leave for Chicago."

"I'll give it to you at the speedway next weekend. After the race. Or maybe before."

He straightened. "You aren't going, Ally. I thought you understood that. Your father made it very clear I wasn't even supposed to mention it to you."

I inched toward the open garage doors. "Thank you, Webster. I knew the Lord would provide." With the flash of a grin, I tried to dispel the fear clouding his eyes. "And don't worry. I won't get you in any trouble about Chicago."

No, there wouldn't be trouble. For either of us. In fact, Mother would be in raptures when I offered to accompany her on another trip to the city.

9

All that night I tossed and turned, worrying about the little lives attached to those precious faces in my photograph. Each body housed a soul. A soul with an eternal future. How gladly I'd sacrifice my few semiprecious pieces of jewelry to give them the opportunity to hear the gospel, to experience the love of Christ through the McConnells. Mother didn't even remember she'd given me those baubles. Besides, unlike my Packard, they were mine to do with as I pleased. And while they wouldn't raise the entire amount, they might at least replace the funds I'd given away.

As the birds started their morning conversations, I forced my tired body out of bed, still cataloging in my head what I could sell without Mother or Father noticing. At my desk, I opened my diary, marking off the past few days. Just over six weeks remained until John and Ava McConnell returned. I pressed the blunt end of my pencil to my lips. There were still a few people in town I hadn't called on to offer my services as a driver. But given the fact that not one person had yet to telephone regarding their need for transportation services, I doubted those conversations would yield anywhere near the entire amount.

A sliver of fear pricked my heart. Would I face the congregation alone and empty-handed? Would I fail John and Ava McConnell? Watch their joyful faces sink in disappointment? I refused to let trepidation take hold. I would trust God's provision. His faithfulness. I shut my diary and opened my Bible instead.

Father's Mercer chugged out of the garage before I dressed for breakfast. Mother met me in the foyer.

"Come take breakfast in the garden with me, darling, before you motor me to the train station." She hooked her arm through mine and led me out the door.

I inhaled the freshness of the morning, wishing I could linger in its embrace. But my feet had to move to keep up with Mother. And my mind whirled with every step. Mother's clubs—both the small one in Langston and the larger one in Chicago—supported a number of causes. Even if she wouldn't lend her name or her effort to raising funds for the Gold Coast mission, she might have some ideas as to how to garner the necessary funds.

Webster's whistle cut across the clear morning, lifting my spirits. At least I had one ally. No, two. Mr. Trotter stood ready to help, as well. I ought to call on him again.

"Alyce?" Mother motioned me to the gazebo as Webster rounded the stand of birch trees, the tune dying on his lips.

The gardener placed a chair near me, and I sat. Clarissa bustled out of the house laden with a full tray, clucking like an agitated hen. A plate of eggs with a slice of cheese and some fresh fruit appeared in front of me. I let my fork wander through the eggs on my plate but didn't bring a bite to my lips.

"Mother, I need your help with something." Father had ordered me not to ask Mother for money for Africa, but he hadn't said I couldn't seek her help in raising the funds.

"Oh?" Her eyes widened and her face took on an excitement I rarely saw.

Clearly, she wanted to help me. And I so rarely obliged. Maybe my request would give us a common bond.

I lifted a forkful of eggs, ready to plunge them into my mouth as soon as the words left it empty. "It's about those children. In Africa."

Mother settled her napkin in her lap and added a dollop of milk to her steaming tea. "I have nothing to give you, Alyce, even if your father hadn't forbidden it."

"I know, but I thought you could at least suggest ways to raise the money. You're so good at that. How do your clubs manage to fund charitable causes?"

"That's different."

"How?"

She sipped her tea. "Why can't you find something more . . . suitable for your efforts? Like those poor Belgian children orphaned by the war in Europe?"

I speared a raspberry and popped it into my mouth. "Plenty of others are championing their cause. These children in Africa have no one else. Or rather, very few others. Can't you help me?"

Her delicate mouth drooped before she set aside her fork. "You ought to be concerned with finding a husband before you take on other people's problems, Alyce. I've tried to explain it to your father, but he cannot be convinced that you must spend more time in proximity to eligible men if you are to marry. After you marry, you'll have plenty of opportunity to do good."

A bee buzzed near my ear. I wished it would jab its stinger into my flesh so I could avoid this conversation. But it bumbled away, off to find a flower to satisfy its hunger instead.

"I'm not missing a thing, Mother. I'm working with the Women's Mission Auxiliary at church. And there's a social planned for later this month. I have other friends, too." *Though none you would approve of.* "I'm satisfied with my life."

Or would be if I had three thousand dollars for the mission in the Gold Coast.

Mother's mouth puckered as if she'd bit into a lemon instead of a strawberry. "You know that isn't what I mean, Alyce. On my last trip to Chicago I met several men who asked to be introduced to you. They are expecting you to accompany me next time. And I'm sure your friends from school miss you, as well. We could go up and stay for a few weeks."

My heart thumped against my chest as I imagined Webster's racing car zipping around the board track just outside the city. "Actually, Mother, I think that's a great—"

"Ow!" Mother sprang from her chair and slapped at her neck. "Get it off! Get it off!" Slap. Slap. Slap.

I caught her hand, held it still. A welt the size of a nickel rose red beneath her ear.

Then her screaming stopped. Her body went limp. I caught her just before she hit the ground.

"Mother?" I eased her to the floor of the gazebo and settled her head in my lap as a bumblebee twitched one last time on the ground beside me. Her eyes didn't open. They didn't even flutter. "Help me! I need help!"

Before my shout died away, Webster lifted Mother into his arms, his eyes locking on mine. I hoped he could read my gratitude.

I phoned the doctor. And Father. Neither hurried to Mother's side. Smelling salts did their job, waking her to a moaning existence. Clarissa made a quick mud plaster, which I dabbed on the sting. Betsy brought Mother a glass of wine to help dull her pain.

Her eyes closed. Her head lolled to one side. The front door opened and closed. Heavy footsteps climbed the stairs.

"Alyce?" she groaned as Dr. Maven stepped into the room.

"Yes, Mother?"

She stretched out her arm. My shoulders slumped a bit as I stepped to her side, holding her hand as the doctor examined the sting.

"Nothing to worry about, Mrs. Benson. Everyone has taken good care of you." He patted her hand and smiled in my direction.

"Thank you, darling," Mother mumbled before turning her head, her face still white and pinched with pain.

"I'll see myself out," the doctor whispered. "Call if you need anything more."

"I will." After the front door shut and the faint chug of the doctor's motorcar died away, I let go of Mother's hand and advanced toward the door. If I knew my mother, this could confine her to bed for a week. And if I couldn't rouse her from bed, how in the world would I induce Father to take me to Chicago for the race?

10

Early Sunday morning, I wrapped my robe around my nightdress and tiptoed into the hall. No stirring in Mother's bedroom. No sound from the floor below. I hurried into the bathroom and then returned to my room to dress. Maybe I could spend some time with Grandmother before breakfast.

Shoes in hand, I crept down the hall, my stockinged feet making no sound on the polished walnut floor. As I passed the stairs, the smell of fresh bread rumbled my stomach.

I pushed open Grandmother's bedroom door. "How is my favorite lady this morning?"

Grandmother chuckled as I made my way to her bedside, kissed her cheek, and settled into my usual chair.

"Did you—were you able—?" She whispered as if I'd taken up something sinister.

For once, I thanked the Lord that she couldn't see my face. "Not much more money. But some."

I'd gone into town for a while the previous day, exhausted my entire list of people to contact, and arrived home with less than two hundred dollars toward my goal.

"You need somewhere to keep what you've been given. Open my armoire."

I did as she bid me.

"Look in the bottom left drawer."

I slid it open.

"The red box. Dig for it."

Pushing aside white undergarments, I spied a bit of scarlet wedged into the back corner. I pulled it out. A square box decorated with tiny beads.

"I purchased it at the Columbian Exposition. I can't remember which exhibit booth. But I thought it charming. And a reminder that the blood of Jesus covered my sins. Take it. For your Africa money. Then I'll feel I have a part in it, too."

I turned the box over in my hands. "It will take time, but God will fill it. I feel sure."

"I hope so." Grandmother's voice shook just a bit. "Yet I fear for you, child."

My chin lifted. "I don't understand why Father's being so stubborn about this."

Grandmother shook her head, tears standing in her sightless eyes.

"What turned him against God, Grandmother? Was it Mother?"

Grandmother turned toward me. "It was my fault, I fear."

"Your fault?" I stroked her hand. "You've never been anything but gracious, even during his tirades and Mother's tantrums."

Her brown-spotted hand reached for the glass of water always on her bedside table. She lifted it to her lips. Once.

Twice. The glass shook in her hand. I guided it back into place without mishap.

"I wasn't always as you've known me, Ally. I didn't come to know the Lord until the year before you were born."

"Yes, I know. At the Columbian Exposition in Chicago. Reverend Moody was preaching under a big tent and for the first time you realized you needed a Savior."

Grandmother nodded. "What you don't know is that those first few years I wanted so badly for your mother and father to come to the same realization. All I could talk about was the peace I'd found in Jesus, the joy I'd never experienced before. And every day—maybe every hour—I asked if they could see that they needed the same thing."

"But surely they understood you just loved them so much you had to share your new faith."

"That was my reasoning at the time. But a wise older woman spied me weeping bitter tears one Sunday after church. I explained your parents' unwillingness to accept Christ and told her I was sure my unlearned words were the cause. She assured me they weren't and counseled me to live out my faith for them rather than preaching to them. She explained that no matter how much I talked or what words I used, Jesus had to woo them to Himself. I couldn't persuade them merely by saying it over and over again."

Grandmother played with the lace edge of the sheet covering her thin frame. "She was right, Ally. It took time for me to admit that. But then you arrived, a tiny bundle of joy with your whole life ahead of you. You didn't know me any other way, so I decided to pour myself into you instead of them."

"But all these years, Grandmother. All these years we've prayed. And nothing changes them." I choked out a laugh.

"Well, maybe they do change. They seem to get further from the Lord."

Grandmother nodded. "Every day that passes they get closer to the end of themselves. That's what I'm believing to be the case."

"Alyce?" Mother's voice drifted into the room.

"Go on now. Serve your parents well, as you always do. And trust God for the rest. Even for Africa."

"I love you, Grandmother." I kissed her forehead. "Pray for me," I whispered as I slipped my shoes onto my feet.

"Always" came the answer.

Behind the wheel of the Runabout, I chugged down the road to church, singing every hymn that popped into my head. By the time I parked, my heart had lightened, my faith had strengthened.

I cut the engine and laid my goggles on the seat before pinning my saucer-brimmed straw sailor hat atop my head.

"Miss Benson?"

I jumped, pressing my hand against my chest.

"May I be of assistance?" Mr. Trotter held out his hand. It seemed a bit ridiculous. I climbed in and out of my automobile by myself every day. Even when Webster stood nearby. But then, Webster wasn't Lawrence Trotter, with his fashionable suit and a tie knotted beneath his chin.

Mother's words about a suitable match flickered through my head. She probably hadn't meant someone like Mr. Trotter. But could she be persuaded to approve?

Sociable. Dapper. Interested in the things of the Lord.

I laid my hand in his and stepped to the ground. A shiver skittered over my arms and down my legs as he slid the duster from my shoulders and tossed it across the seat of my car.

"Thank you, Mr. Trotter." My voice fell to a faint whisper as my eyes met his. Even though I'd sat with him in church for almost two months, I'd never noticed the flecks of green that swam in his hazel eyes, the fullness of his lips beneath the line of fawn-colored hair above them. I remembered visiting with him alone in his office. My heart beat in excited anticipation—but of exactly what I couldn't tell.

"Shall we?" He offered his arm. A smile crept over my face as my heart thumped faster. When I touched his arm, a lightning bolt of thrill shot through my middle, leaving my knees weak.

We walked into church together, whispers trailing behind us. I ducked my head. Did he hear them, too? I glanced up again. His chest puffed out a bit now, and his gait took on a swagger. He obviously felt no shame to be linked with an old maid of twenty-two. One with bobbed hair and a car of her own, who bore the name of the most influential man in town.

Maybe, just maybe, Lawrence Trotter was God's answer to my prayers—in more ways than one.

After the service ended, the congregation buzzed with excitement over Mrs. Tillman's announcement about raising funds for the mission. A Women's Mission Auxiliary meeting was planned for that evening. My palms grew slick with sweat beneath my gloves. I wanted to leave before anyone asked me about the money I'd promised.

"Shall we?" were Mr. Trotter's quiet words in my ear. He led me out the door, around the edge of the crowd. My discomfort eased. We arrived at my motorcar without having to speak to anyone, though I regretted a quick wave to Lucinda and baby Teresa instead of a conversation.

He helped me into my duster again. I pulled my leather driving gloves over my thin white ones, wondering again if God intended more than I'd imagined concerning the man at my side.

He whisked his hat from his head and swept it across his body in a formal bow. "I'd be delighted to take you for a drive this afternoon, Miss Benson. I could deliver you to your meeting this evening, as well."

My heart seemed to stop as my hands stilled. Then my pulse took up its regular beat again. "How thoughtful of you, Mr. Trotter. I think I'd enjoy that."

"Lawrence. Please call me Lawrence." He set his hat on his head with a jaunty tap. "May I pick you up at four? That will give us time for a good long drive."

"That would be delightful. Thank you."

He stepped back. I hit the electric starter and my motor roared to life. Lawrence. Coming to pick me up. At my house. What would Mother and Father say? I pulled my foot from the clutch. The engine quit.

"Lawrence?" Heads turned as my voice carried across the churchyard. I cringed as he appeared at my window. He looked so eager. I couldn't disappoint him. I'd just have to make sure Mother stayed out of the way. And Father, too. At least until I figured out if he and I had any chance at a future together. I relaxed, let a smile frame my innocuous words. "I'll be waiting."

11

The moment I heard a motorcar in our lane, I slipped out the front door and met Lawrence at the gate where our yard met the road. Mother remained abed after her run-in with the bee. Father had shut himself in his study to read, though I'd heard his snore cutting through the air like a saw on logs.

"For you." Lawrence handed me a spray of pink rosebuds, peering past me as if trying to see through the front doors and into the house.

I inhaled the flowers' sweetness. "They're beautiful. Thank you."

"I guess we're ready?"

I nodded, looked up, then gasped. A roadster straddled the line between road and grass, shimmering in the waning sunlight. Red body. Coal-colored running boards and wheels. A sprinkle of brass illuminating the dark trim.

"A Grant," I whispered as we approached.

"Isn't she a beauty?" Lawrence rubbed one sleeve over a dull spot on the hood of the car.

"Indeed she is." I noted the newness of the auto as well as its features. My father evidently paid his employees more than I had imagined. Either that or Lawrence managed his finances well. That would please Father.

Lawrence made the pretense of helping me up onto the tufted leather bench seat, but in truth I'd sprung into the car quite on my own, eager to see inside. I caressed the soft leather, not much different from my Runabout, yet not the same, either. More supple. Like in Father's Mercer.

He placed a lap robe across the pleated skirt of my green silk dress before starting the engine. It felt strange to set my feet against the flat floorboard, to have my hands free of the steering wheel. I tried to ignore the anxious twitch in my extremities.

"She'll do up to forty miles per hour." Lawrence's voice rose above the din as we puttered down the road.

"Will she?"

"Yes, though I'd never presume to expose you to such peril." He glanced at me before his attention returned to the road. "And I'd hate to think what moving at such a speed would do to your lovely hat."

I put my hand to the close-fitting headpiece, pansied and feathered, more ornate than I preferred but one Mother had selected to match the dress. What would Lawrence think if I told him I'd not only ridden at such speeds but also driven in excess of them? A smile tugged at my lips.

I turned my head to watch the trail of houses leading into the center of town. Did Lawrence, with his dapper clothes and smart-looking car, put appearances above people? Like Mother did? Or could he approve of the real me, the one disguised beneath a duster and behind a pair of goggles?

As Lawrence spoke about the features of his Grant, I decided I'd best keep that adventuresome girl hidden from all but Webster Little. At least for now.

After a sedate drive through the countryside, we arrived at the church just before seven o'clock. Lawrence escorted me inside before departing with a tip of his hat. Mrs. Tillman called the Women's Mission Auxiliary meeting to order. I pressed my toes against the floor to keep them from a nervous jiggle, wishing, suddenly, for skirts that hid my feet from view.

My left knee began to bob. I pressed it still, cupping my hands around it and arching my back just a bit.

"We are so happy to welcome Miss Alyce Benson." Mrs. Tillman motioned toward me. The other women nodded in my direction before turning their attention back to their leader. I let out a tiny breath. Relaxed my hands in my lap as I crossed my ankles beneath the pew.

"Miss Benson has given us quite a challenge, ladies. And I intend to see that we help our church meet that lofty goal." Her eyebrows arched. Relief loosened my shoulders. They were willing to do their part.

Please don't let them inquire about mine.

"And to that end, I believe we need a very visible campaign."

A middle-aged woman in a plain dress got to her feet. "We could have a bake sale—or a New England supper. That would raise some money."

Other women nodded as she sat, a quiet buzz zipping through the room.

"Wonderful, Mrs. Graham. We need to consider every possibility so that we will not be found wanting when Miss

Benson"—again Mrs. Tillman's eyebrows lifted while her gaze angled in my direction—"presents her offering."

My mouth went dry. My foot twitched. My knees bounced.

Mrs. Tillman continued. "I've already discussed things with Pastor Swan. He will support all we decide to do toward reaching our goal." She turned a stiff smile my way. "Of course, you will only have the thrill of watching, Miss Benson, with none of the anguish of making it happen."

"Oh, I'm happy to help." My smile quivered. I licked my lips as Dr. Maven's wife rose.

"I will begin our fund with a donation tonight." She dug into her old-fashioned reticule and pulled out some paper money. "For several years now, Mrs. White has offered to purchase my old garnet broach. The Lord convicted me that the children in the Gold Coast need the money more than I need another trinket to gather dust." A light dusting of applause followed her to the front as she placed the money in Mrs. Tillman's hand.

Mrs. Tillman's face softened. "Thank you, dear Mrs. Maven. Your sacrifice is greatly appreciated."

A high-pitched wail cut off her words. Every woman in attendance turned toward the sound. Lucinda's face pinked as she stood in the back, jiggling baby Teresa on her hip. I leapt to my feet and met her at the door.

"Let me take her." I gathered the baby into my arms. "You go on in."

"Are you sure?" Lucinda's eyes flicked from me to the rest of the ladies and then back again.

"I'm sure."

With a weary smile, she gave my arm a quick squeeze before sliding into a pew near the back of the gathered group. The door shut behind me as I carried the screaming Teresa far from the confines of the church building. Lucinda belonged with those women seeking to do their part for the sake of the gospel. I felt like an outsider, the rich girl who could brazenly offer three thousand dollars with no worry at all.

Teresa hiccupped down a sob and quieted.

"There now, you see? Nothing to be so upset about." I kissed her chubby hand and forgot all about Women's Mission Auxiliary meetings and African faces. Instead, I found myself wondering what it would be like to have a baby all my own.

"What a picture you make with that child in your arms."

I whirled around. Lawrence sauntered toward me, one half of his mouth raised in a smile that set my cheeks ablaze.

"I'm just watching her. For a friend."

He put his finger into Teresa's hand. The tiny fist closed around it. My stomach swirled. Perhaps he did find the picture attractive. But which of us beguiled him—baby Teresa or me?

"Do you like children, Mr. Trotter?"

"Lawrence, remember?" He extricated his finger from Teresa's iron grip. "As to children, that would depend on the child."

I studied Teresa. Her bottom lip trembled. Not a happy child. At least never for long. Jaw tight, I waited for her to bellow out her displeasure. But I still wasn't prepared when the noise burst from those little lungs straight into my waiting ear.

Lawrence stepped back, his face twisted into a grimace. I tried to smile as I shushed the baby, rocking her back and forth in my arms. Then I noticed Lucinda hurrying across the yard.

"I'll take her now. The meeting is mostly over." Lucinda held my gaze for a long moment before turning her attention to Lawrence. "Excuse me, sir." She whisked Teresa away, in the direction of her home instead of the church, leaving Lawrence and me in awkward silence.

"Dare I ask if we might extend the evening to include supper?"

For a few moments, my thoughts jumbled together and I couldn't sort them out to speak.

His open smile, the glint of the waning sun lighting his eyes, the offer of his arm all proved too charming to refuse.

"I'd be delighted." And for the first time that evening, I sensed I belonged.

The delightful meal, accompanied by laughter and conversation, almost quelled my unease over the money I needed to raise. But not quite. Lawrence walked me to the front door of our house and then left with a tip of his hat. His engine sparked to life, but the sound quickly faded into the distance.

I tossed my hat onto the small foyer table and sauntered out the back door, into the garden. Starlight twinkled down from the black sky. The wind ruffled my hair, lifted the hem of my dress. I stepped up into the gazebo, leaned on the railing, and filled my lungs with fresh air. There had to be something else I could do, something I hadn't thought of yet. A trail of light across the ground caught my eye, brightness spilling from beneath the carriage house's doors.

Webster? Working on a Sunday evening? Then again, the race was less than a week away. And I'd heard Father mention a breakdown at the factory. Webster would have been called to repair that, as well. I plopped down on the bench beneath the railing. I wanted to watch that race as much as I wanted to raise the three thousand dollars.

Father had promised to take me to see an auto race one day. Why not this one?

I imagined the dust and the smoke, the cacophony of man

and machine at the Chicago Motor Speedway. Closing my eyes, I felt the vibration of the racing car's steering wheel in my hand, the bounce of tires over the dirt oval carved from an empty field.

My eyes sprang open and I leapt to my feet. Father would pay the man who drove the race car. Why couldn't that man be me?

I stared into the heavens. Could I do it? I'd have to have help—both in the driving and in disguising myself to drive, for my parents would never consent or approve. The heels of my shoes clomped across the board floor of the gazebo as shaking legs carried me down the steps, across the path. All the way to the garage. Then my feet refused to move. Was this too much to ask? He'd always helped me before. But this would be far different than driving in the back field, unseen and alone. With a deep breath and a quick prayer, I pushed open the door.

"Webster? You here?"

A muffled reply. I closed the door behind me, took tentative steps to reach the spot where he huddled over the racing car's engine.

"All set?" I peered over his shoulder into the exposed motor.

"Not quite. Need to give her some test runs this week."

"Good. That's what I wanted to talk to you about."

"Oh?" He straightened, crossed to the workbench, chose different parts, and returned to work.

"I can drive her, Webster."

He chuckled. "I know you can, Ally, but—"

I tugged at his sleeve until he turned. "I *need* to drive her."

He straightened, hands on his hips.

I gulped in as much air as my lungs would hold. "I need to drive her in the race."

"You *what?* Oh no. I can't—"

"Yes, you can. Please, Webster? I have nothing else to give. No skill. No possession. You know I can drive. You know I can drive fast. Work with me this week. If by the time we leave, you don't think I can, I won't. But you'll see. I want this more than anything." Tears welled in my eyes, and my throat turned thick. He had to agree. He just had to. This felt so right—a way to use the unusual talent God had given me to raise money for the missionaries.

He scratched his head, toed the ground, cleared his throat. "I just don't think it's a good idea."

"Because I'm not a good enough driver?"

"No." He looked up at me. "You know how they feel about women racing. They won't allow it."

I stepped forward, closing the distance between us. "They let Elfrieda Mais drive in that exhibition in Wichita on the Fourth of July."

"But she's licensed to race, even though they only let her race against Mrs. Cuneo. And Mrs. Cuneo's quit now. Besides, you weren't there that day. I was. The ladies thought her magnificent, of course. But the men?" He shook his head. "I can't repeat their comments about her. I won't subject you to that, Ally. Trust me."

"Couldn't we manage it so no one knows? As long as the car qualifies for speed, why does it matter who drives it?"

He huffed but didn't argue. Then he grabbed my shoulders, his gaze locking onto mine. "What if you get hurt? What then? You could even get killed out there, you know."

I spread my hands, palms up and empty. "My life is all I have to give." My arms dropped back to my sides.

Silence fell between us. I tried not to move, not to blink or to breathe. *Please, God, let him see this is the only way.*

It seemed hours until his shoulders slumped and he ran a hand through his mop of black hair. "All right. We'll try it. But I'm not making any promises. Not yet, anyway."

Wild joy careened me forward, my lips finding his cheek, my arms tightening around his neck. Strong arms circled my waist for a brief moment before falling away. I stood alone. Webster hunched over the racing car's engine again.

"I'll meet you at eight o'clock tomorrow morning," he said. "Be prepared for a long day."

I grinned. I knew Webster wouldn't let me down. I turned and ran back to the house, putting distance between us before I succumbed to the desire to throw my arms around him yet again.

12

$\mathcal{I}$ paced behind the stand of tulip poplars that obscured the carriage house from the garden, stopping every now and again to listen for footsteps crunching over dry grass, batting down the pistons churning in my stomach. If only they would settle. Instead, they stirred up the tea and toast I'd cajoled from Clarissa in the kitchen.

"Come on, Webster. Come on."

Back and forth. Stopping and starting.

Then he stood beside me, his grin cutting through my fear. "All ready, I see."

A quick nod, the swipe of my tongue over dry lips. The jangle of my nerves surprised me. I'd driven fast before. Many times. It wasn't as if speed frightened me. I pulled my shoulders back, stiffened my resolve. "Let's go."

We pushed the race car all the way to the road before I hopped in and he cranked the engine. A short jaunt and we turned off on the small path that led to the track.

Easing onto the smoother surface of the oval, I readied to surge forward, but Webster's hand reached across while his other made a cutting motion across his throat. I let the engine die. Silence engulfed us.

Webster shifted in his seat, twisting his body so he faced me. "Here's what you need to know. First, this track won't be as fast as the board one. Chicago has built a speed bowl, for sure. Resta covered ground on it at ninety-eight miles per hour in June. There's no reason to think this race will be any different."

I nodded, stared down at the speedometer, with its needle pointing to zero. Could I manage the car at speeds of near one hundred? "Got it."

"There will be four heat races first, ten laps each. Then the winners will race for fifty miles. The homestretch is a bit wider than the backstretch, so you have to watch yourself there. The turns are wider still, so there is room for shifting position. Obviously we can't practice banked turns on this track, so we'll just have to do our best for now. If I decide to let you drive—and I'm not saying yet that I will—there will be some practice rounds on the track to work out the kinks."

"Okay." I stared out over the hood of the car. The metal buckles of the leather straps cinched over the hood gleamed in the sunlight.

"For now, let's just focus on speed. Get her up above seventy and then slowly build. Ready?" He pulled his goggles over his eyes. I did the same. Then he hopped from the car and cranked the engine. The roar of it sparking to life chased every last butterfly from my being.

I'd thought all my previous excursions would have prepared

me for our practice runs. I was wrong. By the time we returned home four hours later, my legs shook, my arms ached, my head pounded.

But Webster declared me a success. Now I only had to find a way to Chicago.

It took every ounce of strength and determination I possessed to lift my feet up each step and lumber into my bedroom. It hurt even to press the button to call for Betsy.

"Would you please run a hot bath?" I asked when she appeared in my bedroom.

"Yes, miss." Her eyes questioned, but I avoided any answers.

"And would you bring up a tray of light lunch, please? For after my bath."

"Of course." She disappeared to do my bidding.

I sank to the edge of my bed, fighting the pull of the mattress, the comfort of a short nap. Or a long one. I refused to show weakness. Webster would be watching. I had to revive.

A soak in steaming water soothed my muscles and cleared my head. By the time I consumed the light luncheon on my tray, I felt quite my usual self again. Or at least no more weary than after my typical drives. And I'd come up with a plan.

Webster eyed me as I climbed into my Runabout. I took care not to wince as I lifted my arms. Settled behind the windscreen, I relaxed. At least until Webster appeared outside my window.

He squinted. "What are you up to now?"

"I'm off to secure my trip to Chicago."

His expression turned pensive. He sighed out a long breath. "I guess everything depends on that, doesn't it?"

"Father will concede. I feel sure. He only tried to keep it a secret so Mother wouldn't object. But she's still in bed with the bee sting."

"Whatever you say." He patted the hood of my car as if it were the haunches of a Thoroughbred.

I fired up the engine and took off toward town.

"Good afternoon, Father." I sauntered into his office and planted a kiss on his cheek.

He leaned back in his chair. "To what do I owe this pleasure?"

I sat and smoothed the green silk skirt over my knees, flicked a piece of lint from the fabric. "Actually, I have a request."

"I told you, Ally. No money for that scheme of yours."

I sat silent for a moment, my heart aching. Didn't he care that this was important to me? "Why? Help me understand."

He fished a cigar from the box on the desk. "We've been through this before, Ally girl."

"Not really. Explain why this incenses you so when you don't bat an eye about Mother's charitable work."

He puffed on his cigar. One hand rubbed across his forehead. "I don't trust that man."

"Who?"

"Pastor Swan."

"Did he try to cheat you?"

"No."

"Did he malign you?"

"No."

"What then?"

"I don't know if I can even explain. It's just that my father instilled in me the need to be independent. And it's served me well."

I opened my mouth, but he wouldn't let me interrupt.

"Oh, it's fine for you women, although your mother doesn't see the need for religion to make her happy."

My eyebrows arched. Happy? Not exactly the word I'd use to describe Mother, though I supposed she was happy on occasion.

And then I remembered Grandmother's story, how she'd told Mother and Father again and again. He didn't need another sermon from me. And it certainly wouldn't help my efforts to get to Chicago. I needed to redirect the conversation.

Quick as a turn at full speed, I made my request. "I want you to take me with you this weekend. To Chicago. To the race."

His large hand slapped the desktop, sending papers fluttering to the ground. "I told him not to breathe a word."

"Don't blame Webster, Father. I wheedled it out of him."

His lips twitched. Then he chuckled. "I should have known I couldn't keep a race from you. Especially one in Chicago."

"Of course not." I flashed a saucy grin. "Why else would you have had Webster building that car?"

He huffed and took another puff on his cigar. "The car was his idea, actually. He came to me and asked if I wanted to invest. Some prototype he developed. That man has aspirations far above a mere mechanic."

Webster's design? I kept the smile on my face, but my heart smarted. He'd never told me. But I couldn't think about that now. "So you'll take me with you?"

He lumbered to his feet. "Now, Ally, I won't have time to chaperone you properly. I have work to do while I'm there."

"I don't need to be tended like a hothouse flower. I lived in Chicago. Remember?"

"Yes, but this is different. This is—" A knock at the door stopped his words.

Lawrence poked his head inside. "Oh. I'm so sorry, Mr. Benson. I'll come ba—"

"Wait, Trotter." Father flicked the ash of his cigar into a square of tin. "Are you an auto-racing fan?"

Lawrence swallowed, his gaze cutting to mine before returning to my father's. "Yes, sir. I suppose I enjoy a race as much as the next man."

"Fine. Have you considered attending the event in Chicago this weekend?"

"This weekend? No, I hadn't considered it."

I tapped my fingers on Father's desk. What exactly was he up to?

"Any reason you couldn't go? Social calendar isn't full, is it?"

"No, sir. Nothing to keep me here." He looked at me once more. I gave him a small smile.

"Perfect. You'll accompany us to Chicago, then. I could use your input on a few business opportunities I'll be considering while I'm there. And of course I'll feel better if Ally has an escort on race day."

I suppressed a groan, careful to keep my eager expression intact. Now I had an escort for the day—and one that would report back to Father. How would I escape to drive?

Webster would not be pleased.

But if I balked, Father might turn suspicious. I gulped down my anxiety. I'd have to untangle this mess later. "I think that sounds perfect, Father."

Then a solution burst into my head like fireworks on a starless night. "And if I can persuade Mother to come along, too, she and I could spend some time together." As long as Mother and Lawrence each imagined me to be with the other, everything might work out.

Father grunted and plopped back into his chair. "Persuade your mother to come along, if you like. I doubt it will take more than a suggestion. Trotter, walk her to the car. Then you and I have work to do."

I stooped to kiss Father on the cheek once more before Lawrence escorted me out the door.

"You don't mind coming to Chicago with us, do you?"

Lawrence held the door open as we stepped into the heat of the day. "Of course not. I'm thrilled. Not only to see the race, but to accompany such a lovely lady."

We stopped at my car. He opened the door. I stepped behind it but made no move to slide into the seat. In spite of my need to excuse myself on race day, I found myself warming to him as a companion.

"Have you made any more progress raising your money?" Lawrence leaned across the top of the door.

My heart pumped harder as his face drew near mine. "Some."

"And you haven't given it away yet?"

I laughed. "No, not yet."

He eased back, brushed his fingernails on his jacket, cleared his throat. "So you found a safe place for it?"

"It's in my bedroom, for now. Grandmother gave me a special box to keep the money in."

"Do you think that's wise?"

My forehead crinkled. "Why not?"

"So many people in and out of your room."

"Betsy? She wouldn't think anything of it, even if she ran across it."

"Hmm." Tiny wrinkles framed his eyes, making him look

older than I imagined him to be. "Just be careful, Alyce. I would hate for anything to happen to your money."

"Thank you. Less than six weeks. I need every penny I can get. Oh—and Webster is going to sell some of my jewelry for me in Chicago. It should bring enough to replace what I gave away."

"I see." He glanced back toward the office building, concern rumpling his usually placid face.

"Go on. Get back to work. Father will only be patient for so long." I settled behind the wheel, shut the door, and started the engine. I had a feeling Mother would get over her bee sting as soon as the prospect of a trip to Chicago dangled in front of her. Now to plot my disguise . . .

13

The sharp smell of wet paint enveloped me as I stepped inside the garage.

"Whew!" I flapped my hand in front of my nose. "Why didn't you do that outdoors?"

Webster didn't look up as his brush, wet with white paint, stroked the top of a number 7 on the engine cover. "Too much wind. Blowing grass." He lifted his hand, squinted at his work. "That should do."

He dumped the brush into a can of liquid. "Can't take her out again until this dries. This evening. You okay with that?"

"So you'll let me drive again?"

"Are you going to be in Chicago?"

I nodded. "I worked it out with Father."

"Then I guess you'll be driving." One corner of his mouth lifted as his gaze of admiration fell on the race car and then lifted to my face. "She couldn't be in better hands."

Warmth bloomed in my cheeks as I dropped my chin.

"But don't you think you ought to tell your father, Ally? I mean, secrets can be dangerous things."

My stomach roiled, but at the thought of keeping silent or telling? "Good heavens, no! He'd, well, he'd never allow it. I think it's best to keep it to ourselves. For now."

He wiped the paint from his hands and tossed the rag onto the workbench. "But what if something happens?"

I stepped toward him, thankful I'd put off my silk dress in favor of my driving clothes. "It won't. You'll be there to help me. And the Lord will protect us."

"You sure about that?"

"This is His plan to provide for the work of the gospel. It has to be."

He stared at me for a long moment, much as he had the painted number on the car. Then he knelt on the ground to clean up his paintbrush.

I scooted onto the nearby stool. "There is one little rut in the road."

He stopped working. "How big a rut?"

Setting my feet on the upper rung of the stool, I gripped my knees. "Lawren—Mr. Trotter is coming along."

Scrubbing commenced again, with more agitation than before. "With your father?"

"Yes, but with me, too."

His head shot up. "What do you mean?"

"Father insisted he come along to escort me on race day." I hopped to the ground. My hand found his shoulder, keeping him from rising to his feet. "Don't worry. I'll make sure Mother comes, too. I'll tell him I'm shopping with her, that I'll meet him there later. Besides, Father needs him there for business, too. Not just for me. And if I know my father, he'll mix that business with the pleasure of a day at the races."

Webster's shoulders relaxed a bit. "You sure you can manage all that intrigue and drive, too?"

"You get me to the pits and on the track. I'll orchestrate the rest. Just find a place where I can change clothes—and wash up. Preferably a place no one will notice."

He rose to his feet. I found myself staring into eyes as dark as my morning coffee. And just as warm.

Midmorning on Thursday, Mother and I stood on the train platform as the whistle of the engine screeched through town, calling us aboard the Hoosier Line.

"Hurry, Alyce." Mother stepped up into a railway car as I strained to glimpse Webster supervising the loading of the racer. Perhaps it had already rolled aboard, for I couldn't see either man or car.

"Let's go, Ally." Father looked at his pocket watch. He wouldn't come until tomorrow, but Mother needed no coaxing to leave a day early.

I began to leap up the steps, then paused and did my best to ascend in a slow, ladylike manner. From the platform, Father followed my progress to my seat. I settled next to Mother, who looked regal in spite of the heat and soot. Fresh as a blooming rose, she was, while I already felt as wilted and plain as a week-old daisy.

The train lurched forward. I pressed my hand to my purse. Two of Grandmother's broaches, my three necklaces, a ring, and a bracelet filled the interior. I hoped the trinkets would bring in enough to cover what I'd given away.

The woman across the aisle initiated a conversation with

Mother. I closed my eyes and leaned my head against the plush velvet seat. Never in my wildest dreams had I anticipated returning to Chicago with such enthusiasm. Or with two such friends as Webster and Lawrence. I thought of Webster, somewhere in the freight cars behind. Was he nervous? Excited? Afraid? This car was his creation, though he still remained secretive about that fact. Again, I felt a niggle of frustration. Why hadn't he told me?

Stop it! No time for vain speculation. I'd never known Webster to be devious in any way. He must have had sound reasons for withholding his part in the project.

Heat wafted in through the open window. I closed it and studied my reflection in the glass. Did it matter who built the car—or who drove it? My lips curved into a grin. Or who others thought drove it. The end result would be the same: money to fund the McConnells' work in the Gold Coast villages. A worthy endeavor.

But it wouldn't hurt to have a bit of fun in the process.

The moment we disembarked at Dearborn Station, the bustle of the busy streets energized me. I'd truly enjoyed my two years at the Chicago School of Domestic Arts and Sciences. From cooking to household economy, my classes had fascinated and challenged me. In fact, the only things I had missed during my time away from Langston were my grandmother and my drives.

Ensconced in the hotel, Mother lounged on the sofa, sorting through a sheaf of invitations. How in the world did so many people know we'd be in town this weekend?

"We've been invited to dinner Saturday evening." Mother tossed aside three other cards with barely a glance. "Everyone who is anyone in Chicago will be there."

"Oh?" I peered into the mirror above the dresser and fluffed my curls with my fingers. I knew that those who could afford it left the city for the summer months. Perhaps that meant fewer "anyones" to invite.

"I expect you'll not embarrass us again. Not like you did the last time I took you to a soiree."

I stifled a giggle, giving a generic hum instead, not actually agreeing to her directive. Poor Mother. Instead of flirting with millionaires' sons, I'd found a kindred soul with whom to discuss our faith. Maria and I had hid in a corner and talked the whole long evening.

At least I wouldn't have to worry about my behavior until Saturday night. After the race. I hugged the thought of a first-place win, even knowing it was beyond my skill level. But all I had to do was place first in my heat, reach the finals. Then I would receive at least a slice of the prize money, even if that slice resembled a sliver rather than a feast. Whether or not my purse bulged from prize money by Saturday night, the party might provide another opportunity to garner donations for the Gold Coast.

Fumbling through my handbag, I found the picture, rumpled on two corners now. I pressed them smooth and smiled at the young children I knew by heart. How could anyone resist those faces? I felt sure my picture would find its way in front of the eyes of all in attendance at the party.

The photo went back into my purse. I needed to figure out the way to the track. To Webster. I pinned my hat in place. "I'm off to pay a call, Mother."

"Oh?" She started to rise. "I'll come with you."

"No! I mean, it's been a long day, Mother. And you're just getting over the bee sting. You rest for now."

She settled back down. I kissed her cheek, allowing her to

hold my hand for a long moment before my fingers drifted from her touch.

"Have fun, Alyce darling."

I returned her smile, eager to be off on my adventure. But out on the sidewalk, guilt slowed my steps. If she knew my destination, she wouldn't be so amiable about my leaving. With a tilt of my head skyward, I peered at the corner window on the third floor of the hotel. No shadow of movement caught my eye. I tucked my handbag closer to my body and turned my feet in the direction of an elevated train that would carry me closer to Maywood, home of the Chicago Motor Speedway.

No, Mother had no idea.

Two hours later, I left the racetrack, dejected. Few people mingled in the expanse. Fewer cars. No sign of Webster or the bright blue roadster with the white number 7. I boarded the train back to the hotel but got off at an earlier stop. I needed to walk. I needed air.

My feet scuffed against the steps leading to the street. No Webster. No drive. No reassurance that our plan would work. Even my jewelry weighed heavy in my purse, as I hadn't yet given it into Webster's care.

So much my heart wanted to do for others. So many unknowns littering the path.

Sunlight dappled the walk beneath my feet, dancing with the leaves that shivered in the balmy breeze. Surely Webster hadn't forgotten that I needed to do some practice runs. He did remember that I'd never driven on boards—or over banked turns, didn't he? I turned onto Michigan Avenue. Water lapped the shore across the way, drawing me. Careful to avoid the motorcars and the horses, I hurried over the road. Just as I reached the walk on the other side, a gust of wind wrapped my skirt around my legs. A man bumped my left arm. I toppled and landed sprawled on the pavement, my hat drooping down over my left eye.

Pairs of feet stepped around me. Passed me. Unaffected by my sorry state. Or my father's wealth. Or my mother's social reputation.

For an instant, I lay stunned. Alone. Unable to right myself on the crowded walk. Then a masculine hand reached down and lifted me to my feet. A tip of his hat hid his face as he disappeared into the throng.

Rescued. Not abandoned.

"Forgive me, Lord," I whispered as people surged around me. Doubt might have tripped me up for a moment, but now that I'd regained my feet, I didn't intend to falter again.

14

Before Mother woke the next morning, I traced my path back to the speedway. After talking my way past the guard at the gate, I hid beneath the grandstands. Pushing up on my toes, I peered between the bench seats. Today, drivers and mechanics zipped around the two-mile wooden track. Voices called. Engines started and stopped.

My toes cramped. I bent my knees to look through a lower gap. I needed to find Webster—and our car. A Peugeot skidded around the end of the oval. My stomach lurched. The diminutive driver regained control, hunched further over the steering wheel, and increased his speed on the back straightaway.

Dario Resta. My heart drummed in my ears. Could I race against such men?

I crept to the edge of the grandstand and peeked out. Father would arrive in Chicago today, but would he come early to watch the practice runs? I stepped out a little farther and looked up into the grandstand seats. A few men in suits sat watching, each separated from the other. I shrank back. If Father were here, he would be with those men, the ones whose unsullied hands doled out the money for the cars and drivers and mechanics. The ones who sought glory through the machine their company built.

But none resembled Father. Or Mr. Trotter.

Men hollered to one another. Metal clanked against metal between the growl of engines. A Duesenberg rested a few yards away, the top half of a mechanic's body lost beneath the open engine cover. I stepped closer. The acrid smell of gasoline, burning rubber, and sweat tangled in my nose, sweeter to me than the scent of any Parisian perfume. Then a familiar whistle drifted closer. I ducked beneath the grandstand again. A man swaggered past, dirty rag hanging out of the back pocket of his white mechanic's jumpsuit.

My fingers grazed his sleeve. The whistle silenced as he whipped around, eyes searching. My whole body tingled with warmth—different than the summer heat that dribbled beads of perspiration down the middle of my back. I stepped into the full light of the sun.

He blinked, but then the familiar grin stretched his wide mouth.

"Here I am." My words shook a bit as my stomach swerved like Resta's car on the curve a few minutes ago.

His head turned casually to the left and then to the right, his whistle starting up once more, though quieter this time. He pulled me into the shadows.

While one hand lifted his cap, the other raked through his dampened hair. Both hands fixed his cap back on his head before resting on his hips. "Are you sure you want to do this?"

"I am. Did you square things with the other driver?"

His eyes shifted as his jaw tightened and released. He returned his gaze to mine and gave a sharp nod.

"Oh, I almost forgot." I reached into my handbag and retrieved the jewelry I'd determined to part with. "Will you sell these for me, please?"

He pulled a clean rag from the front pocket of his jumpsuit. "Put 'em here. I'll deal with 'em later."

I dumped the bits of jewelry into the center of the rag. He tied the ends and shoved it into his pocket. "Let's get you dressed." One hand on my elbow, he led me out into the sunshine but then pulled us back into the shade beneath the stands. "One more thing. The race has been moved to Sunday. Some of the drivers are backing out. What about you?"

Sunday? That gave me another day to practice. But ought I race on the Lord's Day? Would it be proper? Should I make a stand to prove my faith to Webster, or was my effort to raise money for those precious people across the globe a holy act, one the Lord would approve of no matter on which day it took place?

Like tug-of-war in a schoolyard, my thoughts pulled back and forth, inching first one way and then the other. Webster waited. I closed my eyes, breathed a prayer, heard only silence. All I knew to do was continue on the course I'd determined. This was my last hope of raising the money I'd committed to give. And with others out, maybe I had a better chance of finishing at the top of my heat and ending with a slice of the prize money. "I'll race."

Webster's chest swelled and then deflated. "All right, then. I've got a place for you to change. We'll practice more than just driving today." With a wink, he crooked his elbow. I curled my fingers around his arm and pranced into the open, determined to appear to all the world as if nothing out of the ordinary were about to take place.

Exhilaration carried me back to the hotel that afternoon. Even after my bath, the excitement of the drive pinked my cheeks. Never had I experienced such speed. And though at first the banked turns sent my stomach careening into my throat, I finally figured out I wouldn't tip over. But could I maintain my speed with other cars fighting for space on the track? All I knew for certain was that I wanted to try.

I joined Mother in our sitting room as suppertime approached. The clock struck six. A few minutes later, Father burst into the room. With long strides, he reached Mother, leaned down, and planted a loud kiss on her cheek.

She blushed, fingers stealing up to touch the spot on her face. "Why, Harry! Whatever was that for?"

He tossed his hat on a chair. "Do I need a reason to be happy to see my wife?"

After making room for him on the sofa, she snuggled into his arms. She looked young again. Not the young of her hardscrabble youth. Young the way she wanted *me* to look. And the light in Father's eyes when he looked at her stirred a bit of that desire in me, too.

Turning to leave them alone with each other, I found myself face-to-face with Lawrence Trotter. "Oh. I'm sorry. I didn't know . . ." I glanced back at my parents, but they'd become oblivious to anyone but each other. "Won't you, um . . ."

Ought I invite Lawrence in or invite myself out?

He took a step backward, into the hall. I followed, pulling the door almost shut behind me. My hands fidgeted as my gaze roamed the empty hall.

"Did you have a pleasant trip?"

He nodded and glanced past me. "Your father invited me to join the family for supper."

"Did he? How wonderful." My mind whirled as fast as tires on a board track. Not only would Lawrence give me a conversational companion at the table, it would afford an opportunity to put my Sunday plan into motion. I had to escape his attention on race day with a legitimate excuse. Or at least a legitimate-sounding one.

My conscience pricked. Lies atop secrets. Was this truly God's plan? It had to be. I could see no other way.

"Should I come back later?"

Mother's soft laughter drifted from the room, followed by the rustle of her dress. I pushed the door open a bit and peeked inside.

"Alyce? We're taking supper in the restaurant downstairs. Is Mr. Trotter with you?"

"Yes, he is." I swung the door wide, revealing us both.

Father reached for Mother's hand, enfolded it within his own, then raised it to his lips, his eyes never leaving her face. "Lead the way, Trotter."

"My pleasure, sir." With a slight bow, he offered me his arm and escorted me to the elevator.

Mother and I sat across from each other at the dining table. We conversed of the weather and Father's work and the hotel, until finally the waiter set our food before us. Toward the end of supper, Mother put on her company smile and turned her attention to Lawrence.

"Mr. . . . . Trotter, was it?"

Lawrence inclined his head.

"So good of you to join us." Her eyes cut to me for only a moment. "Forgive me, but I didn't catch where you and our Alyce formed your acquaintance."

I dabbed my napkin at my mouth as Father cleared his throat and reached for Mother's hand.

"Mr. Trotter is my bookkeeper, Winifred."

"Oh." She drew out the word, as if trying to figure out what to make of that piece of information. I squirmed in my seat. The last thing I desired was a family row over what constituted an eligible beau.

"I asked him to escort Ally to the race on Sunday."

Mother's pretty mouth turned pouty. "Now, Harry. You know how I feel—"

"How was Grandmother when you left?" I kept my voice bright and focused my attention on Father as he answered. But I couldn't miss Mother's pursed lips, then their downward turn.

"I expect you'll meet all manner of eligible men here in Chicago, Alyce," she said.

My eyes cut toward Lawrence, but he didn't appear discomposed. "Yes, Mother."

She turned to Father. "Will you secure us a car for tomorrow evening? I imagine we'll be out quite late."

My back stiffened. Out late. On Saturday night. With the big race happening the next day. Would Mother's party be the undoing of all my plans?

Lawrence stood. "Would you care to take a stroll, Miss Benson?"

He looked to Father for approval and received it with a wave of Father's hand.

"Thank you, Law—Mr. Trotter." I stood. "That would be quite agreeable."

Mother's eyes narrowed, but she didn't object. We exited the dining room, then the hotel. A warm breeze rustled the leaves on the trees as we sauntered toward a small park area.

No better time than now to situate things for Sunday. "Lawrence." I smiled up at him. "I've run into a bit of a snag for Sunday's outing." I stopped walking. "You do know the race has been changed to Sunday?" My heart skipped a beat.

"Yes. Your father and I heard it on the way to town. I hope this doesn't change things. I've looked forward to our day together."

The light in his eyes almost melted my resolve to disappoint him.

He motioned to a bench. I sat, as did he. I laced my fingers, laid them in my lap, and gazed out over the green square of land in the midst of the city.

His arm stretched across the back of the bench, behind my shoulders. I shivered with unexpected delight. He leaned closer to me. "So tomorrow is free—unless, of course, your father requires my assistance. Perhaps we could take in the Lincoln Park Zoo."

I prayed he wouldn't notice my fingers tightening on each other. "What a lovely thought. But I'm—spending the day with Mother. And then there's that dreaded dinner party of hers in the evening." I shuddered. "And on Sunday . . . You see, a friend has asked me to visit."

I swatted back the buzz of my conscience. He didn't need to know that the friend was Webster and our visit would be at the speedway.

His countenance fell. I twisted to face him, my hand lighting for a brief moment on his knee. "But I'd be happy to meet you later on Sunday, at the speedway."

"I don't know. Your father—"

"I'll make sure he understands. Besides, this frees you to attend church on Sunday morning, if you prefer."

His head tipped to one side as he studied me, his face a blank mask. Then his expression opened again. "I'll be happy to see you at whatever moment you choose, Alyce."

A calming wave surged through me. Lawrence might be a different type of friend than Webster, but he remained a friend all the same. I gave him my brightest smile. "I'll look forward to that moment, as well."

15

It was more difficult to slip away with Father around, but I managed. Webster and I zoomed through several more practice laps. Soon I felt more comfortable on the banked turns, but I was still the only car on the boards. When I returned to the hotel, my parents had gone out. I blessed this turn of events and soaked in the tub for an hour, rehearsing the track again in my head, imagining the effort with more noise, more smoke, more dirt.

More excitement.

But first, I had to make it through this evening's party.

After my parents returned, Mother had tea sent up, and we dressed. Father grumbled that it was time to go. Just before we headed out, I slipped back into my room and grabbed the photograph of the Gold Coast children, placing it in the evening bag hanging from my wrist. I promised myself I wouldn't make a scene, but if an opportunity presented itself . . .

The sun slid toward the horizon as we alighted from the hired car on Prairie Avenue, a street lined with grand mansions of the past. But the venerable names no longer lived here. They'd moved north, to the Gold Coast. Not my Gold Coast. Theirs was along the shore of Lake Michigan.

The brick house owned by Mother's friends rose tall, chimneys and dormers jutting up from the rooftop. A flight of wide steps rose to an arch, beneath which the front door remained aloof from the elements. Soft illumination flowed out tall windows into the street below, where we stood after climbing from the car.

Excited exclamations greeted Mother as she swept through the front door on Father's arm. Her face glowed with each press of cheek to cheek, each reintroduction of Father to one of her friends. Her laugh trilled across the room, accompanied by graceful movements and a joy she rarely exuded in Langston. Mother seemed to feel in this environment as I did behind the wheel—as if she were made for this moment.

I trailed my parents through room after room, making polite conversation, until I found myself alone, an untouched glass of wine in my hand. A footman strolled past. I set my glass on his tray. An eyebrow rose in question. I dismissed it with a tight smile.

"Alyce! Whatever are you doing in town?" Lisa Gentry kissed the air in front of my cheek, babbling on as if we hadn't seen each other in years instead of just the couple months since graduation. "Look who's here, girls."

Three or four others joined us. Then I noticed the young men hovering about the edges of our group. Inch by inch, they worked their way in among us.

"What *have* you been up to out there in the country, Alyce?"

Regina batted her eyes at the sandy-haired young man across the circle from her as she spoke.

Lisa took up the refrain, with a shy smile at the dark-haired gentleman at her side. Then her gaze locked with mine. She smiled. I relaxed. It was all the opening I needed. Reaching into my bag, I pulled out the picture of the African children. "I've been quite busy, actually." I held out the photograph. The other girls gathered around, then looked up, each face puckering into a question.

"These children live in a place called the Gold Coast, in Africa. They have need of food and shelter and clothing. But beyond the things needed to survive in this life, they need the gospel of Jesus Christ. I'm raising money to send a missionary couple back to their work among the villages there."

Delicate eyebrows lifted. Gloved fingers tried to block giggles from smirking lips. I stepped back, suddenly feeling as out of place as a horse and phaeton on an auto-racing track. What had made me think they would care about children with hopeless eyes?

Lisa brushed her hand against the dark-haired gentleman's arm, then gazed into his eyes. No, these girls cared only about finding a suitable husband. Perhaps then would they turn their thoughts to others, as Mother had suggested.

I took a step backward. Young men filled in the empty space, crowding me from the circle. I retreated to the wall, watching from afar. The gentlemen hung on the girls' playful words, punctuated by looks stolen from beneath their downturned lashes. My fingers tightened on the photograph. I wished someone would listen to me with such rapt attention.

"Alyce?" Mother's voice carried across the room.

I jammed the picture back into concealment.

"Come, darling. I have someone I want you to meet." She

hooked her arm through mine and led me into the library. Two men I'd never seen before stood conversing near the open windows.

"Mr. Bragg, Mr. Steel. May I present my daughter, Miss Alyce Benson."

We exchanged greetings. Mother patted my hand and then retreated.

They filled in the awkward silence with customary dinner party pleasantries. Mr. Bragg had yellow spun-silk hair and a lean frame. Mr. Steel was a heftier man, but not fleshy. Plainer features. More intelligent eyes. Both impeccably dressed. Obviously these were men of money and culture. Even if their faith consisted only of church attendance on Easter and Christmas, maybe my picture would stir their hearts to help.

If they gave me just one opening in the conversation, I'd dash through it.

A burst of giggles preceded a group of young ladies step-ping into the library. Mr. Bragg's gaze moved idly in their direction. Mr. Steel fought the magnetism a bit longer but finally lost. My enthusiasm drooped. Why couldn't I capture these men the way the other girls did?

Or could I?

Closing my eyes, I imagined the wide eyes in thin faces staring back at me through the miracle of photography. I told myself I would do anything to help them. With a deep breath, I inched closer to Mr. Steel and Mr. Bragg, wearing my most coquettish smile. Their eyes snapped back in my direction. Saucy questions and compliments flew from my mouth. Their attention deepened, even though the other girls stood just beyond the scope of our conversation.

Mr. Bragg lifted his glass and drank deep. Mr. Steel's gaze

wandered over my face. "Tell me, Miss Alyce. What do you find to do in the country?"

I waved my hand. "Oh, this and that. However, I have recently come upon quite a project."

Mr. Bragg took up the challenge. "And what cause has piqued your interest?"

"Why, I can show you." Out came the photograph. Again I explained, but this time with playful smiles and shy glances tempering my usual passion.

Mr. Steel plucked the photo from my fingers. "Interesting way to pass your time."

Mr. Bragg leaned toward the picture, too. The young women around us whispered amongst themselves. Then a petite brunette pushed between me and Mr. Bragg, her arm looping through mine.

"Isn't she a dear to want to help?" She addressed Mr. Bragg, her eyes doelike. Then she turned to me. "I meant to show the photograph to my mother. May I?"

She whisked the picture from Mr. Steel's hand and headed for the door.

"Wait!" I flew after her, colliding with a small reading shelf. Books tumbled to the floor, smashing into my toes. I yelped. Jumped away. Mr. Bragg and Mr. Steel appeared at each arm, helping me limp after my photograph.

As we passed the music room, crowded with guests, I spied her, indeed handing my prized possession to her mother.

"In there." I nodded. We entered. The girl's mother handed the picture back. The girl's lashes shaded eyes feigning innocence, drawing the men from my side to hers. She placed the photograph on the slanted lid of the open piano, her attention fully absorbed by the dance of flirtation around her.

For a moment the picture remained on its precarious perch.

Then a passing guest stirred the air. It slid down the slope and skidded over the wood floor, beneath unsuspecting feet. I followed it with my eyes, then my feet. But every time I neared my treasure, an errant toe propelled it farther from my reach. Back and forth. This way and that. I darted through the crowd, throwing swift apologies.

I tried to catch someone's attention. Mr. Bragg. Or Mr. Steel. Or one of the other girls. But they'd lost interest in me. Again I searched the floor. But the photo had disappeared. I bit my lip and plopped dejectedly into a chair beneath an open window. Then I spied a wisp of something beneath the piano. I leaned down. There, lodged between the instrument's leg and the wall, was my beloved picture. I had to rescue it. A quick glance around assured me that other guests were minding their own conversations, not my actions.

I dropped to my knees and crawled to the corner, my backside in the air. Plucking up my photograph, I sat back in relief.

Then I noticed the quiet in the room.

"Alyce." Mother's hiss.

I crept to the edge of the piano and stuck my head out from beneath it. "Yes, Mother?"

She reached down, helped me to my feet. A buzz filled the emptiness, and I knew Mother felt the sting as surely as she had the bee's in the garden a few days ago.

Her eyes blazed in her white face. Her voice never rose above a whisper. "I'll call for your father to escort you back to the hotel." She turned on her heel and charged from the room.

Tears pushed at my eyes, but I shook them away. I stared at the picture in my hand, the faces marred with dust, the edges crinkled. No one met my gaze as I stumbled into the foyer to wait for Father. At least now I could get back to our room and get some rest before tomorrow's race.

The race. That was why I'd come. Not for the attention of people I didn't know, who didn't know me. Mother wished for my social success. I only wanted to succeed on the track.

I glanced once more at the precious faces before stuffing the picture back into my bag. No matter what tomorrow brought, motoring over the oil-slick boards with smoke in my face would be a cinch compared to this.

16

A yawn stretched my face as I arrived at the speedway Sunday morning. In spite of my early departure from the party, after I'd climbed into my bed last night, sleep had refused to come.

My eyelids felt heavy as I searched for Webster among the bustle of mechanics near the pits—really just space in the infield, off the track. Although I knew the meeting place and the plan, his very presence would settle me like no one else's.

I tucked a curl behind my ear. Just another Sunday drive, I told myself. One I hoped would result in money for my red box.

A three-note whistle. Our signal. I spun around. Webster jumped from the shadows, his usual jocularity turned pensive.

"Let's go." Tight, nervous words. He strode toward the shack where I'd changed clothes for the past two days. I almost had to run to keep up, glancing back over my shoulder every few seconds to make sure neither my father nor Lawrence appeared.

Webster opened the weathered wooden door and nodded. "Remember, I'll knock three times. Your bag is beneath the crate in the back, like before. And the bucket of water and toweling for cleaning up afterward."

Before I could thank him, the door thumped shut and musty darkness surrounded me. I concentrated on a small square of light streaming through a window that sat well above my head. Then I pushed a large box in front of the door before stripping down to my modern underclothes.

A sudden chill shook me. I rubbed my hands up and down my arms. Would I race against Dario Resta? Or Ralph De Palma? What if I panicked? What if I crashed? What if someone figured out I was a woman? My hands turned slick as my head throbbed with the unknowns.

"I can do this. I can." I pulled up my knickers. Dropped the large brown men's shirt over my head, let it drape across my shoulders. Then I stepped into the jumpsuit that identified me as a member of the racing team. It billowed out, disguising my slender frame.

After tucking every strand of hair beneath the tight-fitting driving cap Webster had given me, I positioned the goggles on top of my head, ready to set them in place once I walked through the door. But I still felt exposed. I leaned down, rubbed my hands along the dirt floor, and brushed them across my face.

Better. I took a deep breath. And waited.

Here I am, Lord.

No voice answered, yet I felt only peace.

Three knocks. The door pushed against the box holding it shut. "Ally?" came the whisper. "You ready?"

I shoved the box aside. The door creaked open.

Webster looked me up and down. "You'll do. Resta's small,

too, so you won't look strange. And most people will be too far away to notice anything . . . different. Once you're sitting in the car, we'll be set. You're in the third heat. The mechanical crew has been told that the driver is high-strung and not to talk to him. They're willing but wary. Just play your part. I'll come for you just before start time and lead you straight to the pit area. We'll settle in the car and pull up to the starting line. Rolling start, pace car for half a lap. Any questions?"

A million and one raced through my mind, but I shook my head anyway. No use voicing uncertainties that couldn't be answered. The door clicked behind him, leaving me again alone in the dim and stuffy storage room. I dropped to my knees but couldn't think of another word to say. Even in prayer.

Forever later—or was it a mere minute?—three raps sounded on the door. I grabbed the handle, yanked it open. With no more than a glance in Webster's direction, I strode toward the pits and the bright blue roadster with the white number 7. I knew this car. I knew I could drive it.

Mechanics peeled back, leaving a clear path. I climbed behind the wheel. Webster cranked the engine before jumping into the seat beside me, his grin as wide as Lake Michigan. As I'd done before, I eased the automobile into first gear. My insides jittered with the thrill of competition as the other cars did the same. We all rolled onto the track, followed the pace car, and watched for the red flag to signal our start.

I didn't turn my head to see who I would be racing against. I didn't want to know. Instead, I focused on the track in front of me, at least the bit I could see through the billowing exhaust.

"Steady." Webster's voice seemed a whisper, but I knew he was shouting. "I'll keep up with who's behind you."

"What if I'm the one behind?" I gripped the steering wheel and stared straight ahead.

"No chance, Ally." He leaned into my line of vision. "Flag's up. Get ready. Now go!"

It took only seconds to shift into top gear, throttle open, gaining speed. Like on the track at home, the air slapped my face as the sun beat down on my head. We surged to the front of the pack, only one other car ahead of me. But that car refused to be overtaken. Around the curve. Another straightway. Another curve. Only a ten-lap race. A mere twenty minutes or less. I leaned in, pushed my foot to the floorboard.

Another car inched closer, its front wheels in line with mine. I glanced at Webster, his body twisted to watch behind us. When I glanced again, he faced me, his mouth moving, but I couldn't hear over the roar of the engines. Or was it the roar of my heart in my ears? Knuckles white, I kept one eye on the track, one on the nose of the race car inching ahead of me.

How many laps? I hadn't counted. And I dared not look up at the board that marked our progress. We whizzed past the grandstands, the spectators no more than a blur. Finally, I saw it up ahead—the checkered flag. Waiting.

"C'mon. C'mon." I wished the car could be coaxed to try harder. But nothing I did could spur the engine to a faster pace. In a flash, we passed the flag.

The crowd erupted in cheers. My head turned one direction, then another. Had I won? I couldn't tell. I let off the gas, downshifted, rolled to a stop in the pit. Then my eyes sought the scoreboard.

Runner up. By less than a second.

Just short of the win. Just short of even the smallest share of the prize money.

I wanted to burst into tears. But I couldn't. Not here.

Webster nudged me from the car, his voice near my ear. "Go on. Get out of here. Get changed."

I stumbled forward on legs still pulsating with the vibration of the car, thankful for the muck of oil and dirt that hid my face from recognition.

"Where'd he go?" Father's voice carried over the din, propelling me into the crowd of mechanics and drivers preparing for the next heat. Three strides. Four. Five. I glanced back. No sign of Father. I stalked on through the commotion, the back-slapping, the congratulations, then snaked through the grandstands and back to the storage shed.

The crowd thinned near my changing place. I slipped inside, eased the door shut, and slid the large crate in front of the door before I stumbled to the back wall, eager to relieve my shaky knees. I plopped down on a wooden crate. My chest heaved. My shoulders shook. I covered my mouth and doubled over with giddy laughter.

I'd driven in a race. A real race. And I hadn't been left behind.

Oh, how proud my father would be. If only I could tell him.

Father. Voices outside the small window sobered me instantly. I had to get back to Father. And Lawrence. They'd be expecting me.

Deep breaths slowed my heart as I wiped grime from my hands with a delicate lace handkerchief. I used the shirt I'd worn to wipe oil and dirt from my face and neck before splashing on the warm water. A bird bath to rinse the rest of my limbs. A quick dry with the towel, then I wiggled back into my dress. Driving clothes returned to the carpetbag beneath the upended empty crate in the corner, I eased into the throng of spectators, praying I didn't smell worse than anyone else in attendance.

There was Webster, still in his jumpsuit. He leaned against the grandstand railing, one foot crossed casually over the other. His familiar grin settled me as he offered his arm. "You okay?"

I held my breath for a brief moment. Tingles raced over my arms and legs as his gaze held mine. I almost wished my knees would give way, that his arms would wrap around me, hold me tight. But even that momentary attraction paled against the knowledge of what I'd just done. "When can we do that again?"

His laughter pealed into the air. I pressed closer, my words meant for his ears alone. "Seriously, Webster. I know I'll get the driver's pay for this time, but I could win all the money I need for the McConnells if I could just place in one race."

He stopped, smile fading, eyes searching mine. "You did fine today. Quite well, in fact. But it's dangerous, Ally. And there are no guarantees."

I sobered a bit. "I know. But you'll help me."

He looked away. Why did he hesitate? Did I spy new fear in his face? Fear of my father? Or fear for me?

A cluster of men in suits sauntered past. Webster raised his voice. "Fancy meeting you here, Miss Alyce. May I help you locate your father?"

I bit back a giggle. "I'd be most obliged, Mr. Little. I seem to have lost my way."

He spun me toward the far grandstands, chattering nonsense as we walked. I only hoped Father and Lawrence attributed my glow to a beautiful day and a good showing by our car. For that would be the absolute truth.

A minute later, my gaze landed on a well-dressed man, a familiar figure. Away from the crowd. Conversing with two men in rougher attire.

He turned. Our eyes met.

Lawrence.

I called across the distance and waved. The two men slunk away. Webster let go of my arm, followed a few paces behind.

When I placed my hands in Lawrence's, I breathed relief. "I told you I'd find you."

"So you did." Lawrence glanced backward before linking my arm with his. I bit my lip and peeked behind us. Webster vanished into the shadows of the grandstands.

"Shall we join your father for the final race?" Lawrence asked.

"Of course."

It seemed no time at all until Lawrence directed my attention high in the grandstands. A cigar protruded from Father's mouth as he rocked back on his heels, hands lost in the pockets of his pants, eyes trained on the track. Two dapper men stood in the row just below him. The taller man's mouth moved rapidly, along with his hands. The shorter man nodded on occasion.

Father didn't seem to pay them much mind. Then his big voice carried over the chaos. "Ally, my girl!"

For a fraction of a moment I considered retreating. Then I got my wits about me and hurried up the steps and into my father's outstretched arms.

Laughter swelled from his belly. "Quite exciting to have a stake in the race, even if we didn't make the final round."

The truth threatened to burst from me. But I couldn't spoil it all now. "So true. In fact, it almost made me feel as if I drove in the race myself." I swallowed down a niggle of guilt.

Father chuckled, chortled, then bellowed as he laid his arm across my shoulders. I joined in his amusement. He wiped his eyes as his head wagged back and forth. "I've never understood why other people don't appreciate you, my girl."

I winced. He'd thought my quip about driving charming, but would he find the truth as humorous? My stomach clenched. He might even scorn what I'd accomplished.

The five heat winners pulled forward to the starting line. I sat. Lawrence settled on my other side, leaning forward to hear our conversation.

"Little's automobile held its own. And the driver did well, wouldn't you say?" Father looked like a schoolboy who'd just won at a game of marbles.

"Not in the same class as Resta, of course," I said, "but fine."

Father snorted. "No one's in the same class as Resta. Except maybe Rickenbacker."

"Better not let De Palma hear you say that."

Father chuckled. "That's my girl. But I still wonder that Webster let that other man take his place."

My heart stumbled, then seemed to still. "Webster's place?"

"Of course. He built that car. Who better to drive it?"

Sourness flooded my throat as the red flag flapped. Cars shot around the track. Lap after lap, Resta pulling ahead of Rickenbacker. Rickenbacker surging forward once more. Minutes ticked past. A few laps to go. Then the final stretch.

Rick's Peugeot jerked, slowed, limped to the pits. Resta zipped past the checkered flag to wild cheers. The Gold Cup and the bulk of the five-thousand-dollar prize belonged to Dario Resta.

But that mattered little to me right then. Not in the face of Webster's sacrifice.

17

By the time we boarded the train back to Langston on Monday morning, I longed for the openness of our country home, the breeze that meandered through the tall windows on all but the fiercest days of summer.

The minute we walked through the front door, I tore off my hat and flung it into the morning room.

"Alyce!" Mother scolded. "Do behave yourself."

Without bothering to reply, I charged up the stairs two at a time. "Grandmother? We're home!"

I stopped in the doorway of her room. She lay at an odd angle, as if she'd fallen asleep while sitting and then gradually slid to one side.

"Grandmother?" A step forward. Then two. Wooden movements. Attempting to swallow down my fear. I laid a hand on her shoulder. She didn't stir.

"Granny?" I shook her just a bit.

Nothing.

"Father! Clarissa!" I backed out of the room, stumbled down the stairs, screamed their names again, reached for the telephone. The operator's words jumbled in my ears.

"We need the doctor right away," I told her. My voice sounded too calm. My lips felt dry. My hands like ice. I replaced the earpiece and whirled around.

Mother stood behind me. She laid a hand on my arm. "I'll send the doctor up when he arrives. You go sit with her."

I nodded so many times I wondered if my head would ever stop bobbing. I raced back to the bedroom. Father and Clarissa stood over Grandmother, straightening her body, talking in hushed tones.

"Is she—" Now my hands squeezed each other white as I waited for an answer. Father's pale face frightened me more than Grandmother's unresponsiveness.

"There's still a beating in her chest," Clarissa said. "I put one of her pills on her tongue. I spoke with her no more than ten minutes past." Her lilt calmed me some.

I closed my eyes and dropped to my knees at Grandmother's bedside, tears dampening the sheet. A heavy hand settled on my shoulder. I reached up and covered it with my own, letting my fingers curl around my father's and squeeze tight.

The next thing I knew, Dr. Maven rushed into the room and Mother knelt beside me, her hand gripping mine. I leaned into her, felt her arm cup my shoulder and pull me close. For the first time in many years, I laid my head against my mother's chest and sobbed.

"I can't tell you what will happen next." Dr. Maven's mouth drooped with each word. "Clarissa did right getting those nitrates into her, but beyond that we just don't know."

Father crossed the room, hands behind his back, shoulders slumped. None of his usual swagger or strength. "Who *does* know? We'll take her there. Europe even."

The doctor shrugged. "Even if I knew someone who could help you, she's too weak to move at the moment. You'll just have to bide your time here."

Time. The one thing Father couldn't buy with his money. With the tip of my shoe, I traced a line in the Turkish rug at my feet. How much time did we have? Days? Weeks?

Not Grandmother, Lord. I need her.

I let my lungs take in as much air as they would hold before breathing out again. A whisper floated across my heart. *Trust Me.*

Could I trust the Lord with this? Money, and even my reputation, paled in comparison to my grandmother's life. Gathering every ounce of courage I could muster, I pushed up from the sofa. Grandmother had lived in this house for over twenty years. Not once had I heard her complain of her circumstances. Not her blindness. Or her heart problems. Or the pain that lived in her joints. Not the fact that her son lived for himself and not the Lord. Whatever the issues in her earlier life, by the time I could comprehend her words and actions, she showed only fortitude—and faith. And she'd bequeathed both of those to me long ago.

Circling Father's stout body with my arms, my heart twisted under his tortured gaze. He didn't share his mother's faith, but he loved her all the same.

"We'll take care of her, Father. You and I and Mother. And Clarissa will help, as well. We'll cherish every minute God chooses to leave her here on this earth with us." I knew I'd see her again in heaven one day, but I sensed it wasn't the right time to remind my father of that fact. Instead, I prayed once more for his salvation.

Throughout that night and most of the next two days, I sat with Grandmother. Then on Thursday morning Clarissa ordered me from the room. "Go get some fresh air. Your mother is on her way up to sit with Mrs. Benson."

Yes, I did need to get out of the house. Just for a little while.

Clarissa left the room. Quiet returned, broken only by Grandmother's shallow breaths. The smell of late-summer roses drifted in through the open window, along with distant clanks and clatters from the carriage house.

Webster and I hadn't spoken since I'd joined Father and Lawrence in the grandstand. Not that I'd expected to see him again on race day. But now, after the long hours at Grandmother's side, I remembered my jewelry. Had he managed to find someone to buy the pieces—or had he forgotten amidst the chaos? Perhaps he had the money and was waiting for a private time to settle it in my possession. And what about my pay as the driver? That would be even more significant to my cause.

My mind returned to the race. Driving that car had seemed more right than almost anything I'd ever done before. Like I was born to have a steering wheel in my hand and a gas pedal beneath my foot. But could that be right? If God had intended me to drive a race car, why had He made me a woman?

I'd given my life to the Lord, and His word encouraged me to marry a godly man, to raise godly children, to work in the church. Not to fritter away my time racing motorcars. But so far I had no husband, no children. No important occupation, other than taking care of Grandmother and striving to honor my parents.

And gathering three thousand dollars for the McConnells' mission work in Africa.

I'd never before resented what I didn't have. Now it chafed like a shoe on the wrong foot. And I couldn't fathom why.

"How is she?" Mother's hand rested gently on my shoulder, her eyes fixed on Grandmother's face.

"The same."

Mother studied me now. "You need sleep. Or fresh air. Maybe both." She shooed me from the room, and I found I didn't mind a bit.

After a quick breakfast, I grabbed an ordinary straw hat and scurried outdoors. I needed to see Webster, to ask him about the money, to talk with him about the race. Anything to make my mind forget to worry about Grandmother.

A faint whistle skidded past my ear. I perked up, hastened my approach to the garage. One of the double doors remained shut; one stood half open. "Webster?"

The whistling ceased. Metal clunked against wood. He met me in the dim light, his serious gaze searching my face.

"How is she?" He tipped his head toward the house. "The old lady." His words held reverence, not disrespect.

"She's holding on. We don't know—"

He nodded, relieving me of the need to say more. I cleared my throat. "I was wondering . . ."

Then I remembered what Father had told me—that Webster had been slated as the original driver. Why had he relinquished that role to me? His opportunity for personal glory and monetary gain given to an untested girl who, if discovered, would bring certain disgrace. Would I ever be able to adequately express my gratitude? And would Webster be willing to give up his position to me again?

"Webster, Father said that you were supposed to—"

138

"The money." He turned and jogged deeper inside the building. When he returned, he pressed a fold of bills into my hand. "Eight hundred and fourteen dollars."

"Eight hundred . . ." I stared at it, then at him. That much money for a few minutes of driving in circles with other cars? I felt my mouth hanging open and forced it shut again.

He grinned. "It's for both—the jewelry and the driving. I thought you'd be pleased."

Over eight hundred dollars. Combined with what I'd held onto from before, that put me a third of the way toward my goal—a goal I had less than five weeks left to accomplish. If I could race just two or three more times . . .

The part of me that thrilled at the thought of returning to the track warred with Mrs. Tillman's voice in my head. It wasn't ladylike. Or Christian-minded. It was deceitful, in fact. If Grandmother were well, I'd ask her what to do. But that option didn't exist. I swallowed hard and let go of the words. "When can we do it again?"

Webster lowered his head, peered into my eyes. "The next possibility is Cincinnati, but it's a longer race. Three hundred miles on that brand new million-dollar board track. Should be something to see—or experience."

One hundred and fifty laps instead of ten. Could I drive that long, that fast? My chin lifted. "I want to try."

He toed the ground, studying the dirt before looking back into my face. "Your father came to me on Sunday night asking about the driver. I managed to avoid details." He closed my fingers around the bills. "Just be sure and hold on to that money. If you hope to have it all by mid-September, you won't have many more opportunities to earn it. Not by racing, at least."

Hold on to the money. For me that was easier said than done. I thrust the cash toward him. "You keep it for me. I'll just give it away again. I know I will."

He raised his hands in objection. "Oh no. Not me."

I frowned. Another race, maybe a stronger finish, and I'd be close to the goal. But how could I ensure I wouldn't give it away before the McConnells returned?

"I guess I'll have to hide it from myself, then. But I'll know where I've hidden it, so it won't do much good." I sighed, staring at the bills.

Webster mopped his face and neck with his usual work rag.

My shoulders slumped. "Please help me, Webster."

His face reddened. Was it the heat?

He shook his head, but I read exasperation, not refusal. Then he snorted out a soft laugh. "Do you have some kind of container for it?"

I nodded. "Grandmother—" The word caught in my throat. I pushed past the worry. "Grandmother gave me a box. I'll get it."

I dashed from the garage to the house, scaled the stairs, and flew into my bedroom. Pawing through my clothes, my fingers grazed the raised beads. I pulled out the box, shoved in all the money I'd collected, and replaced the lid. Then I raced back to the garage.

"Here." I thrust the red square at him and then covered my eyes and turned my back. "Don't tell me. If I know—well, you know what will happen."

He led me outside the garage, just far enough from the building not to hear any rumblings from within. Then he disappeared inside, pulling the large door almost shut behind him.

I had no reason not to trust him. After all, I'd handed

him a tangle of jewelry and he'd returned the money it had garnered.

Still, I had to wonder why he hadn't told me he'd designed the race car. Or that he was supposed to drive it. Did his secrets stem from humility—or deception? I inched toward the old carriage house, pressed my ear against the wooden door. If I could hear something I might have an idea where he'd hidden my money. Just in case.

I squeezed my eyes shut as I listened. *Please, Lord. Keep the money safe.*

A touch on my shoulder. I jumped and turned. Then I relaxed. "Lawrence. What are you—"

His gaze slid past me, to the garage. "You going somewhere?"

"No." I waved my hand in the direction of the building. "Webster's hiding my rac—" I gulped down the word that rose to my lips. "The money I raised for the missionaries."

I couldn't meet his gaze, so I stared at the tuft of grass at my feet. If he discovered I'd driven on Sunday, would he applaud my efforts? Commend my bravery and skill in the race? Or would he see me as less of a Christian? Less of a woman? All of a sudden, his opinion mattered more than it had before.

"I thought you were going to let me help you with that."

"Well, I—actually, I—"

He stepped to the small gap between the two large doors and peered inside. I quieted, wanting to ask what he saw, but fearing such knowledge. It was a good thing, I mused, for him to have come along just now. Two people ought to know the money's location. And neither of them should be me.

Then the door flung wide. Webster and Lawrence stood

face to face. Webster's easy expression hardened into a challenge. "Need something?" he growled.

Lawrence gave no verbal acknowledgment of the question as his hand closed around my arm like a vise. "Your mother sent me to find you, Alyce. Your grandmother has taken a turn."

18

Wrenching my arm from Lawrence's grasp, I darted ahead. I burst into Grandmother's bedroom. Father stood near her, his back blocking my view. Then Mother appeared beside me, strong and serene, leading me to the other side of the bed.

"Here she is, Laura."

Grandmother, propped up with pillows, smiled in my direction. "Alyce?"

Her voice sounded as thin as blown glass, but it filled my ears with music. I eased down on the bed beside her and wrapped my arms around her frail body. Her shaky hand stroked my hair as I buried my face in her shoulder.

"I thought . . ." I couldn't say what I'd thought.

A small chuckle in my ear told me she knew anyway. "It wasn't my time, Ally. Not yet."

I lifted my head. How would I bear it when her time came?

I shuddered, brought her hand to my lips and kissed it. "Rest now, Granny. I'll come read to you later tonight."

She closed her eyes and nodded. Mother, Father, and I gathered in the hall, along with Dr. Maven, who I'd failed to notice when I rushed in. Lawrence was dawdling near the staircase, not part of the family, yet seeming to wish to be. I waited until his eye caught mine, hoping he could read my invitation to remain. Then I turned my attention back to my parents.

"And you'll find a nurse for us, Doc? Or two—one for day, one for night? More, if need be. Whatever it takes. We have plenty of room to accommodate medical staff." Father shoved his hands into his pants pockets and rocked back on his heels. "We can make them comfortable here for as long as need be."

Mother's solemn nod comforted me, along with the compassionate knit to her brow. No look of the socialite in exile now. Perhaps she'd just needed a crisis to remind her how much she was needed here.

I pushed up on my toes and kissed Father's cheek. "Thank you."

His fingers reached for the spot my lips had touched. "What's that for, Ally girl?"

I shrugged. "For keeping her here instead of insisting she go to the hospital. She would hate that."

"I know." His voice held a softer quality, not his usual boom of authority. "She despised me for sending my father there." His mouth turned down, and he stared at the floor.

"Oh, Father." I wrapped my arms around his middle. "Not despise. She might have been disappointed about how things turned out, but nothing more. And she long ago asked your forgiveness for her anger. She told me so."

As his cheeks brightened to red, I hooked one arm around Mother's waist, one around Father's. "I'm sure Clarissa has luncheon ready." I raised my voice. "And I'm sure Dr. Maven will be happy to join us."

Father engaged the doctor in conversation as they descended toward the dining room. Mother hurried ahead to alert Clarissa. I craned my neck for some sign of Lawrence. I guessed he hadn't understood my meaning earlier. Disappointment lapped over relief as I made my way down the stairs.

I needed a moment alone. A moment to express my gratitude to the Lord. I stepped inside the morning room and pulled the pocket doors shut. Then I leaned my head against them to pray.

"Alyce?"

I whirled around. "Lawrence."

His eyes searched mine. He took my hand, led me to the sofa, and sat beside me.

"Thank you," I whispered.

His mustache twitched upward. "For what?"

"For praying for my grandmother, for us."

He cocked his head to one side.

I laid my hand on his arm. "You didn't have to tell me you were praying. I knew you were, because you've already shown me the kind of man you are."

Something like fear flickered through his eyes. He needn't be afraid of me. Surely he knew that by now.

Then the look was gone, replaced by a hunger that sent my heart into a wild dance. Maybe God did have a future for me that looked like other women's.

I accompanied Lawrence out to his car after we ate, marveling again that he could afford such a gem as a Grant. Webster stepped around the corner of the house but froze when he saw us, his whistle fading to nothingness.

I smiled and waved as Lawrence climbed into his car with no recognition of Webster's presence. Webster raised his hand in reply, but the line of his mouth didn't bend upward as his eyes met mine. In one swift motion, he hopped into Father's Mercer and drove it down the brick drive toward the garage.

"Didn't you see Web—Mr. Little?"

Lawrence scowled. "I did. But I had no reason to acknowledge him. I don't trust that man."

I leaned into the open window on the passenger side. "Whyever not?"

"Something about his eyes. Shifty. What do you know about him anyway?"

"I know he works for Father, same as you." Irritation sharpened my tone.

"Not the same as me. He's a mechanic, for heaven's sake."

"And what's wrong with that?" My jaw tightened.

One shoulder rose and lowered. "Nothing much, I guess. Just never can tell. That kind roams about a good bit. Often take things that aren't theirs when they move on. People aren't always who they seem to be, Alyce."

My eyes narrowed. "Exactly what are you saying?"

He reached over and patted my hand. "Just be careful. I don't want you to get hurt."

I pulled away from his touch, crossed my arms, and stared down the road that led to town. I hated that his words churned a confused place inside of me. I *didn't* know much about Webster. Not really. He never spoke about his past.

But if he had a penchant for thievery, it wouldn't take long to know it. Not with almost a thousand dollars stashed somewhere in the garage.

If any of that money for the McConnells went missing now, I'd have no one but myself to blame. Again.

19

*W*ebster lifted his goggles from the peg on the wall. "I thought we'd take the Packard today."

"The Packard?" My gaze shifted from my car to the race car and back again. "But I thought . . ."

"Don't worry. We'll do some rounds in the race car tomorrow. Today I'd like to get you used to driving a long distance without stopping. We won't worry about speed, just the amount of time in the car."

I looked down at my unorthodox costume: knickers, shirt, and boots. "But I can't go out in public in this."

He tossed me a duster. I snagged a corner before it hit the ground. After shuffling my arms into the sleeves and buttoning it to the top, I looked down at my boots.

"What if we have to get out of the car?"

"We won't. I filled a couple of canteens with water. And I have extra oil and gasoline and all the necessary tools should a problem arise. We'll be fine." He put the Packard in neutral and shoved his weight against the back, rolling it out into the open.

"Let's go." He hopped into the driver's seat, pulled the brake, and then scooted over to let me behind the wheel.

Three hours bouncing over country roads. If I could survive that, I could survive three hours on a smooth track. I hit the starter and put the car in gear.

"Where to?" I asked as the brick drive met the dirt road that fronted the house.

"Doesn't matter. Just drive."

I turned left, away from town, neither of us speaking as we passed farmhouses dotting fields in various stages of harvest. I kept my speed moderate, so as not to overheat the engine. Still, we'd eventually have to stop to shore up the oil and add gasoline. No getting around that.

"Beautiful, isn't it?" Webster pushed his hat away from his face, his elbow resting on the ledge of the open window.

I leaned forward, trying to see what he saw. Maybe he meant the car. Or the weather. Or me?

The unexpected thought birthed a bubble of yearning that surprised me. What would life be like with a man who knew all of me—my faults, my failures, my secret pleasures? Would it make up for being a working man's wife? I thought of Lucinda and her Billy. It seemed they'd been happy, in spite of their struggles. If only a man like Webster shared my faith. I'd even risk my parents' displeasure for such a one as that.

The car picked up speed. Eyes trained on the road, I counseled my heart to put away fairy tales.

"Careful now. Don't overdo."

For a girl who'd never experienced the need to see appreciation in a man's eyes or hear admiration in his voice, I suddenly found myself imagining such from both Lawrence and Webster. And I wasn't sure I liked the feeling.

"How long have we been out?" I called over the din.

Webster produced a pocket watch. "Close to an hour. You tired?"

I shook my head, forced a smile, hoped he believed me.

Only an hour. My arms jiggled like jelly. I couldn't feel my feet. And my derriere felt like it'd been stuck by a thousand pins. How would I ever survive at speeds of seventy, eighty, ninety miles an hour? And yet there would be pit stops along the way. The thought cheered me, until I realized that every stop increased the chance of exposure. No, the longer I could endure, the better.

Billowing dust and smoke warned me of an approaching auto. I downshifted, eased closer to the edge of the narrow road, and waved as the Tin Lizzie ambled past.

"Why don't you slow for a while? Give the engine a rest."

I nodded and kept the speed steady, puttering along as sedately as any matron.

"Does your father know you're driving in Cincinnati?"

My mouth opened and shut.

"I thought you were going to tell him, Ally."

I extended the fingers of my right hand, then my left, one by one, stretching some feeling back into them. "I'm not sure that's a good idea, not with Grandmother so ill."

"I thought she was better."

My eyebrows sank toward my nose. "Some. But she's still frail. I'd rather not add another burden for Father to shoulder."

He grunted, but whether in agreement or dissent I couldn't discern. I cut my eyes his direction, craving his approval even while wondering why.

We drove on. Perspiration slid down the side of my face, down the backs of my legs. My throat ached with thirst. My legs longed for a short reprieve.

Pop!

My foot jerked from the gas pedal. I downshifted and groaned as the sizzle of liquid on hot metal followed.

"Stop there." Webster pointed to a clear edge of road, just above a lane leading to a sagging farmhouse. He slithered out through the open window, ignoring the door. "I'm sure it's nothing."

After uncinching the leather straps, he threw back the hinged cover and let a trail of steam dissipate before leaning over the hot engine. Then he straightened. Hands on his hips, he stared down the lane before turning to me.

"Why don't you see if you can wait at that house down there? This might take a while." He opened the toolbox bolted to the running board.

"Oh no. You said I wouldn't have to see anyone while I was dressed like this." I pushed open my door. Though the engine had long stilled, my limbs continued to shake with the vibration. I needed to stand, to walk.

Webster appeared and gripped my hand as my feet landed on solid ground. My knees buckled. I fell against his chest. His arms held me upright, his touch caging my breath in my chest.

"See? I knew this would take some getting used to."

I clung to him as my legs steadied, not wanting him to move away. I liked having someone hold me up, if only for a moment.

"Need some help?" A man dressed in dungarees glared at Webster.

Webster let go. I stumbled but then anchored myself with a hand on the Packard as the man's lazy gaze moved in my direction.

"Just engine trouble." Webster pointed to the open cover.

"I see." His eyes narrowed, taking in my bobbed hair and unorthodox clothing. And he'd come upon us in what must have appeared to be an embrace. "You sure you're all right, miss?"

"I'm fine. Just the car. He'll have it fixed soon." My wide eyes pleaded with Webster to hurry. He dove back into the engine. I smiled at the farmer. "Thank you for your concern."

With a tip of his hat, the man sauntered down the lane, toward the house. I exhaled, leaned against the side of the car. Laughter danced in Webster's eyes as he watched the man go.

I crossed my arms and raised my eyebrows. "Back to work, Webster Little. I don't intend to be humiliated again."

He gave me a playful wink before ducking his head over the still engine. Half an hour later, his head popped up again. The cover banged shut. He threaded the leather through the buckles and pulled tight.

"See? Nothing to worry about." He wiped his hands and shoved his rag back into his pocket. His grin warmed me from the inside out.

No matter what Lawrence intimated, I couldn't find any reason to distrust this man. Instead, as I climbed into the car, I found myself delighted at the prospect of two more hours with him at my side.

20

I didn't make it out to the garage until after lunchtime the next day. The sun stood high, scorching all within its reach. When Webster pushed back his cap, a bead of perspiration raced down the side of his face. He wiped it away with the back of his hand. "Speed and duration. That's what we'll work on today."

I climbed into the racing car, thankful Mother was resting in her bed and Father had motored down to the factory after our midday meal, leaving me free. Just over a week until the next race. I needed all the practice I could get.

Webster lowered his goggles as I turned down the familiar track to the dirt oval, neither of us speaking.

Yesterday's jaunt had left me tired and sore. Today would put even greater strain on my body. But I intended to conquer any weakness that threatened my ability to earn the rest of the three thousand dollars. Especially now that the task seemed to be within my grasp.

Exhaust billowed around us as I pressed my foot to the floor to take the first straightaway. With a short track and high speeds, the curves came more often. Round and round and round and round. Until my head and stomach spun in circles, as well. But I kept on. I wouldn't quit. This wasn't about my pleasure as much as it was about the McConnells' mission. And those precious faces in the photograph. I pushed on, teeth clenched. Numb, except for the pounding in my head and the churning in my stomach.

Then the jostle of my shoulder, Webster's concern evident even from behind his goggles. He pointed away from the track. I slowed, pulled into the tall grass. Stumbling out of my seat, I dropped to my hands and knees beneath a small knot of trees and retched into the field. I sat back, chest heaving, stomach roiling.

"Here." Webster thrust a jug of water into my hands. My arms refused to hold the weight. He lifted it to my lips and encouraged me to drink. It dribbled down my chin and onto my shirt, cooling the heat of my skin.

He moved me away from my sickness and sat beside me. Clutched my hand. Stroked it. "You okay, Ally?" Tender ministrations. Anguished words.

Concern for me? Or for his car? My befuddled brain couldn't sort it out, so I simply rested in the comfort of his touch.

I took another drink. My stomach settled. Eyes squeezed shut, I regained control of my brain. "It's the shorter track, all those turns. I think we should concentrate on stamina. The speed is there. We both know that." My eyes opened to find him studying my face. I pushed out a quick breath. "I'm fine. Really. Help me up."

He jumped to his feet. I placed my hand in his outstretched palm and rose.

"Should we chance the open road?" A shaky chuckle punctuated my question.

"Not in that car we won't. You need a break. And something to eat. We can take the Packard out later."

I couldn't argue. Didn't want to. I even let him help me into the mechanic's position in the racing car. I only regretted that I had to let go of his hand so he could pilot us home.

When I arrived at the Women's Mission Auxiliary meeting the next evening, the ladies peppered me with questions about Grandmother. Mrs. Swan's arm circled my waist and pulled me close, shooing the women back to their seats. "I'm so glad to hear she's doing better. May we come visit her soon?"

"I'm sure she'd love that." I sat down and demurely folded my hands in my lap as Mrs. Tillman took her place in front.

"We are well on our way to raising money for those poor souls on the Gold Coast. I'm pleased to announce that between contributions toward this cause and the supper and bake sale held the past Sunday—which Miss Benson, unfortunately, missed—our humble church has raised almost one thousand of the three thousand dollars." Her brilliant smile pinned me to my seat.

One thousand. Near my own amount. Both of us well on our way to providing our part.

Then I noticed all eyes focused on me, as if expecting a reply. "That's wonderful! I'm so pleased!" I cheered a bit belatedly.

Mrs. Tillman's mouth drew in tight but curved heavenward. "Of course it is much more difficult for us to raise such a sum, but we appreciate your encouragement. Don't we, ladies?"

Murmurs of assent all around. I squirmed in my seat. If I told them my father wouldn't give me the money, that I had to raise it myself, would they dismiss it as nonsense? As half-truth, at best? And if I revealed my efforts to raise the money myself—well, they for sure wouldn't approve of my methods. I shivered.

"Is that so, Miss Benson?"

My eyes widened. I'd missed her question.

"Excuse me?" I hated the girlish squeak that edged my words.

"I said, on our trips about town we came across a few people who said they'd contributed already. To you."

"That's correct." My heartbeat echoed in my ears.

"How kind of you to help us reach our goal. I assume you have that money with you tonight?"

My mouth dropped open. I'd collected over three hundred dollars from people in Langston. Well, collected and given away—and replenished through the sale of my jewelry. And Mrs. Tillman expected me to add that amount to their total? I shut my mouth and swallowed, eyes searching wildly for escape as I begged God to provide a diversion.

The back door squeaked opened. Every head—including mine—turned. Lucinda slipped into a back pew, an apologetic grimace on her face, a teary Teresa sitting on her lap.

I scooted over and motioned for Lucinda to come sit beside me. It was the least I could do. Timid steps brought her forward, her face as red as a rose petal. When she sat down, I heard her exhale. All of a sudden it didn't really matter what obstacle Mrs. Tillman threw beneath my wheels. Lucinda and I would endure together.

Lifting my chin, I met Mrs. Tillman's haughty expression. "I'll bring the money to you this week."

"Wonderful. The next item on our agenda is the design and creation of a quilt to present to the McConnells along with our money."

I found Lucinda's hand and squeezed. She nudged my shoulder with hers and I smiled.

In the face of three thousand dollars, what was three hundred more?

It wasn't a long meeting. Afterward, Mrs. Swan told me she'd telephone before presuming to visit. I said that would be fine. Others stopped to say they were praying for "dear Mrs. Benson." It warmed me to know Grandmother was so loved.

I jiggled Teresa in my arms as Lucinda visited with several of the women. But the baby started to fuss.

"Hush now." I swung the child from side to side and paced to the back of the church. But she wouldn't settle, so I whisked her out the door. "Look at the pretty picture God painted for us." I turned Teresa toward the sky, where bluish clouds streaked through the pink and orange canvas.

Lawrence sauntered up beside me. "I thought I'd find you here."

"Just waiting for Lucinda." My gaze fell to the ground. I had no desire to flirt, but his presence did flatter me. Surely he had better things to occupy his time than to find me in the churchyard.

The baby sat with her chubby legs dangling over my forearm, my other arm around her waist, holding her secure. I lifted her toward Lawrence. "Isn't she a sweet little lady?"

He gave me a half smile and seemed to shy away. I pulled Teresa closer to my body and nuzzled her neck.

"There you are. I'm so sorry." Lucinda jogged down the

steps and lifted Teresa into her arms. "I didn't mean to be so long-winded."

"You're fine. I didn't mind." I turned and set my hand on Lawrence's arm. "I'll be with you in a minute." I hoped he'd take the hint and walk away. He did, but not very far.

I lowered my voice. "How are things, Lucinda? I'm sorry I've not been over to visit lately."

"Miss Ben—Alyce, you have so many more important things to attend to. Don't worry about me. And thank you again for the blackberries. We managed both jelly and a cobbler with them."

"I'm so glad. I'll try to bring some more soon." I smiled, coaxing one from her, as well. She filled me in on the rest of the children.

"And how are things at work?" I asked.

She ducked her head, fiddling with the ruffle on the front of Teresa's dress. "I'm getting along fine."

Lawrence inched closer. Something in his manner irritated me. As if he had some superior claim to my attentions. I ignored him. "Mr. Morgan isn't being difficult, is he?"

Lucinda shook her head, still not raising her eyes to meet mine.

"Alyce." Lawrence's hand cupped my elbow. I sighed and then promised Lucinda we'd see each other again soon.

She shuffled from the churchyard as Lawrence led me to the Packard. His hand snaked down and pressed into mine. "I'm sorry, Alyce. I just felt you needed someone to protect you."

"Protect me?" I whirled to face him.

"From the . . . well, from those who seek after your attention and your favor."

People seeking *my* attention? He sounded a bit like Mother now. "I choose my own friends, thank you."

"Now, don't get all ruffled. I wouldn't feel this way if I didn't . . . care."

A small gasp caught in my throat. Were his insinuations about Webster and his dismissal of Lucinda simply misguided actions of affection? I had no idea how to respond to such a declaration, not with Mother's voice and Grandmother's prayers and Webster's whistle all colliding in my head. And over them all arched the thrilling memory of my hands on a steering wheel, my foot pushed to the floor, and the checkered flag waving from the edge of the track.

21

$\mathcal{I}$ parked the Packard in the garage and made my way into an almost silent house. Long pillars of amber evening light spilled through the windows as I leaned my shoulder against the doorframe of the living room. Father looked up from his newspaper and removed the cigar from his mouth.

"There you are, Ally. I was missing you."

I tossed my hat on a chair and sat on the sofa beside him. "So I hear we're racing in Cincinnati on Labor Day." I slipped off my shoes and tucked my feet up on the sofa.

"You heard right. Trotter told you, hmm?" His eyes laughed at me, but I kept my tongue still. I imagined he wouldn't be as amused if I mentioned Webster was the one who kept me informed. "And I suppose you are going to beg me to take you along."

"But of course." I laid my hand on my heart and feigned surprise. "I couldn't imagine it any other way."

His laugher bellowed through the room. "That was quite a ride in Chicago, wasn't it?"

"Yes, quite a ride." My finger traced a circle on the sofa. An oval, really. The shape of a speedbowl. "You know, Father, it might be wise to give that driver a raise after finishing so well. Three hundred miles is much more strenuous. And you wouldn't want to lose . . . that driver."

It was as close as I could come to outright deception, and even as I said the words I doubted it was the right thing to do. But I couldn't retract them now.

"You might be right, Ally. You might be right." He set his cigar on the brass tray on the table and turned a page of his newspaper, but his gaze sidled my way. "You know, I didn't imagine I'd get away without you this time, though I promised your mother—again—that I'd try."

Now it was my turn to laugh. "Don't worry about Mother. I intend for her to come with us."

"To the race?"

"No. Just to Cincinnati. She's been so attentive to Grand-mother. She needs a weekend free. I might even let her take me shopping." I patted his knee and then picked up my shoes.

"Which will most likely cost me a pretty penny," he groused good-naturedly. And though he hadn't committed in words, I knew he'd reward his driver with a bit extra for this race.

"How in the world did you convince Father to leave the Mercer at home?" I climbed inside the low, powerful automobile. No doors, no top. The wooden dash gleamed, and the brass instruments and accents shone bright against the green paint and black trim. One large eyeglass-like windscreen rose up from its place on the steering column. I'd need every bit of cover I could find to not come home with half of Indiana's earth on my clothing and my skin.

"I told him I needed to tweak some things. And I did. I thought this would handle more like the race car, so it would be better practice than the Packard."

I nodded as I tucked the last bits of hair beneath my cap and set my goggles in place. I loved driving the Mercer. Its power had drawn me from the moment Father brought it home. And driving it at our makeshift track taught me that speed didn't frighten. It exhilarated.

"Ready?" I hit the electric starter and steered us down the road. My body adjusted to the feel of the heavier car. My eyes settled on the road while my head chided my mouth for remaining shut. Today I had more on my mind than just driving.

"I have a favor to ask," I called over the clamor of the engine. "Actually, two."

From the corner of my eye I spied his nod.

"First, I need some of the money from my box."

His mouth quirked upward in an I-told-you-so kind of way. I gripped the wheel more tightly. "It isn't what you think, Webster."

"One week. You can't even hold on to the money for one week." His head shook, as did his shoulders. Laughter I couldn't hear but could clearly recognize.

Glaring at the road, I pressed my foot harder against the gas pedal. Webster jerked at the unexpected thrust forward, his hand reaching for the instrument panel. "What'd you do that for?"

"Listen." I had to shout to be heard. "Mrs. Tillman found out about the people who gave me money. The ones in town, I mean. She assumed it was for their collection, not mine. Now I have to give it to her or—" Or what?

"Are you sure you have to do that? Can't you just tell her the truth?" Concern laced his voice, even at its raised volume. Why did it feel so different from Lawrence's consideration last evening?

"I'm sure. I couldn't live with myself if I failed those little children and their families."

His lips clamped shut and I thought I heard him grunt.

People aren't always who they seem to be. Lawrence's words niggled at me again. I slowed the car, my arms suddenly unable to keep the wheel steady.

Webster leaned toward me. "Need a break?"

I nodded as I eased us to the side of the road. Webster hopped from the car and trotted around back.

"Probably wouldn't hurt to add gasoline and oil anyway." His words sounded far away, the thunder of the motor still ringing in my ears. He passed me a canteen from the storage compartment in back. I lifted it to my lips, relishing the wetness sliding down my throat.

With one hand, I released the buttons down the front of my duster and flipped back the edges to let in fresh air. Maybe Lawrence was right in one regard. I ought to know more about this man I trusted with my secrets—and my money. I screwed the lid on the canteen, scooted my knees into the seat, and faced backward. "How'd you end up here, Webster?"

He glanced up, one eyebrow cocked. "You drove me?"

"I mean, how did you end up in Langston? Where did you come from? How'd you learn so much about cars?"

Hands on his hips, he rose to his full height. "Why does it matter, Ally?"

I pressed my lips together. "It's just, well, I know so little about you. For instance, why build a racing car?"

His head jerked to the left, and his jaw clenched. Seconds

ticked by. He cleared his throat. "Just something I always wanted to do."

"So why didn't you tell me it was yours—and that you were supposed to drive?"

He stowed the can of gasoline and picked up the one full of oil. "Didn't seem to matter." He stalked toward the engine, unstrapped the hood, and lifted it.

I scrambled to the ground, facing him across the front of the car. "But it does matter."

"Why?"

Emotion clogged my throat. "Because I thought we were friends."

His gaze pinned me. "We are, Ally. It's just—some things are hard to talk about. Trust me. Okay?"

Trust him. Like he trusted me behind the wheel of his creation. I ground my teeth together to keep tears of frustration from falling. Maybe Lawrence was right. Maybe Webster wasn't exactly the man I thought him to be.

Two hours and miles of silence later, we chugged into the yard. I prayed my face didn't bear the burn of being hatless in the sun. Mother would be sure to scold if it did. Out of the car, released from the heat of my duster, I lifted the curls that clustered just above my shoulders and held them on top of my head, anxious for a breath of air to cool me. But none did.

I hurried across the garden, eager to splash the cool kitchen water against my face and neck. But before I reached the house, I heard my name and turned.

"Lawrence." I groaned, imagining how much dirt clung to my forehead and cheeks. Not to mention my shirt hanging limp and damp around me, caked with dust. And then there was the streak of oil smeared down the left knee of my knickers, a casualty of trying to help Webster plug a leak later in the day.

Lawrence's hands clasped my shoulders, wild eyes searching mine. "What happened? Are you hurt?"

I shrugged from his grasp. "I've been out driving. Nothing more. Now if you'll excuse me—"

His focus jumped behind me, toward the Mercer. "Driving that?" His eyes bulged like a bullfrog's.

"Yes, that. My father's car. Is there a problem?"

"No. I just never imagined . . ."

I sighed. No sense trying to explain it. I remembered how he'd condescended to me about his Grant. Likely he disapproved of all women drivers. But that fault could be overcome. Eventually.

"Why don't I get cleaned up and meet you in the living room?" I put one foot on the bottom step leading to the kitchen door.

"I can't stay. I just—" Once more his gaze roved over my disheveled appearance. I watched his neck pulse with a swallow. "I just came to tell you that your father invited me to attend the Cincinnati race. He informed me you would be there, as well."

I forced a tight smile. I'd have to avoid him yet again, in spite of the fact that a piece of me longed to know him better. "Wonderful. Now if you'll let me . . ." I rose to the second step. His hand settled on the rim of the hat he'd swiped from his head when he'd approached. "I just thought you'd want to know." He looked uncertain now. Skittish almost. He looked to the garage as Webster sauntered out the door, a whistle halting and then resuming on his lips.

I pulled my smile higher, needing to regain Lawrence's attention. "It will be wonderful to have you with us."

He grinned and took his leave, tripping over a stone in the path as he went. But it wasn't until I lay stretched out in the bathtub that I realized he hadn't rounded the corner of the house toward the road. Instead, he'd headed straight for the garage.

22

*W*ebster handed me the money I'd requested first thing the next morning. "Mightn't it be better to just tell the truth, Ally?"

I hurried past him, but his footsteps sounded close behind.

"I can't. You know that. They would never believe . . ." It felt as though the steel frame of the racing car rested on my chest. I pressed my lips together and shook my head.

Why should I explain it to him? He felt no need to explain himself to me. I climbed into the car and we rumbled to the dirt track.

He signaled for me to cut the engine. "I think we need a communication system."

"Oh?" My eyebrows rose. Rich, coming from the man who refused to communicate anything about his past to me.

"Just a few hand signals. You know how hard it was to hear during the race in Chicago."

"Yes. Impossible."

"Exactly. In fact, might be better if you don't even have to look. Maybe we should communicate by touch."

Heat burst into my cheeks as I studied the horizon. Race instructions. Nothing more. Not the tender touch between a man and a woman. So why did the thought of it set my heart pumping? "Why don't we try the signals first? See if I can take them in with just a glance."

He shrugged and leaned down to crank the engine. "Whatever you think. We can try it both ways."

I settled the goggles over my eyes, thankful to be hidden from scrutiny. As we circled the oval again, I forced my thoughts away from the possibility of his touch and focused instead on the money hidden beneath Webster's watchful eyes. Obviously it remained safe; otherwise he would have put me off with excuses, not handed me what I'd asked for. Lawrence's insinuations apparently had no basis in fact.

And yet . . .

What if he had other motives for desiring me to drive? What if it wasn't about helping me raise money for the McConnells at all?

Maybe he meant to blackmail me—or my father—instead.

A turn rose up before me. A poke at my thigh reminded me to glance down. I spied Webster's thumb turned down, his signal to slow. Every ounce of my strength held the wheel steady as the needle on the instrument panel hovered at sixty-five. I breathed relief in the short straightaway. No, blackmail couldn't be it. Otherwise, he wouldn't encourage me to come out with the truth.

Another curve. Another straightaway. Webster's thumb up and then down, his fingers left and then right.

I could think of no reason not to trust this man. His every interaction with me, with Father, seemed the model of

integrity. I'd probably have been smitten with those dark
eyes and that laughing grin if I suspected him to be a man of
faith. But I'd never heard him mention God—or even church.

I pondered as we drove. Fewer laps, more breaks. Our communication system with just the hand signals was working
as planned. Mostly. When we left the track, I felt steadier on
the turns, even if they weren't the banked ones. But I still let
him drive us back to the house.

We roared into the yard. Two figures in the gazebo leapt
from their seats, peering up the drive.

I gasped.

"Mr. Little? Is that you?" Mother's voice.

"Yes, ma'am." He pulled back his goggles while I continued
to study the dashboard and sink deeper into my seat.

"Who's that with you?"

"Just a friend." He climbed from the car and stood in
front of me, blocking their view. "I needed some help with
the race car today."

"See that you don't leave that horrid thing in the yard for
long."

"Yes, ma'am." He lowered his voice. "Walk behind me
into the garage. Just like at the racetrack."

I nodded, but between the hours of driving and the jangle of my nerves, would my legs hold me up? With a deep
breath, I set my feet on the ground. Eyes glued to Webster's
back, I followed as if a rope attached between us pulled me
forward. Just inside the doors, out of view of the garden,
he stopped. Turned. Wrapped his arms around me, his face
just inches above mine. My knees turned as soft as taffy on
a warm night.

His quiet laugh filled my ear, his breath hot on my neck.
"Hold on, Ally girl."

I turned my head. His breath caught, arms dropped. He backed away. My knees stiffened. I reached for the wall.

"That was close," I whispered.

He rested his hands on top of his head, a grin sliding up his face. "I guess you're stuck with me for a while longer today."

I leaned against the wall and ducked my head to hide my answering smile.

Mother's guest finally left. I hobbled to the house, eager for a hot bath.

Just as I stepped inside, the telephone shrilled. I let Clarissa answer as I lowered myself to the bench just inside the kitchen door.

Clarissa's head popped through the doorway. "For you, Miss Alyce. A Lucinda Bywater."

Lucinda phoning? In spite of my stiffness, I hastened to the telephone but covered the mouthpiece and asked Clarissa to have Betsy draw a hot bath. "What's wrong, Lucinda?"

"Oh, nothing's wrong."

My tense muscles eased a bit.

"I wondered if . . . well, I hope you don't think it out of place, but I was hoping . . ."

I switched the earpiece to my other ear. "Whatever you need, Lucinda, I'd be happy to help."

"Oh no, Miss—Alyce. I don't need help. I was wondering if you'd come to supper. At my house. On Friday." She blurted out the last words all at once, as if she feared she wouldn't be able to say them otherwise.

"I'd be honored, Lucinda." My tired brain worked to remember why this didn't seem like a good idea.

Friday.

Cincinnati.

"However, I'll be out of town on Friday. Would Thursday do? I can help with supper. I'm no gilded lily, you know. I can cook and clean up and, well, all sorts of things you probably can't imagine me doing."

Like speeding around a racetrack at nearly a hundred miles per hour.

She sat silent for a moment and then assented. I told her I'd pick her up from work and help her get the kids home from her aunt's house, too. Then I hung up the telephone and trudged up the stairs. By the time I'd removed my clothes and wrapped myself in a kimono, one of the day maids knocked at my bedroom door and announced my bath was ready.

I locked the bathroom door and sank into the water, relishing the warmth on my aching bones. Was this how Grandmother felt on a daily basis? How did she manage without complaint? Too much more of this and I feared I wouldn't be able to move well enough to drive at all.

I leaned my head over the back of the tub. No doubt Webster would make sure he didn't overwork me. I closed my eyes. Dozed for a few minutes. Then awoke with a start.

Swirling my shriveled fingers through the cooling water, I wondered again what Webster wasn't saying. Surely Father wouldn't hire him without references. Could a man be upstanding one moment and sinister the next? Perhaps he deceived everyone. Except Lawrence.

I climbed from the tub and wrapped myself in a towel. I couldn't worry about Webster's past. Grandmother needed my attention. And I had to concentrate on the race. For now, I'd trust that I—and my mission funds—would be safe in God's hands, if not in Webster's.

I slipped into my kimono and padded back to my bedroom.

Halfway down the hall, I stopped. Lucinda. Likely she heard lots of things about people in Mr. Morgan's law office. Maybe she could reveal a bit of Webster's mystery.

At least it wouldn't hurt to ask.

Lucinda and her children piled into my Packard on Thursday, and we motored to her home. Part of a home, actually. An old house divided into two dwellings. It sat on the opposite side of Langston from Mr. Morgan's office, close to Father's factory.

We climbed a rickety wooden staircase to reach a door on the second floor. Lucinda put her key in the lock. "It isn't much to look at, but it's warm in the winter. Mostly." She pushed the door open. Her little boy rushed past us but the girls stood back for me to go first.

"It's lovely," I remarked as I removed my small hat and hung it on a hook I spied behind the door. "So cozy."

Lucinda answered with a weak smile as she placed baby Teresa in her older girl's arms. "You go on into the parlor and sit while I get things ready."

"I'll do no such thing." I tucked the corners of a towel into the bibbed front of my dress. "I told you I'd help. I took several courses on cooking in Chicago."

Lucinda's mouth opened, but I stilled it with a stern look. Her timid directions led me to plates and utensils. Soon the rich aroma of stew bubbled from the pot on the stove. She seemed more comfortable now, more willing to let me be a friend. Together we filled the children's plates, poured their milk, and mopped up their messes, spelling each other to take a few bites of food between times. How in the world did she accomplish it all when she was on her own?

After supper, she instructed her girls to wash the dishes and put them away. The girls didn't protest. She hooked her arm around mine and led me to the parlor before excusing herself to put Teresa and her little boy to bed.

I wandered the room, studying the photograph of her family, husband included. They looked content in spite of their grim expressions.

"That was taken just two months before he died." Lucinda's voice startled me. She sat on the edge of a chair and motioned me to the old-fashioned divan. "I'm glad we spent the money. I didn't want to, but he insisted we should."

Grief-laden silence engulfed the room. Neither of us seemed to be able to find the words to start again. Then I remembered our encounter after the Women's Mission Auxiliary meeting the week before.

"I want to apologize for Mr. Trotter's behavior on Sunday evening, after the meeting. He didn't realize that I didn't feel the need to hurry home."

"Pish." Lucinda waved her hand and scowled. "I don't worry about what that man thinks of me."

My eyebrows drew together as I leaned forward, elbows on my knees. "What do you mean?"

She sniffed and straightened her skirt. "He thinks he's better than most around here, but he isn't."

I stiffened. "Maybe he's just shy and it comes across wrong."

"I don't think so. *Mr.* Trotter lurks in dark alleyways more often than's good for a man, I say."

"What do you mean?" Her words stirred a flurry of foreboding.

"I mean, people like him are often up to no good."

Why did my friends harbor such suspicions of each other?

Webster with Lawrence. Lawrence with Webster. And now Lucinda. Perhaps I'd lived a more sheltered life than I realized. But I knew them, each one. And all of them seemed kind.

"Oh, Lucinda, I really think you've misunderstood. He's a fine, upstanding man. He works for my father. He attends our church."

Her gaze dropped to the floor. Almost as if she pitied me. I wanted to take offense. Then I remembered the hard road Lucinda walked. Would it be surprising to learn some envy fluttered in her breast toward those whose way seemed easy? Could I forgive her that?

I reached across the space and laid my hand on hers. "But I didn't come here to talk about Mr. Trotter. Really. Though I did wonder if you could tell me anything of . . . another person."

Her eyes narrowed. "Who?"

Would she think as unkindly of Webster as she did of Lawrence? Maybe her grief had tainted her view of all men.

I studied my hands. "Webster Little." My head jerked up. "Do you know him?"

Her face relaxed, eyes turning almost dreamy. The stew I'd savored turned sour in my stomach.

"I know him." Soft words. Then silence.

The heel of my boot clattered against the floor. I stilled my bouncing knee with my hands. "Well? What about him?"

Tears filled her eyes. "He's one of the kindest, most giving men I've ever met."

"Why do you say that?" Joy warred with fear in the center of my being.

Her face twisted with emotion, then settled. "I'm not sure he'd care to have his actions bandied about. He acts on the sly."

I cocked my head. "Lurking in alleys, like you say of Mr. Trotter?"

"Oh no. Not that kind. It's just, he'll leave a basket of food for a needy family, maybe some ready money tucked in beneath a loaf of bread or such."

My tension deflated. Not what I'd expected to hear. "How do you know he does that?"

Her face flushed scarlet. "Because I've seen him. And not just at my doorstep, either." She shook her head. "But I never told. Until now."

Webster as the Good Samaritan. It fit what I knew of him, but it frightened me, as well. How did he come by the money for such acts? Was he plotting to rob Africa to feed Langston?

I forced a smile even as confusion spun inside me like a tire in mud. "Thank you, Lucinda. That helps. Now, tell me what the children have been up to."

She stared at me for a moment before her eyes brightened, as if she suddenly remembered that we called ourselves friends.

23

By Friday, I'd packed my driving outfit in an old carpetbag and stowed it with the racing car under Webster's care. At the train station, I flitted from waiting room to platform and back again.

"Sit down, darling. You're making me nervous." Mother patted the hard seat beside her.

I sat, knees bouncing. I popped up again. "I'll check to see if the train's here."

"But you can see—" Mother's voice trailed away as I escaped from the stuffy waiting room and back into the fresh air. My fingers pressed against one another. I straightened my hat. Walked to the end of the platform. Webster waved at me from farther down the line, his backside resting against the white number 7 painted on the hood of the blue car.

If only I could meet him down there. But we'd made a pact to stay clear of each other in public. No use drawing any attention that might ferret out our secret. Or rather, my secret. Webster apparently had different secrets. Ones he refused to reveal even to me.

The deep whistle of the train sent me flying back to the waiting room long before the locomotive chugged into sight. "The train's here, Mother." I grabbed her hand, pulled her up from her seat. But she didn't move quickly enough for me, so I ran on ahead.

By the time the train lumbered to a stop, I was bouncing on my toes, eager to embark.

"If we get on now, we'll just have to sit and wait," Mother said from behind me.

"I know."

Mother's squinted eyes searched my face. "I've never seen you quite so eager to leave Langston."

I licked my lips to get them moist again and forced my feet to remain completely rooted to the ground. *Control yourself. Be careful.* I brushed a curl aside and smiled. "I'm just happy we're all going together."

I linked my arm through hers with a quick stab of melancholy. If Grandmother were with us, it would be a perfect trip.

"Good morning, Miss Benson, Mrs. Benson." Mrs. Swan stood next to us, another woman from my church by her side. Mrs. Swan turned her sweet face in my direction. "Are you leaving us again so soon, dear?"

"Just for a few days. You and Pastor Swan will visit Grandmother while we are gone, won't you? You'll let us know if there is any change?"

"Of course. We are so pleased she is getting stronger. We wouldn't miss our visits with her. I think I draw more from our time together than she does." Mrs. Swan's expression turned wistful. "Laura Benson knows the goodness and faithfulness of our Lord in a way so few of us do. I would like to have her depth of understanding and conviction."

Mother blinked. Sniffed. Turned away. I cringed. But in a strange way, her response brought new hope. She'd heard Mrs. Swan's words. Really heard them. They'd made her feel uncomfortable, not defensive. Perhaps caring for Grandmother during her illness had softened the soil of her heart. Maybe seeds of truth would take root.

I offered Mrs. Swan and her companion a crooked smile of apology.

"Alyce, darling?" Mother stepped up into the train.

"Good-bye." I pressed my hand on Mrs. Swan's before following Mother into the passenger car. Like Mrs. Swan, I, too, longed to be like my grandmother. Gracious and kind. Unflustered by those around her. Always faithful to the Lord.

As I settled into the seat beside Mother, I reminded myself this would be a good opportunity for practice.

I'd promised Saturday to Mother since the race wasn't until Monday, Labor Day. She pulled on her gloves as she turned to me. "We'll go to Mabley and Carew. We must get you some new dresses, though heaven knows they won't be what we could find at Marshall Field's store." She mumbled the last words as we departed the hotel, as if she didn't want the people of Cincinnati to hear her disparage one of their city's shopping choices.

"But I like the clothes I have, Mother. There's nothing wrong with them."

She waved away my protest as the taxicab took us through town. When we entered the massive store, she approached a salesman and announced her name and her husband's occupation, expecting the man to jump to her aid.

I hung back while he bowed over Mother's hand and pressed his thin lips into a smile. "A pleasure to have you with us, Mrs. Benson."

I rolled my eyes. A pleasure to see Father's money, not her. Didn't she recognize that?

"And this is your lovely daughter?" The man came toward me. I stuck out my hand. His fingertips touched my gloved ones for only a moment before he turned his attention back to Mother.

"Mother, I really don't need—"

"Of course you do, darling." She patted my shoulder and continued talking with the salesman, his smile growing wider with her every word. I gave up and wandered to the other side of the store. The money she'd spend today would fill my box for the McConnells almost to bursting. Instead, I would have new clothes to replace ones that didn't even look worn.

I fingered a set of beaded hair combs. *Why, Lord? Why give me this abundance of things I can't even use for You?*

"Beautiful, aren't they?" A young woman near my age stood beside me, eyes shining with delight as her gaze caressed the ornaments in my hand.

"Yes, they are." I set the hair combs down again.

"Aren't you going to purchase them?" she asked.

I shook my head. "I have no need of them." Then I noticed the silky blond hair coiled beneath her shabby hat. "But they would look stunning on you."

"Oh no." She backed away, almost as if she feared I'd fix them on her right at that moment. "I could never afford such an extravagance." She bit her lip as she scanned the room. "I'm here for a new chemise. That's all." Her cheeks tinged as pink as the lone flower on her hat.

I picked up two combs. "Wait here a minute."

"But— I—" She clutched her handbag to her body, her eyes darting back and forth.

"Just wait. Please?"

"Well . . ." She glanced toward the door and then back to me. "All right."

I hastened to Mother's side. "Have the man put these on the list, too." I held up the combs. The salesman scribbled on his paper before nodding at me.

"Pretty little things, darling, but I don't see how—"

I kissed her cheek. "Thank you, Mother." I darted away before she could finish her thought. By the time I reached the blond woman again, she'd inched toward the exit. Grasping her hand, I placed the combs in her open palm.

Her mouth dropped open. She stared down at her hand, then up at me.

"I want you to have them."

Her mouth closed as her eyes widened. "Why?" A whispered, fearful word.

"Because I want you to always remember how much you are loved."

Her forehead wrinkled. "Loved? You don't even know me."

"*God* loves you. He loves you so very, very much."

She turned and fled the store without even purchasing a chemise. I prayed that one day she'd understand the extravagant love of the Lord. Then I thought of Lucinda, the look on her face changing from awe to excitement the day I'd brought her fresh berries.

Lucinda stood only a bit taller than I. A little thinner, perhaps, but not much. And then there was Clarissa's sister. Shorter, but nothing her nimble fingers couldn't remedy. If I gave them some of the dresses now hanging in my wardrobe, they could use their money for necessities other than clothes.

A smile worked its way across my face. How had I never considered such a thing before?

With eager steps I returned to Mother's side. "I've changed my mind," I said. "I do need some new clothes. And shoes. And undergarments. And—"

"Darling!" Mother threw her arms around me, her face displaying the same warmth of feeling as Pastor Swan's when he welcomed a new child of God.

We took a cab back to the hotel. One of the bellboys carried our boxes and bags upstairs. As he piled them in the sitting room, I realized I'd arrive in Langston with an entire new set of clothes—clothes I didn't need. The women at church would peg me as frivolous, not generous. Especially if, dressed in my new finery, I couldn't supply the small fortune I'd promised to the McConnells. They'd believe they had worked and sacrificed and I hadn't taken my own words seriously. With a groan, I fell onto the sofa.

Why couldn't God give me some service for Him that looked normal?

24

On Sunday morning, I crept from the hotel room while my parents slept. Lawrence met me in the lobby and escorted me to a church two blocks from our hotel. It felt odd to worship surrounded by strangers. And yet not strangers, for we shared faith in our Lord. I let the familiar songs wash over me. So much I'd let go in the weeks since I'd decided to race. Too much. My time with Grandmother. My time with the Lord.

I pulled the tattered picture of the African children from my handbag. Did they realize how much my heart yearned for them to know Jesus? By providing those funds, I could help make a difference not just in their earthly lives, but their eternal ones. As the song ended, I slipped the photo back into my purse. But it didn't matter. The children remained engraved on my heart.

The young preacher spoke to us from 2 Timothy 4:5. *But watch thou in all things, endure afflictions, do the work of an evangelist, make full proof of thy ministry.*

It seemed the perfect confirmation. Enduring the afflic-tion of Father's refusal. Working to send the gospel into the world. Full proof of my ministry? I hoped so. I wanted a ministry. I wanted a way to serve. And if that meant hiding myself beneath a cap and pair of goggles to drive a car, I would make that sacrifice.

My gaze roved to the other faces in the congregation. Some attentive, some not, much like our church at home. I twisted my head just a bit to get a view of the back of the church. A familiar tip of the head caught my eye. I stared through the crowd, a round face bobbing in and out of view.

Webster? My heart churned like cylinders in the engine of a racing car. Was it him? I pushed up just a bit, trying to get a better view.

Lawrence hissed my name. My backside returned to the pew as I faced forward once more, suddenly wishing the pastor would bring his sermon to an end.

By the time we reached the front stoop of the church, the dark-haired man had vanished. Had it really been Webster? If only I knew for sure.

"Ready to go?" Lawrence asked, attentive at my side. We shook hands with the preacher before making our way back to the hotel.

Mother was lounging with a late breakfast, a book open be-side her. Father, on the other hand, looked ready for an outing.

"I'm off to the track, Ally." His eyes twinkled.

"May I tag along?" I felt sure a sparkle lit my eyes, too.

"Of course." Father stuffed a cigar inside the pocket of his coat. "And Trotter can join us. I'm anxious to get a look at this million-dollar track."

I held my breath and hid my smile. It seemed too easy. Without any effort on my part, I'd get a chance to see the track and visualize the turns in my mind before my practice time in the morning. And if I could sneak in a few minutes of conversation with Webster, all the better.

"Must you encourage her, Harry?" Mother looked disappointed. As if she'd imagined that yesterday's shopping trip had changed me into the girl she wished I was.

Father patted her shoulder, kissed her cheek. "Don't worry. I doubt any of your Chicago dandies will see her there."

Mother sighed, tutting under her breath.

Father, Lawrence, and I rushed out the door before she decided to object.

The track greatly resembled the Chicago Motor Speedway. Boards laid out in an oval with banked turns. Even the width looked comparable to Chicago. Cars and drivers, mechanics and owners mingled in the pit area. I followed Father across the yard, stretching my neck this way and that to size up the competition. I recognized a few drivers. Resta. De Palma. D'Alene. Father nudged me and inclined his head to the farthest car.

"Rickenbacker."

I stood on my tiptoes but could see only a head of dark hair that poked above the gathering crowd. I frowned. For all I could tell he was the man I'd seen at church. Father pulled at my hand. My feet nearly tripped over themselves trying to keep up.

Then Webster stood before us with his usual open expression and wide smile. Father clapped a large hand on the man's shoulder. "Everything set?"

"Yes, sir." He wiped the grime from his fingers and shoved

the oily rag into his back pocket. "Just learned they've nixed the qualifying heats. Every entered car has run at speeds upward of eighty, so we're drawing for starting positions." His gaze slid to mine but refused to linger.

I turned my focus to the track, imagining the pace lap, the starting flag. The rest of the men consuming our smoke and dust. A real chance at the prize money.

One hundred and fifty laps. Could I do it?

Webster's earnest voice drifted my direction. "Our driver's ready. I guarantee it."

I couldn't hear Father's grumbled reply—and I dared not turn and pretend to be interested. My playacting skills weren't that good. But before I could figure out how long to feign disinterest, Lawrence took possession of my arm. We wandered away from Father and Webster.

"I assume you'll watch the race with us tomorrow?"

"I—" Fingers of panic gripped my throat.

"Unless you are shopping with your mother." He patted my hand.

My eyes widened. Of course. The perfect alibi. Better than an outright lie. But at the same time, his assumption rankled. Did he think I'd prefer a day of shopping to a day at the races? Fury fizzled before it could flame. I'd kept this part of myself from him. Not just the interest in auto racing, but the penchant for speed. So how could he know the insult he'd whipped in my direction?

Maybe he assumed my desire to see the expansion of the gospel of Christ didn't leave room in my life for something so . . . worldly as auto racing. But given our common faith, it occurred to me that if I did tell him of my clandestine activities, he'd likely see the ultimate good, even if my behavior shocked him at first.

If I finished well in this race, maybe I would reveal everything to Lawrence. See what he thought of me then.

We meandered back to the race car. Webster tipped his cap in my direction but ignored Lawrence completely. Then he turned on his heel and disappeared into the crowd.

Lawrence chuckled, his mustache wiggling like a caterpillar.

I cocked my head. "What?"

He turned serious again. "Nothing." He disentangled his arm from mine. "See you tomorrow?"

I inclined my head in answer as an excited shiver ran down my spine. I prayed tomorrow would be the day that filled my little red box to overflowing.

25

*L*abor Day—race day—dawned clear and bright.
And still.
And hot.

My hands shook as I splashed cool water on my face from the sink in the bathroom and then pressed it dry with a towel. The roar of the track filled my ears despite the hush of the hotel room. Excitement and nervousness flip-flopped my stomach.

I dressed and then found Father in the dining room of the hotel. "Do you mind if I meet you at the track later?" I asked him. "I have some things I'd like to do first."

"Of course." He returned to his newspaper. I rode the elevator back upstairs and left a note for Mother, reminding her that I'd be out for the day.

I slipped into the fresh morning. The streets teemed with people, with excitement. Swept up in the crowd, I made it to the train station, ready to ride the sixteen miles out of town to the speedway.

Beads of perspiration trickled down the back of my neck as I reached the grounds. Just after eight in the morning. Already the grandstands held spectators. And more than a few. I gave the gatekeeper my ticket. How would I find Webster in the midst of all these people?

A shrill whistle cut the air. My neck twisted left. Webster leaned against a support pillar beneath the grandstand. He waved.

I waved back but didn't walk straight to him. I moved in the opposite direction, mingling among the growing crowd, letting myself be seen in case Father should ask after me. But I didn't wait long before darting into the shadows behind the grandstands to wait for Webster to catch up to me.

"Good job, Ally."

I whirled to face him, wondering if he could feel my anticipation crackling in the air. He handed me the carpetbag. "Where?"

"There's a small maintenance shed, out a ways. Near where they're parking cars. It's all we've got."

"I'll manage. How much time?"

"Not much. You ready? Still think you can do the whole three hundred miles?"

"I guess we'll find out." I tried to laugh, but it came out as a cough as the enormity of the task settled over me.

Webster studied me for a moment. Then his voice dropped lower. "You don't have to do this, you know."

I shook my head, shook off the heaviness threatening to dampen my enthusiasm. "There's too much at stake to quit now. You know that."

He shrugged as if he didn't care one way or the other. But his expression shouted approval, even in the half-light. "Just wanted to make sure."

I fought a ridiculous desire to throw myself into his arms. Instead, I pulled back my shoulders and lifted my chin. "Show me the way."

And he did just that.

I emerged from the cramped and dilapidated shed into a sea of parked motorcars. Many more than had been there earlier. But no one took notice of me in my crew-member jumpsuit. I ducked my head and concentrated on taking long, authoritative, manly strides, praying no one would stop me. Finally I reached the garage assigned to our car. Lifting my head for only a moment, I stationed myself next to Webster, my back to the mechanical crew that would assist us in the pits.

"Keep looking at me as if we are having a conversation," he said.

"We *are* having a conversation." I tried to keep my face serious.

"Yes, but we don't want others foisting themselves into it. We have to keep you separate. Your clothes might cover most of the issues, but opening your mouth will give you away in a moment."

I clamped my lips shut. So many things could be ruined if someone discovered my real identity.

"Follow my lead. Like before. Nod. Don't speak."

I nodded.

His face screwed into a scowl. "That weasel."

"What?" My neck twisted. I spied a clump of men nearby, no familiar face among them. Until one man bent down to pick up something.

Lawrence Trotter stared back at me.

I sucked in stale air, afraid to move. My heart pumped

faster. Did he recognize me? He'd seen me that day, in my driving clothes. Would his bookkeeping precision add up the evidence and find the sum of truth?

"Ally." Webster's voice near my ear. "Look at me. Pretend you don't know him." The hissed words brought my head around but also fueled the trembling in my hands. If only Webster's strong ones could close over them, quiet the tremors.

"Get in the car." His calmness settled me as I slid into the seat behind the wheel, intent on the instrument panel, the gas pedal, the brake. Other engines ignited. Mine joined the roar. Webster jumped into his seat beside me. I blew out a long breath and set the car in gear. He poked my leg. I looked down. His thumb stuck up from his fist. Good to go.

But I couldn't shake the feeling of being watched. I chanced one glance back. Lawrence stood near the edge of the track. His eyes bored directly into mine.

Over the cacophony of engines and the cheering crowd, I tried to shout.

"He saw me, Webster. He's knows it's me."

Webster didn't hear. Or chose not to. He pointed me to our position, toward the back of the twenty-eight competing cars. Twenty-eight. All racing together. I forced my mind away from the what-ifs and back to our own special racing language. A closed fist to hold steady. A thumb pointed down to pull back, up to move faster. A swipe right or left to move over.

Around the track we started, steady and in order. Wiggles of apprehension worked their way through my stomach as perspiration wet my face. Could I drive for more than three hours at top speeds? I would have to concentrate if I wanted to finish. And oh, how I wanted to finish. But at the end, would Lawrence be there to expose me?

The red flag flapped. Webster's thumb shot up. I kicked us into top gear, nothing else on my mind but the track sliding beneath my tires.

Around. Around. Around.

Curve, back stretch, curve, front stretch.

The sun rose higher in the sky. I kept my eyes on the track to avoid the glare. Fifty miles. One hundred miles. But I never took the lead.

My stomach grumbled from lack of food. My legs felt as liquid as hot jelly. We pulled into the pit, Webster calling out orders. Gasoline. New tires. More oil in his pump tank. He leaned in near my ear, shouting to be heard. "Stay focused. We'll be out of here again in a few minutes."

I nodded, stretching my fingers, flexing my knees, ready to dart back into the fray at his command.

One hundred and fifty miles.

Fewer and fewer cars returned to the track. Oil slicked the boards. Webster guided me through it all. His hand swatted. I jerked the wheel. My car skidded just left of the one in front of me but quickly steadied. I glanced at the speedometer. Eighty-nine miles per hour. We inched forward, pulled even with another car.

Webster's thumb stood in the air. I held my breath, pressed my full weight against the pedal. We jumped ahead of that car and then another. Through the smoke, I counted four in front of me. Air whipped at my face, drying the sweat that mingled with the oil and dirt, though it did little to cool the inferno that encased the rest of me.

From the corner of my eye, I caught the blur of a spinning car. Then it tumbled over itself. My stomach jumped, forcing my heart into my throat. But I swallowed it down, pulled back on the gas, kept my vision roped to the track. We passed the frenetic crowd around the crash. I prayed. Prayed again. And watched for Webster's signals.

My arms joined my legs in their numbness. I fell behind two cars. Rivers ran down the small of my back, pasting fabric against skin. I longed to stand in that dark shed, peel the damp clothing from my body, let the fresh air cool me.

Webster held up one finger. One more lap to go. Seven other cars navigated the final curve. I leaned forward, as if to push the car faster. Webster did the same. Head lowered, I shot out of the turn and onto the final straightaway. Five cars blew exhaust in my face but two others coughed out my dust as the finish line zipped past. I eased off the gas. Webster's fist pumped air as my own laughter rang in my ears.

The roar of the crowd overpowered the whir of the remaining engines. I slowed to a stop. People rushed to congratulate the winner.

"Who is it?" I stepped from the car and bent over, resting shaking hands on tremulous knees. Hands slapped against my back as words of congratulations filled my ears.

"Johnny Aitken and his Peugeot," Webster said.

I straightened, unable to restrain my grin.

Then I remembered Lawrence.

I dropped to a squat behind the car and studied the shredded tire that would not have held for one more lap. I needed to get to the hideaway and change. Unless Lawrence had exposed me already.

A whistle soft in my ear. I stood. Webster's hand pressed at my back, propelling me forward. Long strides around a circuitous route. In and out of shadows. Through the crowd.

"I'll keep watch until you get inside." Webster shielded me

from view with his body. I slipped into the small building, grateful to have made it unseen.

Or so I hoped.

I leaned my back against the door and slowly sank to the dirt floor. Exhausted. Relieved. Exhilarated. Worried. Had Lawrence talked to my father yet?

Resting my head on top of a crate, I thought about what I'd just done. Three hundred miles. One of only a few cars to finish. The warmth of accomplishment surged feeling back in my jolted bones. I removed my driving clothes, toweled my body dry, washed the grime from my face, doused myself with rose water. Slipping into a dress, hat, and shoes, I readied myself once more to meet the world as Alyce Benson and pretend I'd done nothing at all astonishing.

26

$\mathcal{I}$ eased the shed's door shut behind me and wobbled into the crowd. Webster would return for my bag before he took the car to the train station. All I had to do was make an appearance to Father and—

Lawrence. Leaning against a railing, arms crossed, hat pushed back.

I studied the faces around me. No one looked at me askance. In fact, no one noticed me at all, except to tip their hats as they scooted past.

He pushed away from the rail, sauntered in my direction. Dressing my face with a smile, I shook my head, curls bouncing about my cheeks. "How lovely to see you, Lawrence."

His eyebrows lifted.

I sucked in a breath of steamy air laced with gasoline and body odor. He knew. I knew he knew. But had he told? Would he tell?

"You made it, Alyce. Your father wondered where you were."

A forced laugh stuck in my throat, almost choking me. I swallowed it down, brightened my tone. "Wasn't the race exciting?"

"Yes." His eyes narrowed for a split second. "Quite exciting."

I cleared my throat, eager to keep up the pretense. "I suppose I should find Father."

"Allow me to escort you." He held out his crooked elbow. I laid my hand on the sleeve of his jacket and let him lead me through the throng.

"How can he just drive and leave?" Father's voice bellowed above the crowd noise before I spotted him next to Webster, his arms jerking toward the heavens.

Webster, face streaked with dirt, hair plastered to his head, didn't flinch under Father's tirade. His eyes held steady on Father's face. "I told you, he had to go, but I'll give him his money."

"Blast it, Little. I don't like this at all. What's he hiding? I won't stand for a breath of scandal on my name as a businessman or a racing-car sponsor. Do you understand?" He pointed his cigar at Webster, the smoke sending Webster into a spasm of coughing. "And he's not getting another dime from my pocket until he shows his face. Is that understood?"

My teeth sank into the soft flesh of my lower lip. How would I ever get the money now? Webster swiped a filthy rag over his reddening face. His eyes cut in my direction for a swift second. "That's your prerogative, sir."

They stared at each other for a long moment, Father and Webster, while I held my breath. I didn't think Webster would give me away, but Father could be intimidating. And I doubted Webster wanted to lose his job.

"Besides"—Father stuck the cigar in his mouth, his face relaxing back into joviality—"I want to give him a little bonus for a job well done." He extracted some bills from his wallet and slid them into Webster's hand.

I licked my lips, as hungry for that money as a car for gasoline. I had to find a way to get what I'd earned. But how?

"You tell that man—what's his name again?"

"Al—" Webster's face froze for an instant. "Albert. Albert Butler."

Father grunted. "You tell him he'll have to pick up *his* pay in person." He returned the wallet to his inside coat pocket. "We could have avoided all this nonsense if you'd just driven yourself, as planned."

The words hit me again like a fist in the stomach.

Webster shoved the cash into his front pocket. His gaze caught mine. He looked sorry. Almost guilty.

I shoved aside my questions. I'd find a way to appease Father and claim my money. Depending on the amount he intended to give his driver, it might put me one race away from reaching three thousand dollars. And the Harvest Classic would run in Indianapolis this coming Saturday.

Father glanced over his shoulder. "Ally." He opened his arms; I entered his embrace. "Trotter," he said over my head, "you heard me. No money for our driver until the man sees me."

Lawrence's eyebrows arched. "Yes, sir."

I fanned my face, thankful for the heat to disguise my discomfort. Whatever Lawrence knew—or guessed—he obviously hadn't told Father yet. Did that mean he was on my side?

I breathed more deeply, my mouth sliding into a grin. I knew exactly how Lawrence could help me get that money from my father.

We took the late train back to Langston that night, but the moment I heard the faraway rooster announce Tuesday's dawn, I rose. A quick visit with Grandmother assured me she hadn't taken a downward turn. In fact, her cheeks seemed to have more color than I remembered.

"Pray for me, Granny." I kissed her cheek. "I'm off to secure more of our missions money today."

"I'll pray for great success, Alyce." She squeezed my fingers. "Then do come tell me about your trip."

"I promise."

I arrived at the Benson Farm Machinery offices not long after Father did, traipsing into the hallway as if I had nothing better to do of a morning. Yet I felt anything but normal. What would Lawrence say? Would he agree to my plan?

An older man I didn't recognize tipped his hat as he exited the building, letting the door thud shut behind him. I scampered into the safety of Lawrence's small office.

He leapt to his feet the moment I stepped inside, eyes roving past me, to the hall.

I turned to look, wondering if the stranger had returned. But the hall stood empty. "Is something wrong?"

His composure returned. "Not at all. How . . . interesting to see you this morning." He motioned me to the same chair I'd occupied before. I sat, the triangular hem of my new dress tickling my ankles.

Elbows resting on the desk, he tented his hands in front of his mouth. Our eyes met. "Your father doesn't know."

My head wiggled no. "But I'll tell him everything after I present the money to the McConnells."

"You could have been killed out there, you know. Gil Anderson almost was."

The driver who wrecked. I closed my eyes, seeing again the

flash of a spinning car before it turned over. "Is he . . . have you heard any news?"

"No. His mechanic got the worst of it, I think. I'm sure there'll be something in the paper this morning."

My knee bounced. I forced it still.

"What in heaven's name possessed you to do such a foolish thing?"

My chin shot up. "That's exactly what possessed me: heaven. You know I've been trying to get the money I promised the McConnells. But nothing's worked." My shoulders slumped. "Driving is the only skill I possess. Well, the only skill that can make money. Only that's not quite true, either." I pressed my fingers into my temples. "I could have baked pies. Or something. I had a list. But Mrs. Tillman thinks I already have the money, and she would have assumed I was helping them, not raising my own contribution. I had no choice. And Webster assured me—"

Lawrence exploded from his seat. "I should have known that man put you up to this." He paced, scowling. "He coerced you into this because he knew you'd hand him all the money."

I shot to my feet. "You're wrong. I approached him. He simply assured me I had the skill and strength to do it. And he promised to help." I wondered again why Webster didn't fight harder to keep his place as driver. Did he care about the children in my photograph as deeply as I did? I jammed my hands to my hips. "And why shouldn't he help me get the money for Africa?"

Lawrence's eyes grew round, then narrowed. "How did he know you could drive like that?"

I dropped back into the chair and studied my hands, hands that felt so at home on a steering wheel. I pulled in a deep breath before allowing my secret to escape. "My father built a dirt track in one of our back fields. A long time ago. He taught me to drive there. I was thirteen. I could barely see above the steering wheel." I shrugged. "When life gets complicated, I drive. Fast. Webster accompanies me most days. I'm not foolish enough to go out alone. Anything could happen."

"Yes. Anything." Words so cold I tried to rub the shivers from my arms. I had to make him understand.

My fingers clutched the edge of his desk. "I would never have presumed to drive in a real race except for the money. Mr. and Mrs. McConnell return in less than three weeks. I can't stand up in front of the congregation without the funds I promised. I just can't."

"So you drove in Chicago, too?" His fingers stroked the edges of his mustache. I gulped, wishing I hadn't told him more than he already knew.

Please, God, let him understand.

"And have you seen any of your money since you entrusted it to your *mechanic*?" The word slithered out, like the basest of slurs.

"I've seen it. Some of it, at least." I scratched a fleck of paint from the arm of my chair. "I asked for part of it and he gave it to me. Doesn't that prove his trustworthiness?"

"Maybe. Maybe not. But now your father won't give the money from the Cincinnati race to anyone but the driver himself. Or herself, as the case may be. How do you intend to get around that?"

I sat back, settled myself. This was what I had come for. "I thought I'd ask someone else to pose as the driver. Someone familiar with my secret—and my dilemma."

Could he read the unspoken question? I studied his face for any sign of understanding.

"Someone like me." Slow words. Yet a spark in his eyes told me he was flattered, and that he'd agree.

Relief coursed through my veins. "Yes. Someone like you."

If Lawrence asked not to be exposed to the public, Father would honor that request. And he wouldn't suspect anything amiss.

Lawrence shook his head. "It will never work. I went with him to Chicago, remember?"

I rested my head in my hands, thoughts tumbling like Gil Anderson's car. Then I looked up. "Were you with him the entire time? I didn't make it out of the heats, remember?"

"That's true." He leaned back in his chair, laced his fingers behind his head. "And if I remember correctly, I did wander off for a while before the final race. If I can't remember which heat I watched with him, I doubt he will, either."

He smoothed one edge of his mustache. "And I didn't sit with him in Cincinnati. He gave my seat to a customer and sent me to that man's place on the other side of the track long before the race began. I didn't see him after the race until I brought you to him." The corners of his mouth tipped upward as his eyebrows lifted just a bit.

Tingles raced up and down my arms as my smile answered his. "I think we can make this work."

27

I drove back up our lane, past the garden, to the garage, doubting the breakfast dishes had even been washed and put away yet. Lawrence would come for supper tonight. We would approach Father together and reveal Lawrence as the mystery driver. I promised myself again that after the money left town in Mr. McConnell's pocket, I'd spill the truth to Father.

I glanced up at Grandmother's window as I killed the engine. The curtain swayed, but from a slight breeze or someone's hand I couldn't be sure. I climbed from the Packard, but before I reached the stand of trees guarding the garage, Webster's familiar whistle drifted from far away.

With a quick change of direction, I reached the corner of the house and peered up the road. A jaunty figure in overalls strode closer. Had I whizzed past him without noticing? It again struck me as odd that a mechanic by trade wouldn't motor to work. But every time I'd mentioned it, Webster's lips shut tight. Or he changed the subject.

Hands on my hips, I tapped my foot as I waited. He turned in at the gate, walked up the drive. I crossed my arms, raised my eyebrows, and decided to try again. "Remind me why my father's crackerjack mechanic doesn't have a motorcar of his own?"

Webster grinned as he pulled open one of the garage doors. I followed him inside, but he didn't offer any answer, just gathered tools and an oil can before sauntering to the other side of the garage and opening the racing car's hood to expose the engine. His whistle resumed.

I charged across the garage. "Don't ignore me, Webster Little. I'll—I'll—"

The whistling stopped. Languid eyes met mine. My fists clenched.

He leaned against the car, his palms brushing the sides of his trousers. "Why does it matter so much?"

"Because I—" I considered my words. Only Webster knew the location of my money—unless Lawrence had indeed spied the hiding place that day. But if he had, wouldn't he have mentioned it to me by now?

Suddenly I feared I'd been too trusting. "I know Father pays you well, especially now that we are racing. So I just . . . wondered."

He shrugged, returned to his work. "Owning an automobile isn't important to me right now. I have other things to spend my money on."

"Like what?" Not a car. Or clothing. Or a home—Lucinda had mentioned he lived in a boarding house with several of Father's employees. Did he spend all his extra money on anonymous gifts? Was his mother ill? Did he spend evenings surreptitiously drinking or gambling?

Please, God, let him have some worthy cause.

"There are some things a man likes to keep private."

"Even from his friends?"

"Yes, even from them."

Why didn't he trust me to keep his secrets as I trusted him with mine? Brushing back a curl that draped near my eyes, I determined to match his solemnity. "Then I doubt it can be anything honorable."

He stiffened, then stepped closer, his breath warming my cheek. I stared at the stubble on his face, my heart battering my chest. He tipped my chin with one finger, put on his signature smile. "Don't you trust me, Ally?"

I stared into his eyes. Clear and true. Not clouded by hard living and drink. I felt as if I were falling into his deep, dark gaze. I drew in a sharp breath. He backed away. I closed the distance between us again, my eyes locked on his. "I trust you, Webster. Really, I do."

Warmth oozed through me at his nearness. I wanted to reach up, to smooth his unruly hair, but my arms remained pinned to my sides. I hardly dared to breathe.

Tenderness and frustration flickered across his face, as if he wanted to pull me into his arms and push me away all at the same time. Then he blew out a long breath and raked his hands through his mop of hair.

He focused on some point beyond me, his words softening. "Like you, I have a promise to fulfill. It takes all the resources I have—and then some." He blinked hard, his eyes finding my face again. "I need these races same as you. For the money."

My heart tumbled toward my toes. "But you . . . you let me drive. You gave up the chance at the prize money."

He reached for my hand, ran his thumb over the skin just below my knuckles. "Please don't ask me to explain. Not now."

My spirit crumpled as if I'd been suspended over a chasm and then let go. But I pulled myself up quickly. I moved away from his touch, aching at the sudden coldness that engulfed my hand. "I found a way to get the race money from Father."

The tension fell from his face. Suspicion replaced it. "How?"

Caressing the front fender of the race car, I avoided his gaze. "Lawrence Trotter is going to tell Father he's the driver."

"You didn't."

I pulled my shoulders back, wishing I could meet him eye to eye. "I did. He already knew anyway. I told you he recognized me at the race on Monday. Besides, it's a good plan. Father will keep the car entered in Saturday's Harvest Classic once he's convinced there's no scandal. And I'll earn the rest of my money for the McConnells."

Webster stared at the ground, hands low on his hips. "I never thought you'd do such a—"

I sprang toward him. "A what? I made a plan. And a good one, I might add. Lawrence will keep my secret. He and I have the same desire—to see that the McConnells have the money they need to return to Africa and tell people about Jesus."

One of Webster's eyebrows rose. "Whatever you say, Ally. If you trust me, I guess I'll have to trust you. But right now I have to get to work."

I bit my tongue and marched through the garden, into the kitchen.

"Coffee, please, Clarissa. In the morning room." My head pounded with every step. I fell to the sofa and rubbed circles on my temples.

"Good morning, Alyce, darling." Mother swept into the

room and kissed my cheek, then her forehead creased. "Are you ill? And what happened to your new dress?"

"I'm fine, Mother." I fingered a tear in the flimsy fabric. "Must have caught on one of the rosebushes. I'll have Betsy stitch it up."

Clarissa entered with the tray of coffee, left to retrieve a second cup, and returned to our burdened silence.

"Oh, please set another place at supper tonight, Clarissa. I've invited Mr. Trotter to join us."

Clarissa nodded and left.

Mother's head tipped to one side as she sipped her coffee. "At your father's invitation or yours?"

I shrugged. "Mine." I lifted my cup to my lips, but the coffee didn't settle me as I'd hoped.

Mother stared into her lap. "I'm not sure you want to hear this from me, but be very careful, Alyce. I'm not sure you understand—"

"I understand more than you think I do." Pushing to my feet, I banged my cup to the tray, hot coffee sloshing onto my hand. But as I left her there with a look of concern on her usually placid face, I swallowed down the fear that I'd jumped into a pool of water far exceeding my ability to swim.

"I demand he meet with me!" Father's voice crashed through the closed door of his study before supper that evening. I cringed, knowing Webster stood inside. But I couldn't hear his answer, no matter how hard I pressed my ear against the door.

The telephone jangled. I waited for Clarissa to answer, but it rang again. I charged through the hall and picked up the earpiece.

Long distance. Business. I exhaled. It would give Webster a moment of relief.

"I'll fetch him now." I set the receiver on top of the telephone, hurried back to Father's study, and rapped on the door before pushing it open. "Telephone call for you, Father. Long distance."

Father stomped to the telephone. Webster, still sitting in front of Father's desk, wiped a hand across his face.

"I'm sorry." I stepped inside the room, tension still thick in the air. "I'd hoped you wouldn't have to endure another tirade before Lawrence talked to him tonight."

One side of Webster's mouth rose. "It doesn't matter. And I never did tell you—you drove great yesterday."

"Thank you." My hands felt empty and large. I picked up a brass letter opener. My fingers slid down the smooth, dull blade as I leaned against the massive desk.

"I've never seen anyone take to the track as fast as you have. It's truly a gift."

My head sprang up. "Do you think?"

A lock of hair fell across his forehead. He swept it aside. "Most men wouldn't take the chance. And even if they did, they wouldn't know how to handle that machine as smoothly as you do."

I glanced at the floor, suddenly shy in the presence of the only person who knew the whole me.

He looked into the hallway before standing. "Are you sure about this, Ally? I don't trust Trotter."

I ground top teeth into bottom, tired of lies and suspicions and doubt. Webster cleared his throat. I tapped the opener into my open palm as I rounded the desk. I stood near him now, so close I could hear him breathe.

"I know the two of you don't like each other, but this is a good plan. You can trust me, remember?" With a playful look, I pointed the opener at his chest. "You'd better trust me. My father could fire—"

"What's going on here?" Father's bellow cracked through the room.

I jumped back, the letter opener pinging against the desktop before clattering to the floor. "Nothing, Father."

His eyes flashed in Webster's direction. "Is he bothering you?"

Webster paled.

A nervous laugh fumbled from my lips. "Webster? We were just talking."

Father's eyebrows scrunched toward his nose. "But you were pointing that—"

I bent down and retrieved the piece of brass. "Letter opener. I just . . . had it in my hand."

Webster's color returned as Father chuckled away his burst of anger, slapped Webster on the back. "Sorry, old boy. My little girl, you know?"

"Twenty-two," I muttered. "I'm twenty-two, remember?"

"Not a problem, sir." Webster kept his gaze on the floor. "I'd be protective of her myself, if I were you." Then his head rose. "I'll get things settled in the garage before I head home."

"Of course. Of course. Have to be ready for that race on Saturday." Father picked up his cigar. Webster walked away without a look back.

I hurried to the front door the minute the knock sounded, took Lawrence's hat, and placed it on the table in the foyer. Father pumped his hand and led him into the dining room. I followed behind, relieved.

Clarissa's fine meal dissolved all discomfort. Lawrence

seemed quite jovial, not anxious about his upcoming part in my drama. Even Mother participated in the conversation. Maybe I'd finally convinced her I could take care of myself, choose my own friends. Or my own husband.

As we waited for dessert, Lawrence lifted the crystal goblet beside his plate. "An incredible meal, Mr. Benson."

"Clarissa just might be the best cook in the world." Father lowered his voice and his eyebrows. "But don't tell her I said so."

I hid my giggle. Clarissa had no doubt of my father's regard for her. A few moments later, she bustled into the room and served each of us a slice of chocolate cake from the tray Betsy held. I slid my fork through the corner, lifted it to my mouth, and closed my eyes to savor the perfection. Smooth as silk. Sweet as sugar. By the time I returned to the moment, Lawrence and Father had reduced their cake to crumbs.

I set my fork on the edge of my plate. "Father, there's something I—" My gaze skittered toward Lawrence. He gave me a quick smile and nod. "Something we'd like to discuss with you."

Mother's eyes grew wide, but they didn't show anger or disdain. Only fear.

"What is it, Ally girl?" Father's sweet voice. The one I needed to hear. Then he boomed out Clarissa's name, sending my heart into my throat.

Clarissa appeared from the butler's pantry. "Yes, sir? Do you need something?"

Father grinned and lifted his plate. "More cake, please."

She shook her head and tutted her way around the table. "You, as well, Mr. Trotter?"

Lawrence gave a shy but eager nod.

I glanced at Mother, shaking my head, hoping she'd share

my amusement. But she looked pensive, as if she hadn't even witnessed the exchange. I wished I knew what she was thinking.

I pulled my attention back to Father. "I know you've been curious about your driver. . . ."

Father shoved another bite of cake into his mouth. And another. He shook his head back and forth. "Mm. Mm. Mm."

I pinched the top of my nose. Could he not attend to any other subject while Clarissa's chocolate cake sat in front of him? I glanced at Lawrence. He, too, seemed engrossed in the dessert.

Words of frustration filled my mouth, but for once I held them in. I pushed back from the table. "Why don't I meet you in the library when you're finished?" I attempted an alluring exit from the room, but I'm sure neither Father nor Lawrence noticed.

Father's surprised laughter rang through the house after Lawrence's "revelation." Guilt pricked even as I let myself relax. I'd drive one more race and then place whatever money I had into the McConnells' hands two weeks later. And during those two weeks of waiting, I would help the Women's Mission Auxiliary complete their fundraising and pray the Lord would help us secure all the money.

Father wiped tears from his cheeks. "I'll admit, Trotter, I never would have guessed you had it in you. How did you manage to find time to practice? Seems you almost live at the office with me."

Lawrence tossed off a believable answer with an ease that widened my eyes. Then Father opened his desk drawer, pulled out a stack of bills, and slid the bundle across the desk. I sucked in a breath. Lawrence closed his hand over the money my fingers itched to posses. Then it disappeared into his coat pocket.

I swallowed hard, forcing my gaze to Father's face. "I suppose you'd like him to drive at the Harvest Classic on Saturday, right, Father? After such a good showing last week?" My stomach swirled with remorse, but I couldn't find a way to retract myself. I was in for a penny now. Might as well go for a pound.

"Of course he'll drive." Father lit a cigar and inhaled. The tip glowed red. He puffed the smoke into the room and wiggled his eyebrows. "Gives you an excuse for another trip to the racetrack, eh, Ally?"

I nodded, though I wanted to spew my dinner onto the floor. In spite of his lack of faith in God, I did love my father and found no joy in deceiving him.

"I'll trust you with the arrangements, Trotter." And with that, he dismissed us.

Out in the foyer, I curled my hand around Lawrence's elbow and smiled up at him. "You did that beautifully," I said as we stood alone in the shadows, only the faint glow of the electric lamps outside filtering through the window that ran along the top of the front door.

Lawrence slipped his arm around my waist. He pulled me near, our faces just inches apart. I held my breath as his mustache framed his smile.

"We make quite a team, I'd say." He studied my lips. My heart pitched and lurched. He leaned closer, his mustache tickling my upper lip.

A door creaked. Footsteps clomped.

We jumped apart.

My entire body trembled as Lawrence grabbed his hat and slipped out the door. The motor of his Grant sputtered to life and then faded into the distance. I pressed my hands against my cheeks as Father patted my back and mounted the stairs.

I glanced again at the door through which Lawrence had disappeared. Was I in love or embarrassed? Suddenly I realized I didn't have enough experience with men to know the difference.

28

All night long, doubts assailed me. Grandmother had never minced words over sin. She told me when I'd faltered and expected me to repent, to be sorry, but also to change my ways. Was that why I'd kept my activities from her? I'd convinced myself it was to protect her in her fragile state. Now I wondered.

I rolled onto my side and stared at the Bible on the table beside my bed. Or at least at the place I knew it to be. I couldn't actually see the black book in the dark room. But it was there. I knew what it said. And inside its pages rested the photo of Ava McConnell's students, of the children who needed to hear of Jesus. *How shall they believe if they have not heard, Lord? And how shall they hear without a preacher? Without the McConnells?*

I flung back the covers and set my bare feet on the soft rug. If only I could go for a drive, with the stars as my light, the moon as my guide. Thunder rumbled, reminding me that no light existed this night. Just blackness where I longed for illumination. I squeezed my eyes shut.

One more race. After the McConnells left for New York, I'd tell Father everything.

No more hiding. No more lies.

But as I paced in the darkness, new realization dawned. I'd lied long before this moment. For years I'd hidden the part of me that loved speed, the roar of an engine. A lie by omission. And not just to my parents. To everyone.

Everyone but Webster.

Light slashed through my room. A boom rattled my windows. With a long leap, I reached my bed. I wrapped my arms around my legs and held my breath. Rain pelted against the glass. I let out my breath and rested my chin on my mountain of knees.

Lord, I've made an awful mess. Turning the pillow to the cool side, I laid down again. Thunder clapped. I threw the sheet over my head and hugged my knees to my chest before allowing sleep to shield me from the storm.

Sometime later my eyes flew open. Gray clouds drifted across the darker sky, but no patter of rain broke the silence. Something else had awakened me. Something besides the abating storm. A thought skittering just out of reach.

I bolted upright.

Lawrence left without giving me my money.

Just after sunrise, I tiptoed into Grandmother's room.

"Alyce?" She held out her hand toward me.

"How did you know it was me?" I kissed her forehead and perched on the bed beside her.

"I know your step—and I've missed it."

"I'm sorry." I leaned down and pressed my cheek to hers. "I've been . . . busy."

Her smile faltered a bit. "You're being careful with me, aren't you?"

"Yes." My throat tightened. Even when I managed to cover over the truth with my father, I couldn't with her. I doubted she'd read me any better even if she had full use of her eyesight.

"Don't shut me out, Alyce." She laid a hand on her chest. "This heart will stop beating one day. But there's nothing wrong with my real heart, the one that goes on forever. It's the only one that matters. You know that."

"I know." My own heart felt squeezed to suffocation. By trying not to worry her, I'd burdened her all the same. "I'm sorry."

She found my hand. "You're forgiven. Now, tell me what's troubling you."

It didn't take long to spill the story. I told her everything.

Well, almost everything.

I didn't mention that Lawrence told Father he was the driver. Nor did I relate the tumult of emotions when his lips had almost touched mine. Nor the odd need I felt for Webster's approval, and my desire to know more about him. Still, she knew about the money—and the racing.

I watched her face but couldn't read her thoughts the way she seemed to read mine. A gust of wind fluttered her handkerchief off the bedside table. It sailed to the floor. I leaned over and picked it up, rubbed my fingers over the embroidered initials at the corner.

LB. Laura Benson.

She didn't speak often of her life before Grandfather died. He left his son no legacy of money or faith. Only hard work.

Father followed in his stead. After Grandmother embraced the love of the Lord, she hoped my family would eventually build a house on the cornerstone of Christ that would stand strong for generations to come. But it seemed that dream would fall to me alone. Had I failed her already?

I refolded the square of soft cotton and returned it to its usual place. Then Grandmother nodded. Just once, but decisively, as if acknowledging something.

"Esther. And Rahab. Jochebed, the mother of Moses, as well as the midwives that delivered those Hebrew babies. Even Jael. They all concealed something. Sometimes the Lord instructs His people to do a task that seems extraordinary. But always for a reason. Always for the good of His people as a whole."

I squirmed. None of those women lied for the sake of money. To save lives, yes. But my situation wasn't that dire. Nor that straightforward.

"But be very sure that is the Lord's direction and not your own desire, Alyce. Sometimes our motives get so tangled up it's hard to discern the difference." Her brown-spotted hand clasped mine.

I worked to keep tears from slipping down my face. Maybe the Lord had led me to sit behind the wheel of Webster's race car, but I doubted His intention had been for Lawrence and me to sit in front of my father and spew untruth.

"You must pray and then decide what to do, Alyce dear. And I'll pray you have the strength for whatever that is."

But in spite of my respect for Grandmother's opinion, I couldn't bring myself to undo what had been done. I would race on Saturday.

All during breakfast with Mother I prayed for a hot sun to bake the soupy roads. I had to get to Father's office. I had to get my money from Lawrence. Finally, after a light lunch, I donned a wide-brimmed hat and dodged puddles on my way to the garage.

Webster looked up. His eyes shifted a bit before his throat rumbled and his hands danced in the folds of his rag. Whatever was bothering him, I didn't have time to dig it out now. Maybe when I returned. I stepped into the Packard.

"What do you think you're doing?" He stopped my door from closing.

"I have an appointment. In town."

"Not on these roads you don't."

"I'll go slow. I'll be careful." I pulled at the door. He refused to let go.

"I'm not coming to pull you out of the mud."

I sniffed. "I didn't ask you to."

"But you will."

My chin tipped upward as my eyebrows arched. "I can take care of myself, thank you very much."

A prick of conscience reminded me that Webster had proven himself a friend. But I couldn't endure his scolding for my alliance with Lawrence. Our disagreement over that part of the plan still vexed me.

I pulled harder. He let go. The door slammed shut. I ignited the engine and puttered down the drive.

Before I reached the road, my heart condemned me. While maneuvering around a large circle of mud, I resolved to apologize after I motored home again, once the money resided in my handbag. Then I'd ask Webster to retrieve Grandmother's box and the remainder of my money. No more confusion over whom to trust. I intended to safeguard my own funds now.

My back wheel splashed into a hole that was more water than mud. I cringed but kept going, thankful not to fulfill Webster's dire prophecy of needing to be rescued from impassable roads. Then the street turned hard beneath my tires. Hard and bumpy. More like the bricks on the track in Indianapolis.

Would I be able to maintain the speed on brick I had on boards? I didn't know. Perhaps the effort would jar my teeth from my head. Or prove the final surge toward my goal.

I wanted to win. But I only needed a top-three finish to gain the extra prize money. And I believed I could do it.

Sitting in front of Lawrence's desk, my handbag in my lap, I questioned myself. Something had changed between last night and this morning. His eyes seemed . . . hungrier than before. Like a mangy dog eyeing a juicy steak. I didn't know whether to be flattered or fearful.

I took a deep breath and shoved down my discomfort. A product of my imagination after a restless night, for sure. This was Lawrence. My friend. My ally. He'd said we made a great team.

"You forgot something yesterday evening." The tease in my voice declared the situation a simple oversight.

He cocked his head and smoothed one wing of his mustache. "Ah. You mean the money." He opened a drawer, pulled out the bundle of bills.

My smile turned genuine as tension ebbed from my body. I knew I'd guessed right. Caught up in the moment, he'd forgotten about the money. Heat crept up my throat and seeped into my face as I remembered just what that moment had been.

"Thank you." I placed the cash in my handbag and clasped it shut. Would he mention our almost-kiss or did he expect some acknowledgment on my part first? I didn't know. I waited in the silence, my temperature rising under his bold gaze.

"Well." I stood, turned toward the door, waited again for him to say something.

He didn't.

"I best be on my way."

He opened the door, stared down at me with a knowing smile. "And what will you do with your windfall?"

"Put it with the rest, of course."

"You're a fool to trust him. Let me keep it." He stepped closer, his body almost pressing into mine. "If you'll bring me all your funds, I'll hold them for you. I'd hate for anything to go wrong now."

My lungs refused to fill completely, puffing quick breaths in and out as unease clawed through excitement and tightened my throat. "It's only for another couple of weeks."

His face darkened like yesterday's sky. But he stepped away. Shrugged. "Whatever you deem best, but don't say I didn't warn you."

I nodded as I forced my feet forward. Down the hallway. Out the door. Into my car.

Hands and chin resting on the steering wheel, I searched for the window to Lawrence's office. Didn't he think me intelligent enough to recognize a man of dubious character rather than embracing him as my friend? Yet Lawrence claimed this censure to be his way of showing concern, his affection.

I sat back against the warm leather seat and stroked my handbag as if it were a sleeping kitten. If only I could read the situation better. Something had changed between us since yesterday. Of that I was certain.

Setting my purse on the seat, I started the car. What I needed was advice. About love. About men. Perhaps Lucinda had the answers I needed.

29

I knew Lucinda often spent her lunch hour at home, enjoying time with her children, catching up on her chores, giving her aunt a short spell of peace. I prayed she wouldn't be taken aback by my unannounced arrival.

"Alyce!" Lucinda ushered me inside. We sat at the table crammed into her tiny kitchen while she bounced her whimpering baby on her lap. "The doctor will see Teresa again tomorrow, but I'm not holding out much hope that he can help. I don't know that there's anything wrong with her, but I keep trying. I'd hate to think she cries because she's in pain. What if I could help her and didn't?"

Dishes clanked and water splashed behind us as the two older girls cleaned up. The school was close enough that they could walk home for lunch. I wanted to help, to plunge my hands into the water and scrub each plate until it shone. But I knew Lucinda would frown. She wanted a friend, not a maid. As did I.

I reached a finger toward the crying baby. She gripped it and pulled it toward her mouth, forgetting for a moment to wail.

"Lucinda, how do you know if a man is . . . interested?"

A rare smile transformed Lucinda's haggard face. Her eyes sparkled with glee as she leaned forward in conspiracy. "Who, Alyce?"

I glanced back at the girls. Lucinda nodded and pulled me into the small parlor with only Teresa for company.

"Now, tell me everything."

"There's nothing to tell, really. I mean, nothing's been *said*. I'm just starting to get this feeling that there's . . . more. Does that make sense?"

Lucinda nodded and then glanced at the clock on the mantel. "I don't have much time before the children go back to my aunt's." She sighed. "But I can tell you this: Love is about more than how he makes you feel. It comes across in his actions, in his words. The Bible says a man should love his wife as Christ loved the church."

Her eyes turned misty. She shut her mouth, smoothed the feathery hair on Teresa's head. "That's how my Billy loved me. And I knew it not because my heart jumped when I saw him. I knew it because he—" she stared at the floor and blew out a long breath—"he paid my father's debts so I didn't have to worry about leaving my mother without my income." Her head lifted, eyes fierce. "Don't accept anything less."

Did Lawrence love me like that? I didn't know. Unbidden, Webster's face sprang to mind, his love for the car he'd built with his own hands, his willingness to set me behind its wheel. I jumped to my feet.

"Thank you, Lucinda. I'd better be on my way home." I noted the lines creasing her face, and my heart twisted. Could I ease her burden in some fashion? My fingers pressed the edges of my handbag firmly closed. I couldn't give her any more money if I hoped to present the full three thousand dollars to the McConnells. And without money, all I had to offer was myself.

I tossed my purse on the sofa. "Why don't you go back to the office? I'll make sure the girls get back to school and the little ones back to your aunt's."

Hope dawned in her tired eyes. "You would do that?"

"Of course. Go on, now." I lifted Teresa.

Lucinda gnawed at her bottom lip. "If you're sure . . . We're having company for supper and, well, I appreciate the help. Thank you."

"Company?"

Teresa shrieked, reached for her mother.

"Mr. Little, actually."

I bounced Teresa in my arms. "Oh? I'm sure he'll appreciate a home-cooked meal."

"That was my thought, as well. He spends so much time taking care of others and no one takes care of him."

No one. Including me. In spite of all his kindnesses on my behalf.

Teresa's fingers clung to my hair and pulled. I forced a tight smile. "Hurry or you'll be late A few minutes of peace and quiet, that's what you need."

With a faint smile, Lucinda picked up her hat and darted out the door. The baby howled. The older girls stopped washing the dishes to stare at me. Their brother was playing with something on the floor, seeming not to notice anything amiss.

I kissed the baby's tiny palm—such soft skin—and ran my hand over the fuzz on top of her head. "Nothing's as bad as all that," I crooned. "Let's see if we can surprise your mama when she comes back. We'll give her a straightened house. What do you think?"

I jiggled Teresa up and down, finally luring a fleeting smile before she raised another fuss. Holding her on my hip, I picked up strewn clothing and then set her on the floor to scream while I made the bed. When the girls finished in the kitchen, they swept the floors and dusted the furniture before dashing back to school. By the time I dropped off the little ones at their aunt's house, the baby had drifted to sleep in my arms.

Maybe God did intend to use my meager housekeeping skills for something good. And yet as I shut the door behind me, the thought of Webster spending a pleasant evening in the tidy house with my friend skewered my heart.

I wished the Lord would just let me give her money instead.

Ignoring the questions about Webster and Lawrence that twirled my stomach into knots, I motored down Main Street and out onto the country roads. Wind whipped through my curls as I drove. Not at breakneck race-car speeds, but as fast as my little Runabout would go over moist roads. I felt free—much as I imagined Lucinda felt on her short walk alone, away from the responsibilities of her home.

I imagined passing Mrs. Tillman as I zipped along. Her eyebrows would rise, her lips purse in disapproval. I'd already invited her scrutiny for having my own car and driving it myself. I was sure she'd deem my speed unfeminine. And driving on a racetrack, competing against men? Unforgivable.

My parents' reaction wouldn't be much different. Mother would be mortified, embarrassed to show her face among her society ladies in Chicago. And although I suspected Father would be secretly pleased with my success, his aspirations for his daughter didn't involve much more than marrying well. A trophy of sorts. Well dressed. Well matched. Well thought of.

Grandmother and Webster both implied that God had given me this unusual gift as a means of raising money for His kingdom work. Was I wrong to embrace that idea? Even if it were true, I feared I'd overstepped the bounds of God's law by lying and then enticing Lawrence to lie so I could continue. If Grandmother discovered that part of the story, would she reverse her approval?

I feared I'd locked myself in a cage I couldn't escape. I pushed the gas pedal closer to the floor. The Runabout jumped forward as curls danced about my face. A Model T chugged up the other side of the narrow road. With a quick jerk of the wheel, my tires crushed grass, leaving the road to the slower vehicle. I waved as I passed, remembering after I whizzed away that Pastor Swan drove an automobile just like that one.

I reached home, parked my car, and strutted deeper into the coolness of the carriage house.

"I got it!" The money flapped as I raised it over my head.

Webster tossed his rag onto the workbench. "I guess you want it stashed with the rest."

I hesitated, wanting to take back possession of all my money but knowing the flimsiness of my resolve in the face of need. Lawrence insisted I should at least see my money. Perhaps that was all I needed. Assurance.

"I want it with the rest, yes. But I'd really like to see it. You know, just to remember it's real."

He slipped the cash into his pocket, eyes laughing at me as a grin stretched across his round face. His finger wagged in my direction. "You want a glimpse of the hiding place."

I sidled closer, covered my eyes. "I won't peek. I promise."

His laughter filled the cavernous building. "You won't be able to resist."

"But I just want to hold it all in my hands. Remind myself that we're almost there."

He turned serious. Something in his eyes held me still yet made me dizzy. "I want you to succeed, Ally. I want you to drive well, yes, but I also want you to earn your money. I know it's important to you."

"It is important. And you've worked so hard to help." I laid my hand on his arm. "Thank you, Webster. You're a true friend."

He raked a hand through his hair as he plopped down on the muddy running board of my Packard. I sat beside him, our shoulders touching. He turned to me. The anguish framing his eyes squeezed my heart and made me want to guide his head to my shoulder, tell him everything would be all right.

"I would never do anything to hurt you, Ally. You know that, don't you?"

I nodded, suddenly confused.

He held my gaze for a few moments, as if deciding whether or not to say more. Then he jumped up and started wiping the mud from my tires. With stuttered steps, I headed into the sunshine, wishing he felt comfortable talking with me. He obviously needed someone to confide in.

Maybe he preferred someone like Lucinda.

~✺ 30 ✺~

Through the long evening, I stayed at Grandmother's bedside, reading her favorite passages of Scripture, regaling her with tales of the racetrack, all while I wrestled with my feelings. Did I care for Lawrence? Did he care for me? What about Webster? Did I dare think of him as more than a friend?

"Alyce? Are you still here?" Grandmother's warble lifted me into the moment again.

"I'm here. Just . . . thinking." About the dinner happening at Lucinda's house. About my money stowed in a red box in a dark corner of the garage.

Her white head bobbed. "So much to consider. Have you made any decisions?"

I blew a breath upward, sending the sprigs of hair at my forehead wiggling. "I decided to let Webster continue to hold on to the money."

"I think that's wise."

"Do you? Because Lawrence—Mr. Trotter, who works

for Father—doesn't trust him. Says men like him are often drifters and tend to take things that don't belong to them."

Her eyebrows pinched toward her nose. "Have you any reason to suspect such a thing?"

"No. But why would Lawrence cast suspicion for no reason?"

The corners of her mouth twitched. "Could he be jealous?"

"Of Webster? He's Father's mechanic."

She laid her gnarled fingers over mine. "But he's your friend. Has this . . . Lawrence intimated he desires more than friendship from you?"

I pulled my hand away from her touch but didn't answer.

Her unseeing eyes stared at me, her head leaning a bit to one side. "Have I ever told you the story of how I met your grandfather?"

"Yes, ma'am. Many times."

"Oh, I know I told you the when and where, but did I ever explain how I knew he was the man God meant for me?"

I thought back to the old stories. "No, I guess not. But you weren't a Christian then. How could you know he was God's choice for you?"

She smiled. "I didn't understand it then, of course. Do you think the Lord takes note of us only after we turn to Him? No, He woos us through our whole lives."

Woos us. Like a suitor. The perfect suitor. I'd never considered that before. I leaned forward, chin in my hand, elbow on my knee.

She must have sensed my listening posture. "We met a few weeks before the Fourth of July picnic."

"I remember."

"At the end of our celebration of America's birthday, his horse raced against my father's."

"And his horse won."

"Yes, but that's not the point. The point is, after getting to know him, even in that short time, I wanted his horse to win."

"That makes sense."

She shook her head. "Not when you know that my father had promised to give me his horse if it won that race. And all I'd ever wanted was a horse of my own."

I straightened. "So you wanted Grandfather to win even though it meant denying yourself something you'd always wanted?"

"Yes. That's when I knew I loved him."

Lucinda's words about love and sacrifice screamed in my ears. I batted back the noise, eager to hear what Grandmother had to say. "What did your father do with the horse when it lost?"

She shrugged. "Sold him. Spent most of the money on drink in town that night."

"Oh."

Grandmother tried to hold a smile on her lips but didn't succeed. "I tell you this for two reasons, dear. First, so you'll appreciate who your father is, even if he is not who you want him to be. And second, so you will be watchful." Now a real smile appeared. "One day a man will inspire you to care nothing for yourself and everything for him. But of course you'll have the Lord to guide you, as I did not. Wait for him, Alyce. Whomever he may be."

I tried to imagine my grandmother as she said she'd been before she knew the saving grace of the Lord Jesus. But I couldn't.

"I'll be praying for you, dear."

I stood, my fingers curling around hers. "I know you will."

I couldn't settle after the talk with Grandmother. Not even with my tattered copy of *Pilgrim's Progress*, which usually quieted my agitation. Images of Webster with Lucinda's children, of her shy smile as she served him, haunted my imagination. I tried to make myself think of Lawrence instead. But the new look in his eye, his possessive manner, didn't draw those visions close.

Father and Mother went to bed. The house turned quiet. Starlight beckoned me into the garden, and I heeded the call. Roses sent their sweet perfume into the cool night air. I closed my eyes, drank it in. Hands behind my back, I drifted down one path and up another, until I stood staring at the front of the garage, the doors shut tight. But light seeped through between boards and ground.

My heart danced in my chest. Had Webster come back after supper with Lucinda? I told myself I wanted to know if he'd enjoyed the evening. But as the thought of seeing him pulled me toward the old carriage house, I wasn't sure I could find the courage to ask.

But I could ask about the race on Saturday. The potential prize money. The large door swung on its hinges as I pulled.

"Webster?"

I stepped inside, blinded by the glaring light overhead. "Webster?"

All the cars sat in their usual spots. If he wasn't there, why the light? I reached for the string to turn off the single overhead bulb, but it swung away as a breeze wafted in through the open door. Stepping into the void between the cars, the toe of my shoe collided with a solid object. I looked down. Nothing. Had I kicked it beneath the car?

On hands and knees, I peered under Father's car, then my own. Spying a bulky shadow near my rear tire, I reached for it, pulled it into the light.

Grandmother's red box. Open. And empty.

I clawed the ground beneath the car. The money had to be there. It had to. Webster wouldn't have left something so precious to me to be crushed beneath the wheels of one of the automobiles. But no matter where my arm reached, where my hand touched, only a few red beads mixed with earth.

I rocked back on my toes, knees still kissing the ground. Only Webster knew where the box was hidden. Only he could have emptied it.

All of my efforts, all of my desires, stolen in a moment. And by one who'd claimed he wanted to help.

Fury spurred me to my feet. I paced through the garage, beads biting into my hand as I squeezed the box between my fingers. I'd demand he come immediately and explain. I stopped, almost tipping forward from the sudden cease of movement.

I didn't know if he owned a telephone. I wasn't sure which boarding house he called home. I couldn't ask Father how to contact him. He'd ask why. And then I'd have to lie. Again.

Dust tornadoed about my feet as I resumed my frantic motions. I tossed the box into the front seat of my car. I paced across the space and back again, across and back, across and back. Could someone besides Webster have done this? I didn't think so. No one else knew of the money. Or its location.

Webster had said he needed money. And Lucinda had confirmed it by revealing his charitable acts. Clarissa had mentioned such a basket arriving at the doorstep of her sister's temporary home. A basket filled with food and cash.

Fingernails bit into my palms. Lawrence had warned me the temptation would be too great. Why hadn't I listened? And yet, couldn't the Lord have protected my money? His money?

Faces from the photographs rose up before me, souls languishing without the Lord. Would the McConnells be able to return to the Gold Coast without the funds I'd promised? Had I consigned an entire people to eternal destruction?

My throat swelled as I blinked back tears, held in a keening wail. Admitting foolishness in front of Mrs. Tillman and the congregation would be even more painful than admitting failure.

"How could You let this happen, Lord? You knew what that money would do, who it would help. You gave me the desire to give it—even the means to raise it when no way seemed possible. So why this? Why now?" I sat hard on the running board of my Packard, between the car and the wall, hidden from the light, from the door. My own dark corner of mourning. Forehead resting on my knees, I let Lawrence's words play in my ears like a much-loved gramophone record. *"People aren't always who they seem to be."*

The realization slashed across my heart like a knife. The only thing that staunched the wound was remembering that he'd stolen from the Lord, not from me, for my heart and my money belonged to Him.

Deep breaths reined in my emotions. I pressed the heels of my hands into my eyes and pulled a long draught of air into my lungs before laboring to my feet. Tightness in my arms and legs unkinked like a length of rope pulled taut.

A door creaked. I held my breath. Had Webster come to return the money?

Footsteps padded against the ground. I crouched behind the Packard, gathering my skirts and dropping to my knees to peer beneath the chassis. Shoes traversed the space just beyond. But not Webster's shoes. Not dusty and worn. These shone with recent polish. And the pants cuffed above the shoes declared a suit, not overalls.

My pulse bellowed in my ears, drowning out the footfalls.

Not heavy enough to be Father. I kept to the shadows on the back side of my car but inched toward the opposite end, in the direction of the intruder.

Legs in front of my eyes. I lifted my gaze, shot to my feet. "Lawrence!"

I rushed into his open arms, heard breath whoosh from his body as I pressed myself against him. "Thank heavens you're here."

Of all the people in my life, perhaps he alone had the strength of faith to see me through this. Never mind that he'd say *I told you so*. I pulled away, anxious to look into his face as I spilled the catastrophe. His lips curved upward, pulling his mustache with them. But it wasn't a playful grin. Or a soulful smile. It seemed sinister. Leering. That hungry look from earlier today.

He grabbed ahold of my arms. "I always suspected there was something different about you, Alyce. Something hidden from the rest of the world. Who knew you had a passion for money? A passion for driving. What other passions does the innocent Miss Benson conceal?" His gaze wandered down my body. I shuddered as a boulder of fear settled in my stomach.

I tried to pull away. His grip held me fast. I glanced toward the door.

He chuckled low. "No one knows you're out here, do they? We're all alone. You don't have to pretend anymore."

"Pretend?"

One arm circled my waist. A band of steel. Who knew a bookkeeper could be so strong? His breath scorched my face, dried my lips.

"Everyone loves Alyce. But not everyone knows her. True?" One finger traced down the side of my cheek. I jerked my head. He grabbed my chin, forced me to look at him.

His words hissed now, no guise of affection or respect. "A girl with the audacity to drive a race car would have the guts to do other unconventional things, wouldn't she? You didn't find my attention amiss the other evening. What kind of life did you live those years in the city—a pretty thing like you?"

His lips crushed mine. I twisted my head, fought my arms free. "Stop—"

He grabbed my wrists and held them, shoving me up against the wall. "I won't be made a fool. I imagine you've already given every part of yourself to that vagabond thief and liar."

"How do you know he's a thief?" Fear clawed its way up my throat.

"Webster Little puts on a cloak of respectability, just like you." He spat the words. I averted my face. "Ask him what happened to his church—and to their money. I daresay he won't tell you. He's as much a hypocrite as you—and I."

Fire burned behind my eyes. I lowered my shoulder and barreled forward, knocking us both to the ground. My weight held him for a brief moment. Then he grabbed me again and rolled over until he pinned me to the ground.

Tears streaked down my cheeks as anger dissolved into terror. Was this my fault? Me, with my lies and pride? "Please stop. I'm not what you think."

"I know." His knees dug into my waist as he stripped off his coat and tossed it aside.

Sobs tore through my body. *Please, Jesus. Please.*

Then the weight of him flew backward. He landed with a thump. I scrambled close to the wall, drew my knees to my chest, flinched at the smack of flesh connecting with flesh, the oomph of a fist in a stomach, the thud and tumble of two bodies tangled on the ground.

"What is the meaning of this?" Father's voice careened through the building, bounced off the walls. The commotion ceased. Strong arms lifted me, cradled me against a broad chest. Father's chest. His heart stormed against my ear.

"Get out!" he shouted. "Get out and don't ever come back."

Peace rolled over me. My father would protect me against Lawrence Trotter. And rightly so. I turned my head for a glimpse of the man's disgrace.

"Webster." The name sliced like a dagger in my throat as he slunk out the door, overalls smeared with dirt, a river of red dripping from his nose.

"If I even hear of your whereabouts, I'll call the police," Father shouted after him.

"No—" I grabbed at Father's shirt, raised my face to catch his eyes. He didn't look down.

I stared out the door. Webster had come to my rescue after he'd taken my money? I couldn't make sense of it.

"It's a good thing I stopped by to check on the car this evening, sir." Lawrence pressed his handkerchief to a cut on his face.

Indignation flamed within me. Whatever crime Webster had committed, it hadn't been as depraved as what Lawrence had attempted. "Father, it wasn't—"

Steely daggers glittered from Lawrence's eyes, killing my bravado. He could ruin me, *would* ruin me, in more ways than one. Lawrence Trotter had Father's ear as surely as the serpent had Eve's in the garden. How had I ever imagined him kind and good? A man of integrity? A man of faith?

I stared at him through narrowed eyes. He'd twist my accusations, convince Father further of Webster's guilt—and my own. If I hoped to salvage anything, I dared not accuse him until I knew Father would believe me.

But could I truly defend Webster? He'd taken my money, plundered my trust.

Stolen my heart.

My knees wobbled. Father tightened his grip. "I trust you can find another mechanic to ride with you on Saturday, Trotter?"

"Of course." His gaze rested on me, and I knew he wasn't through extracting his price from me. Not yet. He'd insist on Saturday's race to save face, to prove himself in my father's eyes, to cement my inability to prove the truth. And I owned no weapon to wield against him.

31

I haven't heard that young man whistle all morning. I wonder what's wrong." Grandmother fanned herself with one of Mother's old magazines. A drop of perspiration slid down the side of my face. I wiped it away before it reached my chin. The heat of Grandmother's inquiries mirrored the swelter of the day.

"Alyce?"

I reached for her hand, still uncertain how to respond. I had no idea anyone else's ears but mine listened daily for Webster's jaunty tune. He'd betrayed me. Yet he'd rescued me. And because of my deceit, I'd been unable to return the favor.

"Do you mean Mr. Little, the one who works on Father's automobiles?" My voice cracked.

"That's the one. Always so cheerful. He used to stop and talk to me when I could still sit in the garden, while you were away at school. He chased away my loneliness sometimes, even with just his whistle."

I laid a hand on my stomach. Grandmother should never have been lonely. I'd failed her, too.

"Has something happened to the boy, dear?" Her face crinkled in concern.

"He . . . left." Another falsehood piled on top of many. Did it really matter anymore?

"Left? But he seemed so happy here." She turned her head toward the window, as if she could see past the garden, through the trees, and into Webster's domain.

I stroked Grandmother's hand. "What did you and Mr. Little talk about?"

Her smile gave way to knitted brows. "Something weighed heavy on him. He wouldn't say what, but he told me how much it helped him to be here, how this job filled a need in his life."

A need. I pressed my fingers against my forehead. A need for money, apparently. Had he been scheming some treachery long before I plunked cash into his hand? I swallowed, determined to know what game Webster was playing, determined to discover if I could ease my guilt over keeping silent last night.

"Why don't we pray for him, Alyce?" Grandmother groped for my hands, but I feared her touch would undo me. I pressed my palms together, setting the line of my fingers across my tight lips as she prayed. "Father God, we lift up Mr. Little. Whatever his circumstances, show him that You see. You care. Judge his enemies and cover him in the shadow of Your wing."

A small gasp escaped. Why had she prayed that? She spoke as if Webster were one of God's own children. And how did she know he had enemies? Mr. Trotter obviously despised him, but then I'd become his enemy as well for not speaking the truth last night. Grandmother had just prayed God's judgment on me, too.

A lump gouged my throat, cutting off the stale air in the room. Grandmother's frail voice fell silent.

I knew she was waiting for me to pray, as was our habit. But I couldn't. Not when my betrayal of him stung more fiercely than his of me.

My hands fisted. I pressed them into my eyes. With a groan, I groped my way to the windows, clutched at the sill. I needed air. Fresh air. Clean air. "Grandmother, how do you know when you can trust people?"

Her laughter tinkled like a small silver bell. "You can't ever know for sure what people will do. You can guess, given their past behavior. But even then people will often surprise you."

I leaned against the window sill, savoring the bit of cool breeze against my back. "Give me an example."

She turned thoughtful before her face brightened. "When I first met Glorietta Swan, she and I didn't like each other at all."

"Pastor Swan's wife? But she adores you. And you seem to like her, too."

"Of course I do. Now. But it wasn't always that way. For either of us."

I returned to my chair, my attention rapt. "Go on."

"Some things were said about me when I came back from Chicago a different woman. As far as I could discover, the nastiness started with Mrs. Swan. We were much younger then, of course. Her husband new to the church. She had her own issues of adjustment in our town. Your father was successful by then and some people assumed things about me that weren't true. Such as a need to be recognized or to throw money around when they had none to spare. But though I didn't have those flaws, neither did I have a pristine character. I'd spent many, many years believing I was in control of my life."

"What happened?"

"We squared off against each other, each of us bidding for women who cottoned to our side of the story. One day Pastor Swan called us both to the church, sat us down, and made us talk it out." Grandmother's eyes sparkled, as if she could see the scene happening before her.

"Turns out, neither of us did or said or even thought the things we attributed to the other. I believed she couldn't be trusted. She thought the same of me. We were both wrong."

"But what if it had been the other way around? What if you'd thought she was your friend and it turned out she wasn't? What if you discovered it later?"

Grandmother's head dipped toward her chest. "I imagine I would have been terribly hurt. Jesus told us to be as wise as serpents and gentle as doves. That isn't easy. Especially when it comes to understanding people. Including ourselves."

A whistle punctuated her words. My heart hiccuped. A cardinal shot past the window. The whistle faded. With it, my hope.

"What's happened, Alyce?" The compassion in Grandmother's voice scraped across my wounded heart.

I climbed up beside her and laid my head on her shoulder. "I've done such a terrible thing."

"Terrible? I doubt that. But tell me anyway."

So I did. I told her about Webster's theft. About Lawrence's liberties. About my own betrayal of one I'd counted as a friend.

Her face grew serious as she listened. Not hard and condemning but almost as if she was working to keep her heart from breaking. When I finished with my story, tears shone in her sightless eyes and her head dropped in a slow nod.

I pressed fingers to my lips, then to my heart. "Are you disappointed in me?"

"I'm sorry for you, Ally. But disappointed? No. If you had continued on without recognizing your error, then I'd be disappointed. But even when we love the Lord we won't live a sinless life, though we try. The key is recognizing our wrong. Repenting, as you've done. Then moving forward with a lesson learned."

"But how do I move forward? What do I do now?" I wanted to bury my face in her chest as I'd done as a child.

She stroked my arm as her frown deepened. "I don't know. I'll pray."

"But the race is the day after tomorrow." I hated the whine in my voice, like a spoiled child denied a plaything.

"Patience, child. The Lord is never late as we deem lateness. Trust Him to guide you and you'll not make things worse than they are."

"I was afraid you'd say that."

"It's hard, but true."

I kissed her papery cheek, smoothed back her gray hair, and smiled into the sightless eyes that saw so much more than the rest of us. It would be hard to be still and listen to the Lord. But two compelling reasons strengthened my resolve: love for my Jesus and love for my grandmother.

Crashing through the back door into the warmth of the day, I ran past the garden, to the garage. Hands shaking, I hit the starter and ground the gear shift into place. Down the drive. Out onto the road.

I stopped the Packard before I reached the track, flung open the door, and ran to a small cluster of trees that towered over the tall grasses. My chest burned for air, hair tangled about my face. My feet throbbed in my shoes. Reaching for a tree, my palms grating against the rough bark, I pressed my forehead to the trunk, willing the pain to dam the flood in my eyes. But it didn't help. Tears snaked down my face, dripped from my chin.

Stumbling out from beneath the canopy of leaves, I made my way to the center of the oval and dropped to my knees. My fingers tugged at a tenacious clump of grass. "All I wanted was to do something important for You, Lord. To prove my love for You. How did I lose my way?"

A man's heart deviseth his way: but the Lord directeth his steps.

Proverbs. My breathing slowed, though my tears did not. I'd made a grand mess of things by planning my own way. Me, Alyce Marie Benson, who touted herself such a good Christian. A faithful lover of God. I'd woven a tangled web and caught myself in the process. Would the Lord still be faithful to direct my steps? Could I trust Him to lead me out of this quagmire?

"Forgive me, God, for putting myself above You. For running ahead of Your direction. For seeking to fulfill my plans to serve You instead of waiting with an open heart until You beckoned me with Your assignment."

The chug of a slow engine sounded in the distance and then faded as my sin spread before me like a moving picture show. But peace swooped down and dimmed the light, blackened the screen. Peace I didn't understand or deserve.

"Am I forgiven, Lord?" I whispered. No voice replied, but I felt settled all the same. Standing, I winced at the pain in my feet. I deserved as much for my foolishness. I shook the dirt from my skirt and limped toward the Packard, combing my fingers through scattered curls. Anyone coming upon me now would be appalled. Miss Benson, covered in dirt and sweat, but their disgust wouldn't compare to mine.

Yet Jesus had heard my confession. His righteousness covered me now, washed me pure and clean. I still had so many wrongs to right. Those would take time. And patience. Especially if I intended Father to see the truth about Mr. Trotter. My knees quaked at the thought of racing without Webster. But if I refused, I might never get a chance to show Father the truth.

All the way home I prayed. I hadn't been doing enough of that lately. And this time I'd stop and wait for answers at every turn.

32

"Lucinda?" I clomped up the wooden staircase late that afternoon, my arms full of the dresses I'd culled from my closet while Betsy hung the new ones Mother bought in Cincinnati. "Lucinda?" I called. "Are you home?"

I peered through the kitchen window, but before my eyes could settle on the scene, the door flew open. Lucinda fluttered outside, her eyes wide. "Whatever are you doing here, Alyce?" Her gaze darted down the stairs, around the yard, finally back to me. "And what's all this?"

I thrust the bundle of clothes into her unsuspecting arms. "They're for you. New clothes." I shrugged, felt a blush crawl into my cheeks. "Just too many in my closet at the moment."

All of a sudden my plan to help seemed humiliating for my friend. I bit my lip and waited for her response.

"Oh, Alyce," she whispered. "You don't know how much I needed these." A sheen of tears brightened her eyes. She turned away. "Let me set them in the house. Then we can talk. Out here."

I paced the small landing, wondering if Clarissa's sister would respond as graciously to the dresses I planned to give her. When Lucinda returned, I grabbed her hands. "I need your help."

With a glance back, her shoulders hiked a bit higher. "I'd be happy to help if I can."

She sat on the top step. I joined her there, the tread barely wide enough for both of our slim frames. "Do you remember when we talked about Webster Little?"

Did she sigh or was it my imagination? She nodded. I exhaled, wondering how much to say, how much to leave out. But then, leaving out for the sake of gaining was what had led to this snarled situation. Whether she helped me or not, I had to tell her all.

"Webster's in trouble—and it's my fault."

Her eyes rounded. I looked past them, not wanting to read any condemnation of Webster or myself. Not yet.

"He's—that is, my father—" A shiver slid down my back. How did one put such a disagreeable situation into words that didn't sound sordid?

Her hands calmed mine. "I know." She peered back at the door, leaned her head closer to mine. "He told me what happened. With Mr. Trotter."

I jumped up, grabbing the rail to keep from tumbling to the bottom of the stairs. "You've seen him?"

She looked away.

"He's here, isn't he?" I stepped toward the door.

"No. Not here. He came late last night. I patched him up, then he left."

"Did he tell you about the money, too?"

"Money?" Her head tilted. "He didn't mention money. Just the . . . incident." Then her forehead crinkled. "Unless you mean those rumors about him absconding with church funds. But I don't believe any of that."

My heart dropped around my feet like unsupported stockings. It was true then. He'd done it before. I rubbed my fingers across my forehead. But though he'd stolen from me—and, apparently, others—he hadn't attacked my person. And clearing his name of that must come first.

"Will you ask him something for me?"

She nodded.

"Ask him to come to Indianapolis on Saturday. He'll know why. Tell him—tell him I need him. Please." With a click, my pocketbook opened. I pressed the few dollars I'd begged from Mother into Lucinda's hand. "For the trip."

She shook her head, held the money out to me. "He won't take it."

I pushed her hand away. "Then you keep it. I don't care. Just please, ask him to come. And tell him I'm sorry."

"Alyce?"

I turned back.

Sympathy brimmed in her eyes. "I'll do my best."

Father supervised the loading of the racing car onto the train the next morning. Mother and I waited on the interurban platform, ready to depart for Indianapolis.

"I thought you'd be more excited, Alyce, considering this race seems to mean so much to you and your father." She didn't look at me as she spoke, but her tone seemed one of genuine curiosity, not censure.

I shrugged, tried to smile. "I'm excited."

Mother laughed. Truly laughed. Then she patted my hand. "You've never been one to mask your emotions. I won't press you, but I am your mother. If you need to talk, I'll listen."

The interurban car reached the platform. As we waited to board, clouds covered the sun, graying the day. Moisture hung in the air from thunderstorms the previous evening. But at least it wasn't hot. Father had said at breakfast that no more rain was expected. I hoped that to be the case. I feared rain more than heat. Yet the bricks would give a bit more traction than boards when wet, wouldn't they? Again I remembered Gil Anderson's car sliding out of control in Cincinnati and shuddered.

On the interurban, clacking toward Indianapolis, I thought about what Mother had said. She wanted to listen. I wished I could pour out my entire story to her. But I feared she wouldn't understand. Although, for the first time in my life, I felt more willing to open up to her than to Father.

Before I could think through revealing my secrets to Mother, we arrived in Indianapolis. We waited in the lobby of the hotel for Father to arrive, then settled in our hotel room and had a late supper brought up. But I couldn't eat.

"I think I'll walk for a little while." I picked up my handbag.

"You can't go out alone, darling. It will be dark soon."

"Exactly." Father turned the page of the newspaper.

A soft orange hue was streaming in through the windows. Dark wouldn't descend for a while longer. I was a grown woman, not a child. I pressed my lips into a hard line and headed for the door.

A knock stopped my progress.

"I'll get it." Meek words dousing my internal fire.

I opened the door, ready to tell the hotel staff that we were fine and didn't need anything at all. Instead, I stared open-mouthed at Lawrence Trotter.

"Good evening." He swept his hat from his head, amusement twitching his mustache. "I'd hoped to find you in." He peeked past me.

"Trotter, my boy." Father appeared beside me, arm outstretched, and drew the snake right into the room. I wanted to stamp my foot and scream the truth, but Mr. Trotter's cold eyes held me still. I had to wait. Do this right.

Please, God, bring Webster to the race tomorrow. I clasped my hands behind my back to keep them from trembling as Mr. Trotter kissed Mother's hand.

"I thought perhaps I could escort your daughter on a walk through town, ma'am."

My jaw clenched. I would not be alone with that man. I. Would. Not.

"I think we've had enough excitement for the day, Mr. Trotter," Mother said. I wanted to kiss her. But before my elation took hold, Father cleared his throat.

"I think that's a fine idea, Trotter." He shook the paper straight and raised it in front of his face again. "Just have her back at a decent hour. Big day tomorrow, you know."

Mr. Trotter's smirk set my teeth to grinding. I dug my fingernails into my own flesh to calm my words. "I do apologize, Mr. Trotter, but Mother is right, the travel has quite exhausted me."

The newspaper rustled as Father turned a page. "You just said you wanted to get out for a bit, Ally. Here's your chance."

Mr. Trotter's stare pierced like a sharp needle. Then my thoughts changed direction. Perhaps I needed to hear him out, discern his plans. Like strategizing for a race. A race without Webster to tell me when to turn my wheel, pump the gas, and dash past the competition.

"Fine. But just a cup of coffee. Downstairs. In the restaurant." I jammed my hat on my head and marched out the door.

"I mean it," I whispered in the hallway. "Just coffee. In the restaurant."

He swept his hand in front of him and bowed at the waist. I stuck my nose in the air and glided toward the elevator. My emotions ran wild inside, but in spite of Mother's observations this morning, I had no intention of allowing the entire world to witness my agitation. I could be gracious, calm. Listen to what he had to say. Then hear what the Lord told me to do about it.

The elevator operator let us out in the lobby. Seated at a table for two, Lawrence ordered for us—coffee and cake. If he wanted to pay for something I wouldn't eat, I guessed that was his business.

"Now, Alyce." He leaned forward, the look on his face one of tender solicitation. He lifted my hand, stroked it. I eased my fingers from his grasp. Anyone looking on would assume a lover's spat.

His expression and posture didn't change. When he spoke, I had to lean closer to hear.

"You know what you must do tomorrow."

"And what is that, Mr. Trotter?"

An exasperated huff. "Drive, of course. Win, if you can."

"And you'll take the money and the accolades from my father."

He sat back. "Exactly."

The waiter set our coffee and cake on the table. When he left, Mr. Trotter ate and drank as if nothing unsettled him. I added a dollop of cream to my cup. Not having the money and admitting it to the church would be easier than exposing Mr. Trotter's foul behavior. But if I allowed him to escape unscathed, he might attempt such extortion on some other girl, in more desperate circumstances.

I lifted my cup to my lips, letting the coffee slide down my throat as I strengthened my resolve. "And what of Mr. Little?"

"What of him?"

"Am I to drive without him?"

His laughter jolted the quiet room. Heads turned in our direction. I stared into my coffee cup and twirled my fork through the thick icing between the layers of cake.

"That man wouldn't dare show his face around here now. I have a mechanic to drive with you. Don't worry your pretty little head about it. Afterward, I'll explain to your father that I've decided to retire from racing to take on another role. That of husband."

My eyebrows shot toward the ceiling. "Husband? To whom?"

"Why, to you, my dear. *Daddy* is so grateful to me for saving your virtue that he's quite amenable to the idea, as long as you are. And of course you are. Can you imagine the look on Mrs. Tillman's face if she happened to discover how you've been spending your spare time?"

My fork clattered to the china plate. I hurled tight words. "There is nothing immoral about driving a race car."

"Of course not, darling," he purred. "It's just the implication of all those other things that nice girls don't do."

"You wouldn't dare—" I half rose. His fingers clamped around my wrist and pulled me down again.

"Wouldn't I?" he hissed. "Your father won't take notice of the church gossip going around town. And if by chance he did, he'd assume those old biddies were jealous, as they likely are."

Another word and I imagined I'd explode like a can of gasoline exposed to flame. Would God let this man ruin my character? My reputation? I slapped my napkin to the table and stood—quickly this time, jumping out of his reach. I croaked out words for the benefit of those around us. "Thank you for your kind attention, Mr. Trotter. I believe I will see you tomorrow."

He nodded. I swept past him without a glance, determined to remain upright and in control—at least until I reached the sanctuary of my hotel room.

33

*M*r. Trotter arrived at our hotel room early the next morning to escort me to the Indianapolis Motor Speedway, absolving my need to lie to my parents yet again. For that I was grateful.

Scores of people milled about in the crisp morning air despite the fact that the gates had just opened. They filed into the grandstands and onto the infield. Spectators. Mechanics. Photographers. Reporters. The smell of warm grass tickled my nose but was soon replaced with the familiar sharpness of gasoline fumes as Mr. Trotter escorted me toward Gasoline Alley. He thought it best for us to be seen together. I didn't argue. I just followed along, searching the crowd for Webster's face.

A man in a uniform stopped us at the gate leading to the garages. "She can't go in there. Don't you know that?" He yanked up the waistband of his pants and rolled a wad of tobacco into his other cheek.

"She's the car owner's daughter." Mr. Trotter pulled me forward.

The guard blocked our way, eyes narrowed. "Doesn't matter. Don't you know a woman's bad luck on a racetrack? Go on. Take her to the grandstands. Or if she's that important, let her park her own automobile behind the pits to watch like Mrs. Resta does."

Mr. Trotter pinched my elbow as we turned, but I barely felt the pain. Was this the Lord's doing? Would He thwart Mr. Trotter's plan?

Mr. Trotter dragged me past the hospital tent, where a nurse in a starched white skirt, blouse, and cap stood near a motorized ambulance. I couldn't tear my gaze away.

His words rasped into my ear. "You'll have to change clothes to get to the car. I stashed your bag beneath the far grandstand."

I kept my eyes straight ahead, my voice low. "But if they won't let a woman in the garage, how will they feel about me on the track?"

"They won't know, will they? Just like all the times before. Unless you don't live up to your part of the bargain."

I stopped walking. He jerked backward, his grip tightening on my arm. "C'mon."

My feet remained still. "If you expose me, you'll be branded as the liar you are."

His chuckle slithered near my ear. "I'd suffer only a momentary humiliation. Your father, on the other hand, would likely be banned from racing forever. Because of course no one will believe he didn't know his own daughter was sitting in the driver's seat of his car."

My heart sank.

"And don't think you can announce it yourself, either. The fate of your father would remain the same."

I squeezed my eyes shut. He was right. I couldn't reveal my identity. Not here. I'd have to wait until we arrived back at the hotel to confess to Father. But would he believe me without witnessing it with his own eyes?

Mr. Trotter pulled me onward and then stopped us beneath the grandstands, pointed to a dark lump. I picked up the bag. "Where will I change?"

"How should I know? Figure it out. Just get dressed and meet me for your practice laps. Now, get going before too many people arrive."

Yanking my arm from his hold, I straightened my shoulders and tipped my chin upward. "I know what I have to do."

I knew, but could I do it? Could I drive without Webster? Or if he showed up, could I drive with him? Could I sit beside him knowing what he'd done? What I'd done? Nausea worked its way up my throat. I put a hand to my stomach, eager to still its acrobatics, yet all the while wishing I hadn't betrayed the man with the playful whistle and wide grin, in spite of what he'd stolen from me.

With a prayer on my lips, I stumbled into a small lean-to that didn't appear to be in use. I emerged with my figure hidden under a jumpsuit, cap and goggles shielding my face. Arms swinging at my sides, I concentrated on the bit of bright blue winking at me from the track.

Without hesitation, I bypassed the guard and climbed behind the wheel of Webster's racing car, swiping my tongue across dry lips, tasting the salt of the perspiration already beading on my upper lip.

"This is Clint." Mr. Trotter, dressed in a jumpsuit like mine, gestured toward a rail-thin man with shifty eyes and greasy hair. I nodded once, trying to reconcile myself to this man sitting beside me first for the twenty-mile race, then fifty miles, then one hundred miles. I turned away, jaw clenched. In spite of Webster's thievery, I wanted him. Needed him. No one else knew me like he did. And in that moment, I desperately needed to be known.

But I had no choice. I climbed into the car, took it around the track. I watched for Webster's hand signals but quickly remembered they wouldn't be there to guide me. The bricks bumped beneath my tires, but as I gained speed, I hardly noticed. After three passes in front of the pagoda, where the judges and reporters would sit, I declared our practice finished. I climbed from the car. Mr. Trotter reappeared, his face suddenly smudged with grime. My fists clenched at my sides as he chatted with a group of mechanics tending another car.

"So six drivers dropped out after the torture of Cincinnati? I guess the best drivers know how to take care of their machines." The pride in Mr. Trotter's voice set my teeth on edge. Pride that rightfully belonged to me, and Webster, yet Trotter made it his own, in spite of having done nothing to earn it.

I fiddled with my driving gloves as the new mechanic checked the tires. The newest from Goodrich.

Trotter's hand jittered against the side of the car. Was he nervous for me—or for himself?

Ignoring the thought, I peered into the crowd of mechanics and drivers milling about in the pit area, praying for a glimpse of the tattered flat cap over the pleasing round face.

Please, Webster. I need you.

And then, as if by a miracle, he was standing beside me, clad in a matching jumpsuit, hands settled low on his hips.

"Webster." A whispered word amidst the pandemonium of sound, but he turned, his eye catching mine, quieting my heart and setting it sprinting at the same time. Until my gaze roved just beyond him, to the infield grass.

Lucinda.

A faint blush stained her cheeks, sending my unreasonable hope whirling into a concrete wall and dissolving in a column of smoke. I ducked my head. She couldn't recognize me. And I had no time to dissect my feelings over her presence here. With him.

I had to race.

I had to win.

A quick vision of flashing camera bulbs and crew members pulling me from the car in congratulations stopped that thought quicker than pulling a hand brake. I couldn't win. If I did, everyone would know. How had I not considered that before?

Webster leaned near. "You need anything? Race time's still a few hours away."

I pushed up on my toes, leaning my mouth closer to Webster's ear. "You are here to help me, right?"

A flutter of activity drew my attention.

Father.

I couldn't move. He pushed through the crowd, calling for Trotter.

Webster nudged me forward, shielding me from those behind. "Where'd you change?"

"A small building in back of the grandstands. Southeast corner, I believe."

"Go there. I'll bring some food. You can hide out."

I nodded and strode toward my hideout, praying the Lord would bring something right out of all my wrongs.

The lean-to held the heat like a cast-iron pot. I was too warm and too nervous to eat what Webster brought, though I tried. I wiped my forehead once more, wishing I could splash water on my face. But of course Mr. Trotter hadn't bothered to supply any. Not like Webster usually did. Webster had promised he'd try to bring some the next time he came. If he didn't, I'd be hard-pressed to clean the muck from my skin before finding Father after the race.

Three quick knocks stole my breath. I opened the door. Webster handed in a bucket, water sloshing from its lip. I set it in the corner, slipped into the sunshine, and shaded my eyes with my hand as a gentle eastern breeze cooled my face.

He turned and charged back through the crowd. I kept my eyes on the collar of his jumpsuit, where cloth and hair and flesh met. Webster would ride beside me. We'd finish the race. Then somehow I'd make Father believe I'd driven, not Lawrence Trotter. No matter the consequence.

The noise of brass trumpets blaring and drums banging rose above that of the crowd and the cars as local bands wandered the infield. We easily slipped past them and arrived at the bright blue race car on the track.

Then Webster's hand landed on my shoulder and pushed me into a squat on the side opposite of the automobile. Father's voice boomed above the chaos, questioning Trotter. The man hemmed and hawed. At least I could enjoy his discomfort. Finally Father's voice faded away. I stood. Circled the car with my head down, as if inspecting each detail. Then I climbed into the driver's seat.

The other drivers sat ready. Two rows of four followed by my car and another. Still no mechanic in the seat beside me.

Panic rolled through me like a wave. I had to have a mechanic or I'd be disqualified. *Please, Lord, don't abandon me now.*

Then Clint the mechanic romped toward me. I looked at Webster, nodded toward the interloper. Webster leaned down and the steel frame came alive beneath me. I closed my eyes, breathed in the tainted air, and gripped the steering wheel. Despite everything, I'd miss this. Miss the rush of wind in my face, the competitors hemming me in on either side, the roar of the engines and of the crowd. I'd miss being caught up in the moment, the release of all that sat heavy on my shoulders.

But if sacrificing the bit of joy I felt in a fast-moving car would lead me back to a life of truth, I'd do it.

Or at least I would try.

Webster bounded into the seat beside me, pulling goggles over his eyes. His thumb poked up from his fist as his full lips spread into a grin. I shot a quick thank-you heavenward as the howl of engines screamed in my ears. Although my heart pounded louder.

We started around the track. Fifty yards following the pace car. Then the starter flapped the red flag from high on the suspension bridge. My foot jammed the gas pedal. The car jumped forward. The roar of the crowd surpassed that of the engines. My tires slid over the brick track with ease.

One lap down. Then another. I inched toward the leader. I wanted to be on his tail. And soon.

Two other cars drifted behind me as we rounded the curve. Again and again. And again. My head dizzied with the count. Webster poked my leg. I glanced down. Thumbs up. The needle on my speedometer already hovered over ninety. Did he really think we could do better?

I threw my weight against the accelerator as Webster pumped oil to the engine.

Another straightaway, the grandstand looming to the right, along with the inner wall. Then the tail of my car pulled left. My muscles tensed. I tightened my grip on the wheel, ground my teeth together. I could get control. I'd done it before.

Webster's hand in front of my face, thumb down. Slow. Slow. But the rear wheels refused to respond. I fought with the steering wheel, but the back end took control. Swerved. The smell of burning rubber stung my nose. A gray wall of concrete hovered near the hood of the car. I yanked the steering wheel to the left, toward the infield. We skidded across the expanse of track, other cars missing us by inches. Then the world spun. Tilted. I wanted to let go, to cover my head, but I couldn't pry my fingers from the wheel.

A sickening thud. A mass of arms and legs. Pain and a snap near my shoulder. The squeal of metal scraping brick. We screeched to a halt.

Shouts. The rush of feet. Pain throbbed through my body with every heartbeat, held me still even though I wanted to move.

"Webster?" I wasn't sure I spoke the word aloud, though I tried. I tumbled from the car lying on its side. Searing pain shot through my left arm. I remembered the ducks, the barn, the fall from my childhood. I clamped my arm to my side, held the elbow still with the opposite hand. Something wet dripped from my face, landed red on my jumpsuit. I tasted metal in my mouth.

Where was Webster? I limp-crawled through the haze, tried to wave it away with my uninjured arm. Coughing shook me, sharpened the agony. Hands helped me to my feet, dragged me from the roar of approaching motors.

A shout near my ear. "We've got the driver."

Relief that still no one had guessed my identity. But fear that I still couldn't find the face I sought.

Another shout. "Over here! Help me move him!"

"Webster!" I shook myself free. One wobbled step and my legs collapsed. The torment in my left arm created havoc in my stomach. Strong arms lifted me, a shoulder lending support. Half carried to the infield, I found Webster. Prostrate. Groaning.

I dropped to my knees beside him. His eyes fluttered open, head lolled to one side. "Go." At least that was what it looked like he'd said. I heard nothing but the whine of the engines circling the track. Then his eyes drifted shut.

Go? I couldn't leave him. Salt stung my lips even as it occurred to me that a man wouldn't cry. But I couldn't stop. I had to help Webster—the one who knew me, who defended me, who came back when I needed him. I clawed at my goggles and leather cap with my right hand, my left arm hanging useless. But I couldn't get them off before hands lifted Webster, settled him on a stretcher, and carried him away. I stood. Swayed. Arms caught me from behind.

"Can you walk, son?" Gravelly words in my ear, the edge of cigar smoke wafting near my nose.

I turned my head. My knees buckled.

Father was staring down at me.

"It's me." I prayed the words actually left my mouth—and that he could hear them in spite of the noise.

His eyes widened. His grip tightened. He lifted the goggles from my eyes. "Ally?"

I whimpered. "They can't know. You'll be disgraced. But Webster. Get him help. Please."

Father's mouth dropped open, his jowls quivering. "Webster Little?" He looked past me, fury staining his neck scarlet.

I yanked at his shirt with my good hand. "It's not what you think. He tried to help me. He's always tried to help." My chest caved with sobs as Father glared back at the confusion. Then I felt myself lifted from the ground. We surged forward, away from the fray.

And the world disappeared to black.

34

A low hum pierced my darkness, muttered words drifting about me like clouds of smoke. I wanted to bat them away, but it hurt to move my neck, and one of my arms refused to work. My eyelids felt nailed shut, but I forced them to rise. Light slammed them closed again.

I lifted my head off the pillow in spite of the pain. "Father?"

Lips pressed against my forehead, large hands encased my free one. Now my eyes opened in earnest. I tried to hide a grimace of pain but saw my discomfort reflected on Father's face.

Another man stood near, a long white coat over his suit. Then I remembered. The crash. Had I been exposed? And what about Webster?

I tried to smile, but the right side of my face felt stiff. I wiggled my fingers free of Father's, touched the spot. A bandage covered a patch of skin beneath my eye. Thank goodness I'd never been a beauty. Maybe a small scar would add more interest to my face. "I'll live, then?"

The doctor's eyes crinkled with a sympathetic smile. "I think so. A few lacerations and bruises. You'll be stiff and sore for a while. And that broken collarbone will need to heal. We've immobilized it. It needs time to knit itself back together." He wrote on the pad of paper in his hand. "I'd like to keep you here a few days, just to make sure everything's as it should be."

Relief washed over Father's face, flushing it with color again.

Light reflected off the doctor's round spectacles. "And you be more careful on the road, young lady."

My gaze shot to Father. He chuckled, but tight lines framed his mouth as beads of sweat glistened at his temples. "I'm sure she will, Doctor. Thank you."

The man left us alone.

Father pulled a chair close.

"He knows?" I whispered.

Father shook his head. "Only that you've been in an automobile accident." His lips twitched, seeming to fight a grin. "I cleaned up your face, but of course your clothing was a bit . . . unconventional."

I giggled, imagining my father whisking me from the speedway to the hospital, removing my driving jumpsuit to find my knickers and shirt concealed beneath. "How did you . . . we . . . get here?"

He grunted. "I didn't let anyone stop me, that's how. I couldn't take you to the medical staff there. If the speedway officials heard you'd driven . . ." His head swished from side to side. "We'd have been more than banished. We might have been lynched."

I cringed. So many chances taken, not just with my own life and reputation, but with those I loved. "I'm sorry," I whispered.

"I know." He pressed a limp handkerchief to his red-rimmed eyes. "I'm just glad my girl will be fine."

"But what about Webster?" I wished I could snatch the words out of the air the minute I spoke them, for Father's face roiled like a thundercloud as he stared at the far corner of the room.

His fists clenched. Then his eyes found mine again. "What was he doing in that car, Ally? I thought I made myself clear. Did he force his way in? Did he put you up to this stunt?"

I groaned. "Don't you understand? I've been driving all along, Father. Since Chicago. Webster and I. Trotter never had anything to do with it, other than posing as the driver to get my money from you." My voice faltered, fell away. It all sounded so . . . sordid.

His eyes narrowed, then widened as the truth sunk in. "You drove those other times?"

I nodded.

He rubbed a hand across the back of his neck as he stood and paced beside my bed. When he stopped, laughter and anger vied for reign. "You do beat all, Ally. But why?"

I picked at a loose thread near the top of the sheet covering me. "I needed the money."

"The money?" His voice rose. A nurse peeked around a partition and shushed him.

"For Africa—the mission in the Gold Coast. Remember? I promised to help them."

"But racing?"

"I tried more conventional ways to raise the funds, but the ladies at church were using most of those. Then I thought of driving. Turns out Langston is too small for a taxi service, mostly because no one wanted to pay me to do it. I guess they assumed I had enough money and didn't need more." I tried to shrug but cried out in pain instead.

Father's face paled again as he plopped into the hard chair beside me.

I smoothed the blanket with my free hand until the pain lessened. "When I heard you'd entered the car in Chicago, I asked Webster if I could drive for the pay."

"You could've been killed out there, Ally!"

"I know. But I love to drive fast, Father. And I felt helping those children and their families was worth even my life." The shock on my father's face drove me forward. "I don't regret the driving, though I do regret not telling you what I was doing. Well, that and . . ." I could only force out a whisper. "And not realizing what I asked Webster to give up for my cause."

He shot to his feet. "I don't understand your loyalty to that man. If Trotter hadn't—"

"If Lawrence Trotter hadn't taken liberties, Webster wouldn't have had to defend me." I said each word firmly, staring into Father's eyes. "Mr. Trotter assaulted me, not Webster." I ducked my head in shame. "Webster only came to my rescue."

"But I saw—"

"You saw them fighting, nothing else. Please believe me. I'm telling you the truth."

A nurse in pristine white stepped into the room. "A Mr. Lawrence Trotter is outside asking to see you, miss."

Father's face went slack. A war flickered behind his eyes. He wanted to believe me. I knew he did. But would his pride win out over the truth?

"Please, Father. Please believe me." And yet why should he? My many lies now lay uncovered before him.

I let the pillow fully cradle my aching head as his shoes clacked across the room and out the door. Only in the silence did I allow the first tear to fall.

I must have drifted to sleep, for by the time I woke, a shade covered my window and electric light glowed dim behind a partition in the far corner. The chair beside me sat empty. I wiggled and then yelped at the pain that shot through my arm. A nurse stepped around the screen, her stern expression melting into compassion.

"They'll be so glad to hear you're awake."

"They?"

The nurse helped me sit up. "Your parents."

Mother was here. I squeezed my eyes shut for a moment. Father would have told her the same as the doctor. An automobile accident. I groaned. She'd begin a diatribe of my unfeminine ways.

"And a friend of yours is with them, too, I believe."

A friend? My forehead puckered for a quick moment. Then I grasped at her sleeve. "Don't let him in here. Please."

Her laugh trilled. "It's a young lady, miss."

"Oh." I leaned into the wall of pillows she'd set behind me, no less disconcerted. Who in Indianapolis would know—

Lucinda.

My heart soared with joy but quickly sank in despair. She'd accompanied Webster to the speedway. Was there more than friendship between them?

I stared at the ceiling, begging God to dull the pain in my heart. I should be happy that my two friends had found love.

"Do you feel up to seeing them?"

"No. Yes. I mean—how is Mr. Little?"

"That mechanic who was thrown from his race car?"

I swallowed past the lump banked in my throat. "That's the one."

"He's still unconscious. Concussion. And a leg broken in two places." She patted my hand. "I'll send in your visitors."

A few minutes later, footsteps stopped at my door. Every muscle in my body tightened. I couldn't look up.

"Oh, my darling." Mother suffocated me with her nearness, stroking my face, kissing my hand, holding a glass of water to my lips.

Lucinda lingered behind. After a few minutes, my parents moved away, their voices quieting to a murmur. Then Lucinda approached the bed, grabbed my right hand, and pressed it to her cheek. "Oh, Alyce. I'm so glad you're okay. I couldn't believe my eyes when I saw you climb out of the wreckage."

I hissed and beckoned her closer, shooting a glance toward my parents, who now stood behind the partition. If Lucinda had guessed, how many others suspected?

"You recognized me?" I whispered.

She smoothed her skirt, settled into the bedside chair, and leaned close. "Why didn't you tell me?"

"You would have thought me mad."

She laughed, leaned closer. "You're right, of course. But whyever did you do it?"

The partition rustled. My parents were conversing with the nurse. I swiped my tongue over cracked lips. "For the money, Lucinda. For Mr. and Mrs. McConnell's African mission."

Her eyes grew wide. I inhaled as deeply as my sore ribs allowed. "How is Webster?"

Her face contorted as her hand let go of mine.

My heart pummeled my chest. "Please tell me."

She stared at her lap. "They haven't let me—us—see him

yet." Her head rose. Tears stood in her eyes. "He asked me to come here with him, you know."

I nodded, determined to keep my emotions in low gear. "I never meant for anything like this to happen, Lucinda. You've already had so much tragedy. I hate to think that because of me you again face losing—" I swallowed hard—"losing someone you love."

She frowned. "Love?"

I blinked. "Isn't that . . . isn't that why he came to your house? Why you came here with him?"

Her face softened. "He helped me—and let me help him—because of my Billy, not because of any romantic feelings for me. And I finally told him I knew about his secret gifts to those in need."

The thought of my missing money made my heart sink again.

"Besides," Lucinda said, laying her hand on my arm and smiling, "I have a feeling his heart is already accounted for."

"Oh . . . I see."

"Do you?" She looked amused. But for the life of me I couldn't figure out why.

Lucinda darted from the chair to a spot near the door when Mother swept around the partition and back to my side. "Your father and I will go find supper for ourselves, but I'll make sure they get some up to you soon." She kissed my cheek and reached for Father's hand.

"Wait." I swung my legs over the side of the bed. "I have to see Webster." Pushing to my feet, I leaned into Father's sturdy body.

"Webster? Who's Webster?" Mother peered at Father, then me, then Lucinda.

I shuffled forward. "Where is he, Lucinda?"

She shook her head. "I don't know. They won't let me see him."

"Ally girl. You need to get back to bed. I'll find out about him. I promise." With gentle pressure, he lowered me back to the bed.

"Who is Webster?" Mother was more insistent now. Father swung my legs up and covered them with the sheet. Lucinda inched toward the door, face white, eyes wide.

"I said, Who's Web—"

"Our mechanic, Mother. Mr. Little. He works for Father. He built the race car. Father agreed to sponsor it. He . . . I . . ."

Father cupped Mother's elbow. "Come, Winifred. I'll tell you all about it over supper."

I sighed, wondering how Mother would react to the news. But at least we'd be done with the secrets.

"And you'll tell the nurse to take me to Webster before you leave tonight?"

Father pushed my hair from my face, kissed my forehead. He still smelled of burning rubber and gasoline. "Tomorrow, Ally. I promise."

Nothing prepared me for the pain of Sunday. Not even driving the three hundred miles on the track in Cincinnati. Every inch of me hurt. No one had to force me to be still. Since I couldn't go to Webster, I sent Lucinda and Father in my stead, charging them to report back to me on his condition.

Mother sat beside me, fussing over my every move, my every need. She didn't want to leave my side. Exactly as she'd done with Grandmother.

Grandmother. Had she heard the news of the crash, or my

injuries? Could her heart stand the shock? She expected us home today. Had Father telephoned to say we wouldn't arrive?

"Does Granny know?" I asked.

Mother glanced up. "Know what, darling?"

"That we won't be home this evening."

"Yes. Your father telephoned Clarissa."

"But he didn't say anything about me?"

"Of course not." She straightened the sheet around me.

"But Grandmother will be worried."

"Whatever for? She knows you are with us."

I swallowed. Mother wouldn't like this. "She'll worry because she knows. About the racing."

Mother's shoulders drooped as she let her back rest against the slats of the chair. "Oh, Alyce. You do realize if this gets out you'll never find a man who will marry you."

"Or maybe I'll find the perfect man, Mother—the one who loves me for who I am and who appreciates how God made me."

Someone like Webster.

How could my heart still hold such feelings for him when I knew he'd taken my money? In spite of the evidence, I wanted to believe him innocent of breaking my trust, for the more I thought about it, the harder I found it to fathom a thief returning to protect his victim. If he really had taken my money, he must have had a reason he felt I would understand.

He'd sacrificed so much for me. Everything, actually. And as clearly as the red starting flag cutting through a mountain of exhaust smoke, I knew I loved him—and I believed in him, just as he had always believed in me.

35

I have to go to him." I set my feet on the floor, grimacing as I stood, and then swaying a bit as I straightened.

"Alyce. Please." Mother gave a gentle push and I sat back on the bed again. Mother leaned out the door to call for a nurse.

Father hurried to the bed. "What's wrong? Where do you hurt?"

I shook my head. How could I explain? "Where's Lucinda?" croaked from my throat.

"I sent her home. Back to Langston. She'll assure your grandmother that you are well."

"I have to talk to Webster." With sheer determination, I pushed to my feet again. Father grabbed my waist, held me steady.

"I don't think this is a good idea," he grumbled.

I waited for Mother to concur. She didn't.

"I don't think it's allowed, miss." The young night nurse inserted herself into the conversation.

"I don't care if it's allowed or not. I need to see him. Now."

"But—" Her eyes grew round. I shuffled forward, careful not to jostle the arm bandaged to my side.

"You can take me there, or I can go on my own."

"Harry?" Mother this time. Her expression both soft and chiding. "Help us."

Just before I thought I'd slither to the floor, Father's eyes cut toward the nurse. She frowned. "Sit down. I'll go get a wheelchair."

I sat. The nurse returned. Father helped me into the chair, pushed me on a brisk journey down the hall and around a corner. Mother held my hand the entire way.

We entered a darkened room. The chair stopped moving. Rhythmic breathing whispered into the blackness. Then a shaft of light illuminated a round face. Swollen and bruised. Deathly white around the edges. Chest barely rising and falling.

"I'll be back shortly." The nurse turned on her heel and hurried away.

"We'll be outside, darling." Mother pulled Father from the room.

I leaned as far forward as I could, my heart crying his name as I smoothed a lock of hair away from his forehead. "I'm sorry, Webster. For everything." I watched his closed eyelids, anxious for a flutter of recognition or understanding.

Nothing.

A lump swam up my throat, lodging in the middle of my neck. I tried to swallow it down, but it refused to budge. "I should never have let Mr. Trotter bully me into silence. I should have shouted the truth to Father no matter what Mr. Trotter told him in return." His face blurred. I leaned closer to his ear. "Please don't leave me, Webster. I need you."

If God took my only true friend, how would I survive?

I will never leave you or forsake you.

I closed my eyes. *Yes, Lord. I know that.* I wanted it to be enough.

Even if I couldn't give the McConnells the money I'd pledged to their ministry.

Even without Grandmother's presence to buoy me.

Even if I lived my whole life without a man who shared my faith and understood everything about me.

My eyes roamed back to Webster's face. Maybe it was better to let him go. Lucinda had said his heart was already taken. And even if it were free, he'd betrayed my trust by taking my money. He'd never given any indication he shared my faith, though he'd never scorned God in my presence, either.

An ache pulsed up my arm, across my shoulder, and into my temple. Then it shot across my forehead and wrapped around my skull like a turban of steel.

"I think you should rest now, Alyce." Mother pressed her cheek against mine. I assented with a slight nod. But until sleep claimed my mind, I prayed the Lord would have mercy on my friend.

Mother found me in Webster's room early the next morning. "How is he?" she asked before she kissed my forehead.

"The same."

She pulled up a chair and sat beside me, both of us staring at his unresponsive face.

"You know who he reminds me of?"

My head jerked in Mother's direction. Instantly, I regretted the motion, biting my lip, waiting for the pain to subside. "Who?"

A smile played at the corners of her mouth. "Your father

272

when he was younger. Full of big ideas. Big dreams." She glanced at me and then back at him. "Not handsome to everyone else, mind you. But his face fluttered my heart."

I held my breath. Could this possibly mean she approved of Webster? Or at least that if he was my choice she wouldn't oppose it? Of course she had no idea of his thievery. Or that I'd allowed Father to think him guilty of forcing himself on me. Or that he didn't share my faith.

For a long while Mother and I sat in silence, nurses and doctors bustling around us. This new territory of sharing my heart with her didn't come easily.

"Where's Father?"

"He had some business to tend to. He said he'd be here later today."

I nodded, strangely relieved.

The hours ticked by. My stomach rumbled. Then Father appeared in Webster's doorway, face ashen, eyes blank. Hat clenched between his hands.

"What's wrong?" My heart leapt into top speed.

Fiery eyes glared past me as he slowly crushed his hat into a ball. He growled out one word. "Trotter."

I couldn't swallow. Couldn't breathe. I staggered to my feet, fell back into my chair again.

His shoulders hunched. Red anger faded to a bloodless complexion.

"Darling." Mother reached his side. "What is it?"

His mangled hat fell to the floor as he knelt in front of my wheelchair. "He's a liar and a thief."

My eyes widened. "But he isn't. I told you that already."

He shook his head. "Not Little. Trotter. You were only part of his plan, Ally. Maybe an impulse, a trinket he couldn't resist. I guess because you belonged to me."

A low moan skittered across the silence. Or had I imagined it?

Father raked a hand through his already untidy hair as he paced the small space beside Webster's bed. "How could I have been so stupid?"

"Harry, Harry." Mother crooned his name as she placed her hands on his cheeks. The scowl on his face disappeared. "I'm sorry, Winifred. I should have been more careful."

"But what happened?" I looked from Father to Mother and back again.

He grasped Mother's hand as if all of a sudden he needed her strength. "After what you told me, I hired someone to investigate Mr. Trotter." His mouth turned downward. "It wasn't that I didn't believe you, Ally girl, it's just that I needed to know the truth for myself. And I discovered him a worse scoundrel than I imagined. He wanted to hurt me—for what reason I still don't know. So he used you. Now he's vanished. And so has my investment capital."

Capital? "What do you mean, Father?"

He rubbed the back of his neck, suddenly resembling a small boy caught in mischief. "I'd culled the profits from the last year into a special fund. We didn't need the money to live on anyway. I wanted a new challenge but wasn't sure what. So I gathered a good bit of ready money, intending to invest."

"Forget the money, Harry. We've survived on so much less." Mother laid her head on Father's shoulder while I marveled at her words. "At least we still have our girl."

"I'm not concerned about the money as such. It's what I'd intended the money to do."

My mouth went dry. Had he meant to give it to me? For Africa? "What did you intend to do, Father?"

His look slid past me, to the still form on the bed. "I was going to tell Little after our success in the Harvest Classic, but then that scene in the garage . . ." He wiped his hand over his face, took a deep breath. "I wanted to invest in a new venture: manufacturing Mr. Little's cars."

I gasped.

"Why I didn't see the truth that night, I don't know. Little is a man with a vision, a man who'll go far. I wanted to be a part of that. But I trusted Trotter, too. Or maybe I saw what I wanted to see. I don't know. I guess when he claimed to be the driver of our car, I assumed he had a hidden talent. And I liked that. And if Webster trusted him with his car, well, that just boosted my consideration of him."

Suddenly I recalled again the night Mr. Trotter came upon me in the garage, remembered he'd known about the cash money in my box, perhaps even spied on Webster as he'd hidden it. And now Father declared Trotter a *thief* and a liar. I bolted from my chair. The world spun. I reached out to steady myself. My hand landed on Webster's broken leg.

A guttural groan accompanied the roll of his head to one side. Father scooped me up and deposited me back into my chair, and then leaned over Webster, obscuring him from view.

"What's happening?" I pulled at the back of Father's coat.

Another moan. Louder this time.

Father stalked to the door. "Nurse! Get in here!"

Within moments, nurses and doctors shoved past us. The fear in their eyes unnerved me. We moved away from Webster's bed. I gulped in air, praying this wasn't the end—and if it was, praying I wouldn't wither in the face of calamity. I'd always asked the Lord to allow me to show my parents His presence and power in my life. But I hadn't meant like this.

A doctor approached. "We've given him more pain medication, Mr. Benson. He'll go back to sleep again. We'll decrease the dosage throughout the night. Perhaps by tomorrow he'll wake more fully. Then we can assess the leg. We'll need to take some X rays to determine if the break warrants surgical intervention."

"Whatever needs to be done for him, Doctor, I'll make it good."

The doctor nodded. "Fine. I'll keep you apprised of the situation."

He left the room. One by one, the nurses returned to their other duties, as well.

I sat by the bed again, longing to stroke the hand that lay atop the white sheet, to tell him what I knew now, to ask him to forgive me for ever suspecting him. But I couldn't. Not with my parents watching and listening.

"Father, why don't you ask if I can go back to the hotel with you tonight? I've felt much better today."

"I think that's a good idea, Alyce." Mother's agreement warmed me. She and I seemed to have reached some new place of understanding.

"I'll find someone right away." Father charged toward the door.

"Wait."

He turned.

"Go with him, Mother. I'll wait here."

She looked past me, to the man on the bed. When her eyes met mine, they softened. "Of course, darling. Take as long as you need."

The door clicked shut.

We were alone, Webster and me. Well, as alone as we could be behind our partition of thin muslin. He in his drug-induced sleep. Me with a heart fully awake.

I hung my head and prayed for courage. Courage to stand up in front of my church without the money for the

McConnells and their mission. Courage to let go of Grandmother when the Lord called her home. Courage to convey the love of Christ to my parents. Courage to accept the possibility that Webster might not care for me as I did for him.

By the time my parents returned, my heart had emptied of its cries. I studied Webster's face one last time before we left, silently promising I wouldn't ask more of him than he could give.

36

*F*ather escorted me to the hospital the next morning and then left to meet with his attorney about Trotter. Mother stayed at the hotel, packing our things, though I'd refused to leave Indianapolis without Webster. Just before noon, a light step sounded on the floor behind me. I twisted in my chair and then hobbled to my feet. "Lucinda!"

She rushed forward, pressing her cheek to mine, careful not to jostle my arm. "You look much better today, Alyce."

"What are you . . . You can't afford a day off work."

Pink stained her cheeks. "Mr. Morgan, well, he's, um . . ." Her face turned scarlet as her gaze locked on mine. "I may not have to work much longer." A shy smile transformed her face.

"You and Mr. Morgan?"

She nodded. "After you and I talked—about men—I realized I'd ignored those same signs myself. Afraid, I guess. I thought he was just being nice." She giggled. "I guess working for Mr. Morgan was exactly where I needed to be."

I squeezed her hand as tears pricked my eyes. Lucinda deserved every bit of happiness she could find. Mr. Morgan would treat her well, and she wouldn't have to worry anymore about feeding and clothing her children.

"But I didn't come to tell you about me. How's Webster? I've been so anxious."

"He woke a bit last night, and he's stirred some this morning. But he hasn't fully returned to us yet." I eased back into my chair, suddenly tired again.

"Do you know what I learned about Webster this week?" Lucinda asked gently.

I shook my head.

"He's a preacher."

"A what?"

Webster moaned. I searched his face. Anxious. Eager. But he stilled again. I turned back to Lucinda, pondering her revelation. I couldn't make sense of it. Webster had always supported my faith, but he'd never acknowledged his own. "I think someone must have told you wrong. Webster builds cars. Fixes machinery. He doesn't preach anywhere. I'm not even sure if he believes in God."

Lucinda shook her head. "I had Clarissa's sister in the other day. To help with some cleaning. She and her family might rent my house after Mr. Morgan and I . . ." She cleared her throat as her cheeks once again blazed scarlet. "Anyway, her husband ran into a man who knew some of Webster's history."

I bit my lip, afraid to hear more. But I couldn't stop listening.

"Remember how I told you I'd heard about him being linked with money missing from a church?"

My stomach clenched. I remembered all too well.

She took a deep breath. "Apparently he'd held the pulpit

at that church and had just resigned. That's why suspicion fell on him. Though as I told you before, I never believed he could do such a thing."

But I had. Shame heated my face.

"He didn't take up preaching as a living again. He came to Langston and went to work for your father. He lived in the midst of the factory workers and such. When someone hit a rough patch, he tried to help. He prayed with them. Studied the Scriptures with them. Told them about God's love. And, of course, left those baskets of food and money when he heard of a dire need."

I wanted to shake Webster awake, to demand he tell me everything. He knew I would have embraced this. Even helped. Legs trembling, I rose from the chair. Lucinda caught me by my good arm. I couldn't believe the fury inside me didn't scorch her at the touch.

Then she gasped. Pointed.

I froze.

Webster stared up at me, blinked. Breath caught in my chest. My heart seemed to stop mid-beat.

"It's you," he said, his voice gentle.

Tingles chased over my arms, down my legs—until I realized that Lucinda was standing behind me. Whom did he mean to address?

My tingles turned to chills as Lucinda ran for the nurse. By the time the room emptied of her, he'd fallen back asleep.

Father insisted I go out to dinner with them, but in spite of my tangled feelings, I couldn't abandon Webster. Not even for a few hours. My parents finally left me to my solitary vigil.

I scooted my chair closer to the edge of the bed, night creeping in around us. I ached for Langston. For home. For Grandmother. But I burned to hear Webster's voice once more, to lose myself in his dark eyes.

"Come back to me," I whispered. "Please come back to me."

A cart rumbled through the room. Soft voices questioned and answered. Electric light chased shadows into dark corners.

Was my vigil a foolish one? The doctors claimed to be more hopeful now. But what if they were wrong? Could I sit by and watch him fade into eternity?

I walked to the window and looked down into the graying street. I stretched my right arm, shook feeling back into my left foot before returning to my chair. I closed my eyes, but no words of petition bled from my heart.

A clammy finger touched my wrist. My eyes flew open. He stared at me, chest rising and falling faster than usual. Was he in pain? Ought I go for help?

"Should I—"

"Don't leave."

Our words overlapped, but I heard his above my own. I laid my palm against his cheek. "I won't leave you."

"Good." An unhurried grin traveled across his face, lighting his eyes. He reached up at the same leisurely pace and curled his fingers around mine. "Good."

His eyelids fluttered shut, but he never let go of my hand.

I thanked the Lord for the interurban, which transported Mother and Father back and forth from Langston with greater regularity and less hassle than the train. Each evening one of my parents would come to stay with me. Each morning one would return to Langston after settling me beside Webster's bed.

X rays proved the necessity of surgery to set the bones in place to heal properly. Lucinda sat with me through the surgery, which Dr. Oliver assured us went well.

Webster's smile came more frequently now, as did his lucid moments, though the pain in his head and his leg often tightened his jaw. By Sunday, just a week after the accident, he sat up in bed and ate under his own power.

"Why don't you rest now, Webster."

"I've slept too long. When can I get out of this bed?"

His grousing awakened my guilt.

"I'm so sorry. You wouldn't be here if I hadn't—"

His eyes softened. "It's not your fault, Ally. It could just as easily have been me driving." He stared at the ceiling now, his Adam's apple bobbing in his throat. "I knew what I was getting into the first time I let you take the wheel. But I didn't mind. I knew you could do it. I knew you *needed* to do it."

I shook my head, studying the open, empty hand in my lap. "No. My impulsiveness drove me into a situation I couldn't handle."

"I don't agree." He leaned forward. "Maybe you shouldn't have so flippantly committed your father's money, but maybe, just maybe, the Lord used this situation to show you something about yourself. Something important."

"Like what?"

"Like the fact that you have the guts and the strength to drive farther and faster than most people would ever dream possible."

My mouth turned down as I shook my head. "That isn't important."

"Why not?"

"Because it's . . . it's . . ." I remembered again crushed steel, a concrete wall, the unforgiving brick of the track. Our very lives at stake. Did God really lead me to that place, or did I move forward with my own plan without seeking His blessing?

Webster closed his hand around mine. My stomach spun with fear and delight, reminding me of everything I still needed to talk about with him.

Can't we just go on like this, Lord? Everything seems good. Almost like before.

I breathed in the aroma of ammonia and freshly laundered sheets. "Webster?"

"Hmm?" His head fell to the pillow propped up behind him. The look in his eyes threatened my resolve.

"Can you ever forgive me?"

"I just told you, it wasn't your fault."

"Not the accident." I slid my hand from his grasp. "Will you forgive me for not defending you to Father—that night?"

His jaw twitched as fire leapt into his usually peaceful gaze. "He wouldn't have believed you. He'd already made up his mind about me."

"That's not true. He trusted you completely."

"Except when he found me with his daughter."

"But don't you see? Even that was my fault."

A nurse walked in to check the bandages on Webster's leg. When she was satisfied, she popped a thermometer in his mouth and checked it a few minutes later. The moment she rounded the partition, I leaned forward, my voice low. "Father assumed you trusted Trotter enough to let him drive."

"But then supposed I would attack his daughter? Don't try to excuse it, Ally. It can't be done."

"He knows the truth now. He's trying to make up for it."

He turned his face to the window. "I don't need his charity."

"But you give your own quite freely."

His head whipped back toward me. "What did you say?"

I wedged my hand between the seat and my thigh. "You give your charity freely."

His eyes narrowed. "How do you know about that?"

"Lucinda."

He lay still, eyes shut. Had he fallen asleep? Just as I reached to shake him, he pulled in a deep breath.

My shoulders sank in relief. "Father thinks the world of you, Webster. Really he does. He even—"

His hand rose. I stopped speaking. His brows drew toward his nose. "I'm sorry, too, Ally. I should have told you more about myself from the beginning of our friendship, but it was easier not to. It wasn't shame that kept me silent. It was fear."

"Fear? Of me?" My chest ached with the weight of his words.

"Not fear that you'd reject me—I knew that almost from the moment we met in your garage two years ago. But the more you talked of the Lord, the more I feared if you knew, you'd push me to do the uncomfortable, to embrace the vision the Lord has given me for my life, unusual though it may be."

"What vision?"

A wave of pain crossed his face, but whether pain from his leg or a pain in his heart, I couldn't discern. "I graduated from seminary. Preached in a small church on the other side of Indiana. But after a year or so I became dissatisfied, as if I'd missed something. I prayed and prayed for contentment. But the more I prayed the more uncomfortable I became. God seemed to be calling me to something . . . different.

Finally, though, I couldn't embrace the new, and I realized I couldn't remain in the old. I resigned from my church and wandered westward."

He scratched the back of his neck and then smoothed down the ruffled edges of his dark hair. "I'd been interested in automobiles ever since I saw my first one as a boy. And I'd become quite good at tinkering with them. So when I heard of your father's need for a chauffeur and mechanic, I applied for the job. Of course after he hired me, he decided he liked driving his own car. So he gave me extra work at the factory. I settled in town, among many of his other employees, and just . . . lived.

"But I discovered that whether I preached with words or not, people were drawn to me. I helped them in any way I could, including introducing them to my Savior or leading them into a deeper relationship with Christ. Lives changed. I began to wonder if God's hand had brought me to Langston for His purpose instead of my own."

I squirmed, imaginary needles poking into my legs.

"As I maintained your father's cars, I began to wonder if I could build my own. Then he found me late one night in the factory, tinkering with something I'd put together. He gave me permission to use spare parts when I needed. I showed him the engine I'd built. His eyes lit up. It occurred to me that this might be the future God intended."

"God wanted you to build racing cars?" I rubbed my forehead, fearful my head would explode with all this new information.

He chuckled. "Not racing cars necessarily. But cars. I began to consider the possibilities. If I could pay my workers a fair wage to produce a quality product, I might gain credibility with them, incite them to live lives that pleased

God in the process." He grinned but then ducked his head. "Crazy, I know."

Prickles raced through my chest, swam into my extremities. No wonder I loved this man. I'd never known a heart like his, though Grandmother's came very close. Someone who wanted to live a life that led others to God. I reached for his hand, threaded my fingers through his. "Not crazy. Amazing. Like your own little mission field."

His face clouded. "But Trotter was right when he said the funds at my church went missing."

My hand went slack as I slurped in air. "You took the money from your church?" All the old doubts assailed me. Who had my money? Webster or Trotter?

One corner of his mouth lifted. "No. But it disappeared just after I resigned. There were insinuations. I didn't take it. I don't have any idea who did. But I determined I would pay it back anyway."

I couldn't make sense of his story. "So you took my money to pay back your church?"

"*Your* money?" He stiffened. "What happened to your money, Ally?"

"You don't know?" My lips trembled. "That night—that awful night with Trotter—I went to the garage. Late. I wanted to . . . I don't know what I wanted to do, exactly. The light was on. I thought you were there. I found my red box on the ground. Empty."

"That blackguard."

"Who?"

"Trotter, of course."

"Yes. I think it is safe to assume he took it."

"Then he hung around and waited, so he'd have some sort of alibi."

"So he could accuse you." Warmth lit my cheeks. "I'm not always as good at reading people as I am driving cars."

He looked at his leg and then back at me. "Sometimes you aren't so great at driving cars, either."

I tried to frown, but a smile won. His finger trailed across my cheek, teasing the corners of my mouth upward. His dark eyes held mine. "But don't worry, Ally. I wouldn't ride with anyone else."

37

D r. Oliver plastered Webster's leg on Wednesday—eleven days after our crash. By Thursday afternoon, my arm had been freed from its prison of bandages and housed in a simple sling instead. And Webster had been cleared to leave the hospital. Though he and I had sorted out some of our misunderstandings, we hadn't spoken of our feelings for each other. We circled around them as if they comprised the infield of a racetrack.

"It will be good to get home," he said as I fussed over him on our way back to Langston.

"You won't be going home," I told him. In the sway of the interurban car, I jostled his outstretched leg. He hissed. I winced. We did look like a pair, each with an immobile limb. But I had to wear the sling only for a couple of weeks. His plaster would remain in place for months.

"And where would you propose I go?"

"You're coming to our house. You don't have a choice."

I turned to the window, my heart dancing as the Langston station drew closer. I recognized Mother and Father huddled on the small platform, along with Lucinda and her children and Pastor and Mrs. Swan. Oh, how I'd missed them all!

Father jumped aboard once the other passengers exited. He helped Webster thump down the steps. Beads of sweat were clinging to Webster's gray face by the time he got settled in the waiting wheelchair. Mother flitted about me, but I brushed her aside and squatted beside Webster. "Are you all right?"

He nodded, lips tight.

Father and Pastor Swan worked together to get him from the wheelchair and into the back seat of the Packard. I squeezed up front with Mother. "Now, Father, go slow."

His belly shook with laughter as he put the car in gear and pointed us toward home.

Bursting through the front door, I rushed up the staircase and straight into Grandmother's bedroom, stopping just short of the bed.

"Ally?"

"It's me, Granny. I'm home."

Tears filled the wrinkles around her eyes like spring rains in dry creek beds. "I was so worried."

I eased down on the side of the bed, reached across her with my free arm, and hugged her frail shoulders. "I know you were. I'm sorry." I pulled away.

"Your friend was here. Sweet girl."

"Lucinda?"

"That's the one." Grandmother chuckled. "Very talkative."

My mouth turned down. Lucinda? Well, my grandmother often brought out the best in people.

"And is your young man with you?"

"My . . . young man?"

"Mr. Little."

My lips twisted into a frown. "I sent Lucinda here to tell you I was okay and to ask you to pray."

"And she did both of those things." Grandmother groped for my hand. "I've been praying the Lord would give you someone to take my place."

I blinked at her. "But no one can take your place."

"I won't be here forever, dear."

Fear careened through my body. "Is something wrong? Have they kept it from me?"

"No." Contentment covered her face. "But an old woman knows when her days are drawing to a close. And she doesn't mind. Not when she feels sure of the faithfulness of God toward those she loves."

For the first time since the McConnells had appeared at our church, I felt only peace.

Mother followed me to my room that evening and helped me undress. I slid beneath the cool sheets, sheets ten times more comfortable than those in the hospital or at the hotel. I must have been more tired than I realized, for when I woke and threw open the shutters, the sun splashed yellow light far across my floor.

I spent the day between the two sick rooms but found more and more excuses to be with Webster.

"This isn't much better than being in the hospital." He shifted a bit, trying to settle himself upright.

"At least you get to eat Clarissa's food."

"Well, there's that."

I fought a grin. "Besides, here you get to open the window and breathe fresh air." I poked my head into the sunshine, whiffed farmland and flowers on the warm September breeze. Gratitude swelled my heart. Whatever happened from here, I could never deny God's existence in my life. His protection. His provision. His love.

All the things I wanted others to experience, too.

Pulling back into the room, I turned to Webster. He wanted that for others, as well. Really wanted it. Not like Lawrence Trotter, who'd pretended in order to win my favor. But even if Webster and I desired similar things, did that mean we were meant for each other?

"Thinking about Sunday?" His voice startled the question from my head.

I eased into the upholstered chair at the opposite end of the room. No sense torturing myself with his nearness. I slid the crinkled photograph from the pocket of my skirt.

Those same faces stared back at me. People I felt as if I knew. Shy, yet bold. Courageous, yet wary. They needed a lifetime of Ava McConnell to demonstrate God's unchanging love.

"It won't be easy. I know that." My fingers skittered across the surface of the picture. "I feel bad for the McConnells, mostly. They were counting on that money."

"Maybe your father will give it to you now. If you ask."

"Oh no. I couldn't ask. He's just lost all that money . . ." My words faded into silence.

"Lost? Oh. You mean what he shelled out for the hospital and my operation." His shoulders sagged. His despair pulled me from my chair. I perched on the edge of the bed.

Father had asked me not to tell Webster anything of the capital he'd intended to use to finance Webster's car-making venture—felt he didn't need another disappointment. Or was it just Father's pride standing in the way?

To tell or keep silent? *Please, Lord, help me know what to do.*

"There you are, Ally." Father loped into the room, nodded at Webster.

I rose. "Did you need something?"

"Your grandmother is asking for you." He led me to the door. I glanced back at Webster. He smiled my release.

We stepped into the hallway. "Father, you have to talk to Webster. You have to tell him about the money."

"We already discussed this, Ally. I think it's best to say nothing."

"But he thinks— You see, I just mentioned . . ." I wanted to make things right between them. A deep breath cleared my head. "He still thinks you don't trust him. He doesn't like accepting your 'charity.' He needs to understand the truth: that you respect him and believed in his dream long before you knew of Trotter's duplicity."

Cigar-scented breath tarnished the air. His head wagged as he considered what I'd said. "When did you grow up, Ally girl?" His hand cupped my cheek. I leaned into its strength.

"Go on, now." He nodded toward Grandmother's room. "I'll take care of the rest."

In my usual place at Grandmother's bedside, I read from God's Word. We talked about it, prayed together. She asked about the race, the crash, my parents' reaction to my startling revelation. And she asked about Webster.

As we finished talking, Mother took possession of me,

whisking me to the dining room for supper, insisting Grand-mother and Webster would be fine for a while with the nurse.

Mother, Father, and I sat at the table together, as we'd done so many times before. Mother full of plans for next month's club meeting in Chicago, Father full of indistin-guishable grunts in her direction. I sighed and pushed my plate away. How could so much have happened to me yet my daily routine change so little? Was this really all God had in mind for my life?

As soon as I could, I escaped from the table. But when I reached the upper hallway, the nurse shut Webster's door behind her.

"He's sleeping, miss. Finally. Best leave him until morn-ing." She flashed a stern scowl, almost daring me to defy her charge.

I made my way to my own bedroom instead.

I bounded from bed the next morning, checking first on Grandmother and then tiptoeing to Webster's door. Still shut. I turned. My gaze met the nurse's as she climbed the stairs. I headed in the other direction. A walk in the garden, but not to the garage. A cold luncheon with Mother, Father remain-ing locked in his study.

Every time I ventured near Webster's room, the door re-mained closed, and I dared not open it. Just before supper, I approached again.

The door opened.

Father stood before me.

"I'm sorry. I didn't know . . ." I tried to peek around his wide body to see if Webster was dressed.

"Go on in," he grumbled as he stalked past me.

I watched him jog down the stairs. What had he done now? I rolled my eyes and steeled myself for whatever foul mood my father had incited in Webster.

But Webster greeted me with his biggest grin. "There you are. I missed you last night."

Indeed his manner had changed. But I hadn't expected it to be for the better. Wary, I tucked my feet under me and sat in the faraway chair.

"Mother wanted us to have supper at the table. Like normal." I laughed. "Or as normal as we get."

Webster chuckled, too, his eyes never leaving my face. I squirmed a bit beneath the pointed gaze. "So what did you and Father find to talk about?"

He shrugged. "This and that."

I waited. Surely he'd tell me more. But the silence lengthened.

I cleared my throat. "Did you get things settled between you?"

"Settled?" His head tipped to one side. "I guess settled is a good word."

Frustration boiled inside me like water in a kettle. If he didn't say something soon, I knew it would pour out through my spout.

"How's your grandmother?" A mischievous glint in his eye.

"Fine." Through my clenched teeth.

His grin grew wider, his look more tender. I wanted to grab him by the collar and strangle him. Or kiss him. I wasn't sure which.

I pushed up from my seat, passed near the bed. "I guess you're tired already, so I'll stop in later. If you want me to."

He grabbed my hand and pulled me near. I didn't want his touch to dissolve my anger, but it did.

"I'll always want you beside me, Ally."

My heart raced like a car in sight of the finish line, but I jerked the wheel and it swerved aside. If he still couldn't share openly with me, we had no future together. Ever. I extracted my hand from his grasp and left the room, shutting the door firmly behind me.

38

Although part of me wanted to throw the covers over my head and disappear on Sunday morning, another part was ready to get the ordeal over with. Once I told the truth, I'd have done my part. I couldn't worry how other people would react or what they would assume. Though I imagined the gossip would hurt all the same.

I planned to get to church early and confess to the McConnells in private before announcing my failure to the congregation. I threw my robe around my shoulders and started toward the bathroom at the end of the hall. No stirring sounded, abovestairs or below, though I knew Clarissa was bustling around the kitchen at the back of the house.

I bathed and dressed with as little movement of my arm as possible, then set it back in its sling. Balancing my handbag and small hat atop my Bible, I descended the stairs. Setting my Bible and purse on the table, I stared at myself in the mirror in the foyer, attempting to pin my hat in place with one hand. Gray shadows lined the skin beneath my eyes. I could have covered them with cosmetics, but I decided to let my flaws show. Perhaps my appearance would elicit a bit of sympathy. Prove that, despite the wealth of my father, my life was not unmarred by trouble.

If they only knew.

I jammed the hat pin in place and tried to smile. The words of Psalm 42 came quickly to mind: *Why art thou cast down, O my soul? and why art thou disquieted in me?*

Why indeed.

I shrugged into one sleeve of my duster and buttoned it closed one-handed. Handbag hanging from my arm, I cradled my heavy Bible, and then decided to leave it. I slipped out the front door. The sun hovered just beneath the tops of the trees that lined our lane. The low iron gate opened with a push. I followed the rutted road toward town. The road Webster walked almost every single day.

I glanced up to the window of the room where Webster was sleeping. Morning light hit dew on the grass, transforming heaven's teardrops into an endless field of polished diamonds.

The chug of a motor sounded behind me. I moved into the weeds that edged the road. The car slowed. The night nurse leaned through the open window over the driver's door. "Need a ride?"

Not one other conveyance sat beside the little white church when I climbed from Nurse Amy's Brush Runabout. Not even Pastor Swan's old Tin Lizzie.

"Are you sure you want me to leave you here?" she asked.

"I'm sure. Thanks again for the ride. I don't know that I'd have made it on my own."

She shook her head, trying not to laugh. "You do have pluck, I'll give you that." She put the car in gear and chugged away.

A few minutes later, the putter of an overworked engine carried on the crisp September breeze, and a cloud of dust moved in the distance. Pastor Swan's Model T rolled near the building. The engine sputtered and died. Ava McConnell's laugh wafted from the car. I shuddered beneath my linen duster, one sleeve limp and empty. The moment I'd dreaded had finally arrived.

Give me courage, Lord.

With firm steps across the damp grass, I met the Swans and McConnells at the car.

"My dear girl. You're here early." Mrs. Swan's gloved hand reached for mine and then paused. "Should you even be out yet?"

My stomach tumbled, and I glanced at Ava McConnell's confused face. Evidently no one had informed them of my injuries.

Pastor Swan led me up the steps, into the church. "Should we drive you back home again?"

"No. I need to talk to you. All of you."

"Of course." Pastor Swan's footsteps echoed through the sanctuary. We followed him to the back of the building, where his small office crouched in a corner. Mrs. Swan's delicate forehead wrinkled in confusion as her husband unlocked the door.

Two chairs—one behind the desk, one before it—were offered to the ladies. I proclaimed my preference to stand, though I did position myself against a bare spot of wall for support. Pastor Swan wedged his body behind his desk chair, hands resting gently on his wife's shoulders. Mr. McConnell stood close beside his wife, as well, his large hands perched on the back of her chair.

And all looked at me with a disconcerting expectancy.

"I have a confession to make." I ducked my head, counted the scratches in the wood floor beneath my feet. Deep gouges, presumably made by desks and chairs of rectors past.

"No one here will condemn you." Ava's angelic voice made me wince. Best not to linger. Best to face it now, all at once.

The smell of musty books tickled my nose as I pulled in a breath big enough to push out the unpleasant words. "I don't have three thousand dollars."

Silence.

In agony, I lifted my eyes to the face of my grandmother's former-nemesis-turned-trusted-friend. No shock registered on Mrs. Swan's face. "Whatever amount you have, dear, will be appreciated all the same. Isn't that right, Ava?"

My shoulders sagged. "No, you don't understand. I don't have any of it. Nothing." I opened my empty pocketbook. "I thought Father would give it to me. He wouldn't. Then I tried raising the funds myself, but—" My voice faltered. I stopped, steadied it. "But I kept giving the money away. To meet other needs in our town."

Mrs. Swan's lips twitched. Almost as if she were holding back a laugh.

"Then I—" My voice lowered. "Then I earned some money. In a race." I held my breath in an effort to diffuse the sting of their displeasure.

Pastor Swan's eyebrows shot upward. "You bet on a horse race?"

"No!" I gasped out, head shaking, curls bouncing. "I'd never gamble!"

"Oh." Pastor Swan and Mr. McConnell looked visibly relieved.

I swallowed, reminded myself that I drove my car around town all the time and no one minded. Much. Only the venue had changed.

"I earned the money driving in an auto race. At Speedway Park in Chicago. Then in Cincinnati. And Indianapolis." There. I'd said it all.

Mr. McConnell's eyes stretched wide. "You raced against Dario Resta?"

Now my lips twitched. I pressed them together, demanding sternness. "Yes."

His eyebrows lifted. "And how did you fare?"

This time I couldn't quell my smirk. "Not well enough."

Mr. McConnell's laugh shook the room. I reached for the wall as my knees quaked with the vibration. Ava McConnell leaned toward me, a twinkle of humor in her eyes. "But what happened to the money, Miss Benson? You did say you won some?"

Her words sobered me in an instant. "I earned some for driving. Unfortunately, the money was stolen from me just before the race at Indianapolis."

Mr. McConnell's gaze took in my limp sleeve and the half-healed cut on my face. "And you crashed at Indianapolis."

My mouth dropped open.

He nodded at my sleeve. "Even missionaries read the newspapers, Miss Benson. And since auto racing fascinates me, I read the accounts of it in particular. Though I would never have taken you for Albert Butler."

I cringed.

"By the way, how is your mechanic? The last I read, he remained unconscious."

"Much better, thank you."

Mrs. Swan looked at her husband. He cleared his throat.

"You knew all along?" I thought of the Swans helping Webster back to our house.

"Not the whole story, certainly," Pastor Swan said. "We knew Mr. Little had been injured at the Motor Speedway in Indianapolis. As for you, your father left the details sketchy at best. I might never have suspected if I hadn't seen your Packard tearing up the roads around town on occasion."

I grinned. Gooseflesh pricked my arms and legs, but not from fear. From the unexpected wonder of forgiveness and grace. However, I had no illusions that everyone in the congregation would be so kind.

Ava reached for my hand. "The Lord will provide for us. Don't you worry." She glanced back at her husband, his face still transformed by awe over all I'd done. "And my guess is you've given my husband and me some much needed joy— both by your unusual story and by your generous heart."

I squatted beside her chair, looked into the serenity of her face. "But the children . . . I wanted so much to help them."

She laid her hand on my cheek. "And you will, Alyce. I believe that. But right at this moment, the Lord has more important work for you."

My heart raced. "What work?"

"The work of character. Of surrendering your pride to His loving hands. Allowing Him to mold and shape you in His way, not yours."

Her words soothed my soul with a peace deeper than I'd ever known. I let my empty handbag slide to the floor and clasped her fingers in mine. "I'm ready."

39

The Swans and the McConnells prayed for me before we made our way into the half-filled sanctuary. Mrs. Tillman, swathed in blue, barreled in my direction, as unstoppable as a touring car on snow-slick roads. I retreated to the outer wall, pulled my duster around my sling-clad arm, and pretended to be looking for someone.

Muscles tense, I waited for her to swoop in and start interrogating me. But she never arrived. I glanced over my shoulder. Mrs. Swan and Ava McConnell stood between us, engaging her in conversation until organ notes resounded in a call to worship.

After Mrs. Tillman returned to her pew on the opposite side of the room, I slipped into the space between Mr. and Mrs. McConnell on the front row. Ava held my hand as we focused our attention on Pastor Swan.

"Today we will be giving John and Ava McConnell a generous send-off as they return to their work in West Africa. At the end of our service, we will take up a special offering and pray for them. But first, Miss Benson has something she'd like to say to you all."

I rose, knees unsteady but heart determined. When I reached Pastor Swan's side, he anchored me with his arm about my waist. Even if my earthly father couldn't understand this part of my life, God had given me a spiritual father to uphold me in his stead.

Familiar faces stared up in expectancy, followed by bewilderment. I followed their stares to the limp sleeve of my duster. With as much grace as I could muster, I unbuttoned the coat and slipped my right arm free. Murmurs and gasps of dismay littered the room as Mrs. Swan took my wrap and sat back down. I filled my lungs and emptied them again, praying for the strength to say it all.

"Most of you sat in these same seats seven short weeks ago, when Mr. McConnell stirred our hearts with stories of their work. His words and pictures burned in me a desire for the African people to know Christ. So I committed three thousand dollars toward their mission—and encouraged you all to join together and do the same."

My heart pumped with more speed than Dario Resta's Peugeot while inadequacy and humiliation bore down on me like racers eager for the finish line. I glanced down at Mrs. Swan. She nodded, smiled. With a final push, the words tumbled from my mouth. "I stand before you today with empty hands."

A buzz of astonishment swept through the sanctuary as my chin met my chest. I stared at the floor for a few moments before raising my head, determined to accept their expressions of disgust.

"I'm sorry," I whispered. "I committed money that was not mine to give. After I raised a portion of the funds, I—"

"Her compassionate heart took over." Pastor Swan's voice filled the room. "She heard of needs in our own community and wanted to help. Did help. Though she ought to have consulted with those who had donated before making that decision."

Words cloaked in gentleness, but I felt their censure all the same. And I reflected that my actions, however well intentioned, appeared too much like Lawrence Trotter's than I cared to acknowledge. My gaze landed on Lucinda, wearing one of my old dresses, seated next to Mr. Morgan. She nodded, wiped a tear from her cheek. Teresa sat peacefully in her arms, and I smiled. Then a blur of robin's-egg-blue silk darted toward the platform.

My stomach clenched, but I refused to shrink back. "Mrs. Tillman, I do hope you and all the members of the Women's Mission Auxiliary will forgive me for not fulfilling my obligation."

Mrs. Tillman stopped so fast she almost reeled backward. She blinked as if I'd struck out at her instead of spoken words of humble repentance. "Of course you're forgiven," she stammered. Then her usual authoritative tone returned. "I wanted you to present this quilt to Mr. and Mrs. McConnell." She looked down at the folds of fabric filling her arms and then at the sling that hung from my shoulder. "But I guess you'll need some help to do that."

She unfurled the patchwork quilt. The congregation gasped. Names stitched in colored thread wound through the entire design, culminating in an outline of Africa stitched in the center, *Alyce Benson* emblazoned across the continent in letters twice as large as the rest. My cheeks burned.

"I'm so sorry," I whispered again.

"Whatever for?" Mrs. Tillman motioned Mrs. Swan up to

the front. Together they held it open and aloft. "Go on now, Alyce. Make the presentation."

I swallowed down my own emotion. "Mr. and Mrs. McConnell, the Women's Mission Auxiliary of Langston wishes to extend to you the fruits of our labor. Between bake sales and suppers and the donations of generous members, we wish to present to you this quilt in commemoration of those who sacrificed for the cause of Christ."

"And three thousand twenty-six dollars and fifteen cents." Mrs. Tillman's face lit as brightly as an Edison light bulb in a dark room.

Faces young and old reflected the awe I felt—awe that God would allow our small congregation to participate in His work in such a big way.

The McConnells stepped forward, Ava weeping with abandon. A man's voice rose from the back of the room. "Could we take that offering now, Pastor?"

"Offering? I think that's a fine idea." Pastor Swan motioned for the deacons to pass the plates. I stumbled back to my seat, thankful for the Lord's provision for my friends, even if it didn't come through me as I'd hoped.

Organ notes rose and fell with intensity, but as the final sounds faded, the squeak of rubber on hard floor caught my attention. I turned.

Webster was sitting in a wheelchair, his plastered leg propped up in front, Mother and Father walking behind.

My body refused to obey my commands.

"Did I hear the collection plates are being passed already, Pastor?" Webster's strong voice carried across the stunned silence. "Because I have something to put in."

He laid a white envelope on top of the bits of cash already inside the plate.

I sucked in a trembling breath. Webster lured my gaze to his. My hand gripped Ava's until I felt sure the bones in her hand would snap.

"May I?" He motioned to the front pew. I nodded. Father parked the chair in the aisle, and he and Mother took a seat in the pew behind us.

Pastor Swan remained open-mouthed on the platform. Clearly they'd not prepared him for such an incident in seminary. Finally, he gave a slow nod to the deacon holding the offering plate. The man slipped behind the sanctuary, into the pastor's office, I assumed. I turned my attention back to Pastor Swan. Standing behind the pulpit, he found his composure again.

He opened his Bible and began to preach. But while his words reached my ears, they penetrated no farther. Instead, I kept sneaking sideways glances at Webster from beneath my lashes. My fingers twisted in my lap while my legs tingled with the need to move, and my mouth twitched to spill out the swirl of questions in my head.

After what seemed ages, the rustle of the congregation alerted me to the end of the sermon. The prayer ended. The deacon reappeared, surrendering a fat envelope into the Pastor's outstretched hand.

Pastor Swan looked down. Cleared his throat. When he raised his head, his eyes were glistening with unshed tears. I held my breath as he motioned John and Ava McConnell to join him up front. He handed the envelope to Mr. McConnell.

A grin transformed Pastor Swan's wrinkled face into a picture of pure joy as he slapped a hand on Mr. McConnell's back. "Combining the Women's Mission Auxiliary's gracious contribution and the generous offerings of this morning, Langston Memorial Church is pleased to present to you all that God has provided for your work in the Gold Coast. Six thousand, six hundred forty-two dollars and twenty-four cents."

Mrs. Swan handed me a handkerchief before she wrapped her thin arms around me, guiding my head to her shoulder and telling me it was okay to cry. They were tears of joy, to be sure, joy and gratitude for the Lord's mysterious ways. When I finally composed myself, I noticed Webster's chair no longer rested at the end of the pew. I looked around and saw that Mrs. Swan and I were almost alone in the sanctuary.

"I'm sorry." I blew my nose once more. "I'll return this to you when I've washed it."

Mrs. Swan chuckled. "I'm not concerned about a scrap of cloth, Alyce. I'm concerned about you." With a gentle whisk of her fingers, she pushed one of my curls from my face. "Why don't you join your parents and that nice young man? I believe they came here today for your sake."

I nodded, studying the delicately embroidered edge of the handkerchief. Small purple flowers on a vine of green. *I am the vine, ye are the branches* came quickly to mind. A branch accomplished nothing on its own power, but when connected to the vine, it produced the fruit or flower it was created to provide. My job was to abide and let the Vine do its work.

"Miss Benson." Mrs. Tillman's prim voice stiffened my spine. In spite of her graciousness to me in front of the congregation, I feared a scolding remained to be endured.

I turned. Her gaze swept over my immobile arm, and her eyes softened.

"I apologize again, Mrs. Tillman. Especially since you made my name such a focal point on the quilt." I tensed, waiting for the smack of her words.

"I won't pretend I'm not disappointed, Miss Benson." She

fidgeted with the purse hanging from her arm. "But I have to admit, your pledge, however rash, stirred the rest of us to action. And in the end, I do realize that your desire is the same as mine—to send the gospel into all the world." She sniffed as if the admission had cost her dearly.

"As it stands, Miss Benson, you are welcome to continue to be a part of the Women's Mission Auxiliary. In case you wondered."

"Thank you, Mrs. Tillman. I appreciate your consideration, both now and in front of the church this morning."

She dipped her head in acknowledgment before darting up the sun-drenched aisle.

A few parishioners lingered in the yard as Mrs. Swan and I stepped outside. Webster stood propped against the trunk of a large tree while Father and Mr. McConnell strapped his chair to the back of my Packard. Lucinda's face danced with excitement as she jiggled Teresa into silence.

Eyes trained on Webster's face, I stumbled over the sprawling roots of the tree and tumbled into Webster's arms. He tilted. Mr. McConnell caught his arm, held him until he found his balance again.

Mr. McConnell stepped away, and Webster grinned at me. "I've been hoping to hold you in my arms."

"I'm sure you shouldn't even be out of bed yet," I said, moving from his grasp, letting him anchor himself steady against the tree once again.

A slight bend at the waist brought his face closer to mine. "When your father told me where you'd gone, I knew I didn't want you to face it alone. I just wish we'd have arrived sooner. I'm sorry." The backs of his fingers grazed the side of my face. I wanted to catch them, hold them. But not in front of all these people.

Father cleared his throat. Webster's arm fell back to the tree trunk as I forced my gaze to Father's face. He looked as giddy as a child with a bag full of sweets. "You'll never believe it, Ally girl."

"Believe what?" Hope sprang into my heart. Had the Lord answered Grandmother's and my long-standing prayer?

"I have a new business partner." Father beamed as he landed a light clap on Webster's shoulder.

Mother came up beside him, her face transformed with the glow of excitement. "If your father intends to manufacture cars, Alyce, I suppose you'll have to teach me to drive one. Will you?"

My head whirled in complete disbelief. "I . . . of course I will."

"Why don't we give Webster a few minutes to explain?" Mother pulled Father away, but he winked at me before striding back toward the small gathering of the Swans, the Mc-Connells, Lucinda, and Mr. Morgan.

I lowered my voice. "You and Father?"

Webster's grin stretched the fading bruises on his face, but I'd never seen a lovelier sight than that smile. "Your father already has the factory facilities and the labor. We'll just shift our focus a bit. From farm machinery to automobiles. Besides"—he lifted my hand, studied my fingers as they rested in his palm—"family should stick together."

"Family?" My heart battered against my chest.

"Your father gave his permission for me to marry you. That is, if you agree." His dark eyes stared into mine, strong and soft all at once. I wanted nothing more than to scream yes, but too many questions crowded my head.

I gently rested my head against his chest. "Are you sure? Some people will guess about the racing, eventually."

One of his arms slid around my back; the other tipped my chin upward. "That won't matter. I'll see to it that everyone recognizes my wife's amazing talents."

"What?" I pressed my hands against his solid, strong chest.

He shrugged. "Every time you get behind a wheel and do what you do best, it'll boost our business, even if it's an exhibition instead of a real race. Think how many women will want to drive our cars once they get a look at how much fun you have behind the wheel."

"But people will think it's not feminine." I lowered my voice. "And what will Mrs. Tillman say?"

His laugh wrapped around me. "Things will change. We'll make them change."

I thought of Mother, of our conversation about Webster in the hospital. Of her wanting to learn to drive. Things were changing already.

"Just think, Ally. We'll have our own little mission field, not only at our manufacturing plant, but at the tracks, on the racing circuit."

Could this be what the Lord had planned? After all that had happened recently, I didn't trust myself to know. I noticed Mr. McConnell lingering within earshot. "What do you think of his outrageous plans, Mr. McConnell?"

Before he could respond, Ava tucked herself under her husband's protective arm and pressed into his side. "People thought we were crazy to leave all we'd known and travel halfway around the world to preach the Good News. Some may wonder at your choices, too, but you can't let that stop you. We all have a call from God. And it will always seem a strange call to some. But that doesn't mean it isn't our purpose and calling. And it doesn't mean it isn't a valid occupation."

Her delicate face seemed to shine with ethereal wisdom, this fragile woman who lived and worked in a place that would defeat many. Maybe Webster was right. Maybe God was calling both of us to a life of unusual service to Him. Or rather of ordinary service—simply living the life He gave to us, serving as His beacon of hope and truth to whomever crossed our paths.

"So are you resolved to accept me now?" Webster's jaunty grin weakened my knees.

I pushed up on my toes, ready to press my lips against his. But just as his breath hit my face, I pulled away. "Wait. You never told me about the money."

"What money?"

"The money for the automobile business. Where did it come from? And how is there enough?"

The corners of his mouth lifted. "Things'll be tight at first. Your father is going to sell off a few assets to raise the capital, but since he already has the space and the labor, we won't need quite so much."

My eyes narrowed. "So then . . . what did you put in the offering plate?"

His gaze flicked to the McConnells. "I knew how much this meant to you, Ally, and I couldn't stand for you to be disappointed. I've been saving everything I earned, from working for your father and from our races." His cheeks colored pink. "I wanted to replenish the funds at my old church, but your father discovered that the money had already been returned. Or rather, rediscovered. A clerk made an error, and gossip spun it out of proportion. Nothing more." He shrugged. "So I gave what I'd saved to your missionaries instead."

I leaned into him, as close as my sling would allow. "But you could have used that money in the business. You wouldn't have needed Father as a partner. You could have done it yourself."

He cupped my chin in his hand. "Remember what I told you I wanted from this business? To make cars, yes. To make money even. But also to live out the gospel in front of my employees." His gaze traveled in the direction of my father. "And my partners."

My chest ached with a prayer of gratitude. I didn't deserve this man, this happiness. "I love you, Webster Little."

His arms tightened around me. "You should have let me say it first, you know."

My mouth dropped open. "I-I'm—"

He chuckled, his finger brushing my lips, hushing my stammered words. "I love you, too, Ally. Just the way you are."

And my heart revved faster than any engine I'd ever known.

AUTHOR'S NOTE

While this is a work of fiction, a few real-life facts made it into Alyce's story. All the racetracks, drivers, and races mentioned in the book are real. The Chicago Motor Speedway is long gone, converted to a military hospital during the Great War, just a few years after it opened. Of course the Indianapolis Motor Speedway still remains, though the Harvest Classic race in September of 1916 is only a brief footnote in its century-long history. And yes, red flags, not green, signaled race starts at this time.

Around the time of this story, Elfrieda Mais and Mrs. Cuneo were licensed to race by the Motor Contest Association and raced against each other in exhibitions. At the Indianapolis Motor Speedway, women were strictly forbidden to be in the garages or pits until well into the twentieth century.

The British colony formerly called the Gold Coast, in western Africa, is present-day Ghana. I am grateful to Cheryl Read for taking my daughter, Elizabeth, with her to work among the northern villages. I'm so inspired by the work that continues to go on there because one woman answered God's call.

Not being at all familiar with old cars or auto racing when I started this story, I so appreciate Donald Davidson, official historian of the Indianapolis Motor Speedway, spending time on the phone with me at a very busy time for him. He pointed me to some great resources, including the IMS Hall of Fame Museum. In a providential meeting at the museum, I became acquainted with the gracious and knowledgeable Fred Harris. His grandfather was the mechanic on the car that won the 1922 Indianapolis 500. Fred gave me information I couldn't find anywhere else and was so patient with my lack of knowledge about cars and racing! Everything I got right is due to him.

Many thanks to my friend Becky Hurst, who accompanied me on my research trip to Indianapolis, acting as another pair of eyes and ears as we explored the speedway, old newspaper articles, and the Indiana State Museum. I wouldn't have accomplished so much in such a short amount of time without her.

As always, my prayer team has been invaluable. Thank you, Mom, Dad, Debra and Kirby, Dan and Jen, Dawn and Billy, Jeff, Robin and Bill, Mary, Leslie, Cheryl, Cherryl, Becky, Becky, Jill, and Andrea.

My critique group, Leslie Wilson, and Mary DeMuth keep me chugging down the right path in writing and life. Thank you!

I'm so grateful for my editor, Charlene, and all the others at Bethany House. Their suggestions always make the story stronger. And the art and marketing departments are an awesome force to have behind a girl. Thanks, y'all!

Elizabeth, Aaron, and Nathan, I couldn't ask for more

understanding and supportive kids. A special thank-you to Aaron for sharing his graduation month with my need to be with Alyce and finish her story.

As always, my husband, Jeff, keeps me grounded and helps me soar. I couldn't do this without you. I love you.

And thank You, Jesus. It's all by You and for You.

ANNE MATEER has a passion for history and historical fiction, a passion that often rears its head during family vacations. Thankfully, her husband shares and indulges her love of the past. She and her husband live near Dallas, Texas, and are the parents of three young adults.

Learn more about Anne and her books by visiting her blog and Web site at *www.annemateer.com*.

If you enjoyed *At Every Turn*, you may also like...

Rebecca's heart is set on aviator Arthur Samson and big adventure. But will mounting obstacles force her to choose between escaping life on the family farm and the unexpected love that could change the dream of her heart?

Wings of a Dream by Anne Mateer
annemateer.com

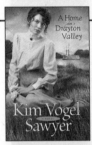

When tragedy strikes on the prairie, throwing Tarsie and Joss into an unexpected arrangement, can they trust God with their dreams for the future?

A Home in Drayton Valley by Kim Vogel Sawyer
kimvogelsawyer.com

In the picturesque Amana Colonies, two very different young women are looking for answers. But secrets run deep there, and the truth could alter everything.

A Hidden Truth by Judith Miller
HOME TO AMANA
judithmccoymiller.com